copycat

A Jake Lydon Mystery

JOHN
OWENS

Author of *JACKPOT*

OTTAWA PRESS
AND PUBLISHING

MYSTERY

ottawapressandpublishing.com

Copyright © John Owens 2022

Print Book ISBN: 978-1-990896-00-2
Ebook ISBN: 978-1-988437-99-6

Cover and page design: Glenn Torresan

This is a work of fiction. All characters, places, names, incidents, organizations, and dialogue in this novel are either products of the author's limited imagination or are used fictitiously.

Also by John Owens

Historical Fiction
On the Rails
The Sixth String

Jake Lydon Mysteries
Connecdead
Machete
Bushwhacked
Jackpot

To Steve McGill, for forty years of beer, yuks, and friendship

The man ain't got no culture.
- Paul Simon

Wish I didn't know now what I didn't know then.
- Bob Seger

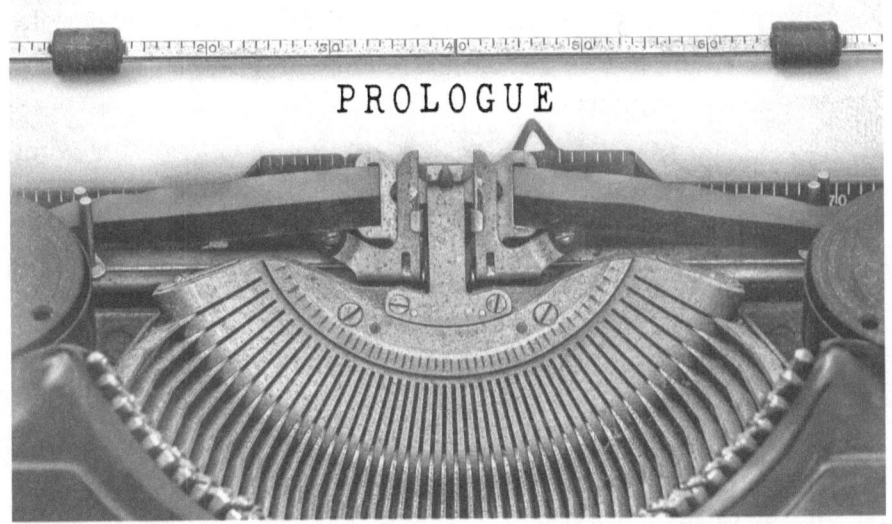

PROLOGUE

He was feeling pretty pleased about the way the seminar had gone as he walked to his car in the dark parking lot. After years—no, decades—of teaching the same material to new crops of students he could recognize a turning of the tide. His students were getting it.

But *as* he fumbled for his keys while juggling papers and books, his immediate irritation returned. Ordinarily, he wouldn't even be on campus for the class but rather his twelve attendees— he referred to them as My Half-Assed Apostles—would just then be leaving his comfortable living room in town holding all that red wine and wisdom he'd passed on to them.

His annoyance grew. And just why was he out here now? His attendance, the department's attendance was expected just so they all could listen to that charlatan's guest lecture on the patent-ly obvious, and then pretend to be adoring at a reception for him afterwards. Bah! And worse, this fake was now to be writer-in-res-idence for the second semester. Favourite son, indeed. More like a chicken come home to roost.

He was angry at himself too, for not having the courage to confront him in front of all those academic and literary grandees. He needed a new plan.

He pushed his bile down, seized by his intentions for what remained of his evening. Home to a fire, a little jolt, and a return to writing his next book.

The trunk of his aging Corolla popped open, and he leaned over to pile in his books and essays. That's when he felt the sharp pain in his troublesome lower back. But instantly, he knew this was different, stabbing, searing. He fell to his knees. Papers scattered in the warm breeze. Then came the next electric agony. And the next.

His last thought was of his image as a supplicant, worshipping at the altar of his car's rear bumper.

CHAPTER ONE

It was a dark and stormy night.

Wait. Check that. Notwithstanding the fact that pretty well all nights are dark, it actually wasn't. Downtown Boston's streetlights combined with all the illuminated office buildings and store fronts and bar signs produced a bright artificial halo. And now that I think about it, there were only a few random raindrops.

So, to recap:

It was a semi-dark and slightly damp night.

Alexandra and I had just left a swanky Italian restaurant on Franklin Square. In a way, it was a make-up dinner for the scene I had caused in front of her place earlier in the day.

Without letting her know I was coming, I had just flown to Boston from my newly inherited Florida hovel-by-the-sea in Indian Rocks Beach south of Clearwater. Rather than give her a mid-afternoon surprise at the ethical investment brokerage that she ran, I cabbed it to her place in Framingham. I sat on the front steps and waited, looking habitually shabby, smoking, and generally driving down property values in her upper-scale neighbourhood.

In an hour or so, I saw her green (of course) Prius roll up and pull into the driveway. Heart soar like triumphant eagle when I saw her. Then heart plummet like suicidal condor when a sporty black Mercedes followed her up the driveway.

She got out, looking more surprised and awkward than delighted to see the worthy object of her adoration (that would be me, in case you missed it).

At about the same time, a spiffy-looking lad, maybe twenty years younger, a couple of inches shorter, and a whole lot more fit than me got out of his Benz and hurried to Alex's side.

"Everything OK here, pal?" he asked me, puffing up all manly and defensive.

"Everything's hunky-dory, Chad or Muffy or whatever the fuck your name is," I answered, a rush of anger washing over me. "Just came to see my lady," I added, trying to put an arm around Alex's waist.

She shook it off and glared at me.

"Alex?" he asked.

"It's fine, Mark. I'll see you tomorrow at work. We can go over the reports then."

With some hesitation, this Mark disappeared, and I was anticipating our slightly delayed but happy reunion. Wrong, moron! (That would be me again, in case you missed it).

"What was that Neanderthal bullshit?" Alex demanded.

"What was that preppy-asshole-showing-up-for-a-evening-with-you bullshit?" I countered.

Turns out this clever answering-a-question-with-a-question strategy of mine was ill-advised. Alex was red-faced furious, the angriest I'd ever seen her.

I started looking around for a sword to fall on, pretty sure that Alex would supply one if she had one.

"I honestly don't know, babe," I managed.

"Well maybe you ought to find out."

"In my defense…," I started to say, but the look on Alex's face very plainly indicated I should abandon any weak-ass self-justification.

"…OK, there is no defense," I said. "It was a childish display of automatic jealousy and suspicion. I didn't plan it and it surprised the shit out of me too. I haven't had that feeling since high school; I swear."

All of this was true. What I didn't say was that I was a teensy-weensy bit pleased with my reaction. In my head and my heart (or any other organ you care to name) I knew that I loved this woman. But there was something elemental, primal, about my roaring jealousy that sealed the deal. You can't fake that shit.

It was chilly in the house. And not because the furnace hadn't kicked in.

"C'mon, ya big lug," I said. "I'll buy you dinner downtown. You pick the restaurant. C'mon, whaddya say?"

I'm something of a professional cajoler. It worked.

Judging by the elegant surroundings of the Italian eatery she selected, the punishment for my asinine exhibition wasn't yet over. We were seated by a suitably snooty be-tuxed waiter. I looked around for a loans officer when I read the menu.

I don't often feel embarrassed for anything I say, do, or look like. But I did feel a little more than underdressed in my worn black sweatshirt and track pants, the only warm clothes I owned at that moment. If you asked me—which nobody did—there were altogether too many neckties and dresses (although not on the same patron) among our fellow diners.

Alexandra ordered a glass of chianti (hold the fava beans, for the moment) and I had to settle for a bottle of Peroni as Italian beer was my only choice. (Hey, *mi amici*, stick to winemaking, not limp-dick lagers). I had to stop Signore Snooti from pouring it for me. He was pissed.

By candlelight, Alex looked tremendous as she leaned in.

"Do you want to know a secret?" she asked.

"I promise not to tell." I answered. (Quoting sappy Beatles' lyrics proved I was still in full grovel mode.).

"I don't quite understand it," she almost whispered, "but deep down, I was…a little bit…I don't know… pleased at your chest-thumping."

"Sort of like watching a teen gorilla and an old silverback about to bash heads over you?"

"…Yeah, I guess," she smiled.

"Well, all I gotta say is you should be ashamed of yourself for that 'My Boyfriend's Back and you're going to be in trouble' shit, you sexist, you," I said. "Oh, and I would've beaten the chicken soup out of him."

She didn't order anything listed on the menu at the always-ominous 'Market Price,' so I figured I was getting time off for good behaviour.

The meal was spectacular, our surroundings rococo plush, the ambience wonderful, right down to the gentle piano tinkling going on in the background. But the waiter's sullen service would put every stereotype of an arrogant Paris server to shame.

Good time to have a chat with the lad, I thought. But Alex beat me to it.

"Say, pal, can I ask you a question?" she said as he presented the check.

"Yes, madam?"

"What the fuck is your problem?"

I was startled. He was startled. He glanced at me, or rather at my clothes, but didn't say anything.

"Just so you know," Alex said. "My friend is coming from his oceanside estate in Florida, on his way to his lakeside mansion in Canada. Now run along."

"Estate? Mansion?" I said, after the waiter slunk away.

"With a little work."

I reached for the check, but she beat me to that as well.

"My treat. I was advising my rich Canadian client."

Later that night, she advised my brains out and all was right with our world again.

CHAPTER TWO

It doesn't take me long to develop habits. At the first dizzying cigarette in the high school smoking square, I knew I had found a hopeless, lifelong (however short that might be) addiction. Here in Boston in chilly late April, I soon reverted to a ritual that was just a year old but showed promise. I was restless and petulant—and forced to wear fucking socks. I didn't fit in yet—and perhaps never would. Mercedes Mark aside, I was an interloper in Alex's upscale universe. I knew she was slumming it by being with me at either of my hovels, but she seemed fine with it, even enjoyed going waaaay down-market. But I was incapable of gettin' my hoity-toity on there. I'd left that corporate world decades earlier and didn't miss or want it back one fucking bit.

"I gotta head home, babe," I finally said, after three days of jonesing to hear loons again.

"I know," she said, "I've been meaning to talk to you."

I had been low on dread ever since that gunplay that concluded my stay in the tiny Hovel-by-the-Sea in Indian Rocks. Suddenly, I was fully topped up with the aforementioned dread.

She seemed reluctant to speak.

"What is it, Alex? Just say."

"I know you have your habits. But would you mind if...if I came with you?"

"Are you fucking kidding me?!" I nearly shouted with relief. "You betcha!"

"We can rent a car at the airport, finally drive up *together*....," she said, already in full planning mode.

"Whoa, I don't think that'll work. Carl's gonna be pissed."

Carl, my seventy-something neighbour, and I had an arrangement. For the last six years, I put the NHL and NFL packages on his cable account so he could spend the winter watching all things football- and hockey-related on my huge, big screen that I boat over to his place on the small island offshore from my property. In return, he looks after the Hovel-by-the-Lake and gets my mail after taking me down to the Toronto airport in early November and before retrieving me in April.

"Nonsense. We'd be giving him a break," she insisted.

"He won't see it that way."

I e-mailed him, telling him that Alexandra and I would get a car and not to worry his pretty little head about sweating through Toronto traffic. He wrote back a few hours later. I showed Alex his short but to the point response.

That's not the fuckin deal, son.

Master of restraint, I resisted the childish temptation to dance around Alex chanting "I told you so! I told you so!" Instead, I booked flights to Pearson from Logan, wrote Carl with the arrival details, and off we went.

I was so delighted to have my lady accompanying me that I didn't really mind the usual egregious profiling I received at Canadian Customs, where I was—yet again—hustled into a windowless room to watch as they tore apart my trusty bowling bag searching for all the drugs this shabby old hippie was surely trying to import.

Outside, I was equally delighted to watch Carl wrap his giant arms around Alex in a bear hug that I assumed he usually reserved for hugging bears in a death grip. It was a very big deal for me that those two get along.

Sticking to the script we wrote six years ago when I first started fucking off south for the winter, we didn't say much as my ageless classic Pontiac Vibe chugged out of Toronto. Once clear of serious traffic, Carl began intermittently filling me in on the major events of the past winter

"Lake's high….Lotta snow melt….Already started two more houses on the west side….They raised the price of a goddamned beer at AA by fifty cents…."

"Those thieving bastards!" I said of the owners of the Angler Arms, the finest cottage country bar in the world™.

"Oh, and didja hear a professor at Trent got himself dead about a month ago?" he said.

I hadn't. My Canadian news-weather-sports-gathering had tailed off, as it usually does the longer I'm away in the south frying my skin and brain cells.

"Any idea who?" I asked.

"An older fella. Ned Tromly, Fred Burley, something like that."

"Ted Bromley?"

"That's the one."

"Christ, I took a course of his, back when there were a lot fewer books to study. Not too surprising he's gone to the great library in the sky; he had to be pushing eighty," I said, hoping to get a rise out of Carl who himself was north of three quarters of a century on the planet.

"Hey now, steady on, son," Carl said. "And it weren't natural causes."

"What happened?"

"Stabbed to death in a parking lot."

"Downtown?" I asked as we were passing through downtown Peterborough.

"Fuck, no. Out at the main campus."

That took me aback. I couldn't imagine anything nasty happening on the university's idyllic main campus that covered fifteen hundred acres of mostly bush and river and featured its very own drumlin.

"Catch the guy?" I asked.

"Not that I heard."

Just then, we were coming up on the sign for the university where I'd spent three years after a disastrous first year in Toronto. I always had liked the logo. Simple hunter green and white, part of a sword—majestic looking handle, hilt, and start of the broad blade—rising out of stylized waves. Everybody assumed it was Arthur's Excalibur levitating out of some goddamned mythic English lake. The sign was all you saw of the sprawling campus from the main road because it did all its sprawling out of sight, tucked in behind that big drumlin rising out of the post-glacial Canadian Shield.

I stared at the big, treed hill as we passed, wondering about Bromley's death on the other side of it. Just then, Alex reached over from the backseat and gently but firmly squeezed my shoulder. She knew what I was thinking, and she was showing her concern. I had almost fucked things up between us a few weeks earlier after I had been involved in a shoot-out with a man who was really keen on killing me. I hadn't told her about all the details of the major brouhaha I was knee-deep in that led up to me nearly dying. Or any specifics about the actual gunplay. She was, to put it mildly, not amused when she read about it in a newspaper.

"So, anything else happen?" I asked Carl and her grip relaxed.

"Nah. Couple of elections is all. Bunch of new arseholes got in."

We pulled off the main road and onto the dusty track that led to the lake. I saw that the new town council had quickly changed its name from Edgewater Lane back to the very elegant Fire Route 162 to erase any reminder of the embarrassing (not to mention deadly) real estate development shitshow from the previous summer.

We indulged in a slightly modified version of our normal deck ritual. As usual, after we dumped our baggage, Carl and I—along with Alexandra now—headed out to the deck overlooking Mississauga Lake. Alexandra and he sat in the two Adirondack chairs while I, gallant bastard that I am, perched on one of those wobbly fold-up director's chairs. Also as usual, we drank one beer and shivered as we stared at the big block of ice that was Mississauga Lake. I was encouraged that spring had started to defrost its edges.

Compensation came later that night after Carl left as I nestled with Alexandra like crazy under the comforter. Gosh, what a lovely thermal aid.

But I didn't fall asleep right away. I thought about Professor Bromley again and his untimely death. He wasn't a favourite of mine when I was being schooled forty years ago. Yes, he was earnest about his subject, and I always like anybody who's enthusiastic about his work. I just didn't care for his rhapsodizing about the budding local and expatriate writer community in the drug- and booze-fueled Paris at the turn of the 19th century, before all the drug-and booze-fueled Brits and Yanks showed up in the 20s. Turns out they were mostly shitty writers—in my never humble opinion.

I only had the central fact of his death: a violent killing.

And I had one overarching question: Who the fuck murders an old professor of English literature?

CHAPTER THREE

The great thing about thoughts is that you get to have them alone. You can also function doing something completely unrelated while you're having them—except neurosurgery and maybe air traffic control.

All I was doing at this thinking time was my homecoming ritual of cleaning up mouse turds, souvenirs from the little bastards' all-expenses paid, winter-long indoor vacation. So I drifted back to my university days.

Those days had started out shittily enough. In my first and only year at the University of Toronto, I was allowed to take just one English course even though I had long made up my mind that I was only interested in studying fiction. So I randomly picked introductory courses in political science, history, sociology, and philosophy to fill up my course load. Fifteen hours of lectures a week in total with a minimum of a hundred students per lecture, some of whom actually took notes.

The problem I had with all the non-English courses was that I had already earned my PhD in Cynicism and I was a card-carrying atheist by the time I left high school. Plus, I was a budding simpleton, prone—as I still am—to sweeping, dismissive generalizations about things that don't interest me.

So, as far as I was concerned, political science became merely the convoluted explanation of the main point of politics: to get and keep power. History was the record of how monarchs or despots got power then either kept it or lost it, usually after the violent and huge pointless loss of life, while sociology attempts to explain how we let generals, dictators, and politicians get power and keep it.

My career as a philosopher-to-be was the shortest-lived.

Our philosophy prof was a bird-like man with a huge head teetering on a slender neck. He'd walk into the lecture hall and demand silence. "I have to think," he'd say. After his second lecture, he announced: "What I just spent an hour and a half telling you, I could've properly done so in four minutes."

I stood up, seeking clarification of that remark.

"Then why the fuck didn't you?" I asked.

When a goddamned answer to my simple goddamned question wasn't forthcoming, my only remaining move was to pack up my things and leave. To a smattering of applause, may I add.

That childish display left a hole in my timetable that I filled with a poetry writing workshop. In the main, this year-long credit course consisted of us aspiring laureates anonymously submitting a poem we'd written to be dissected by the rest of the class. I have kept some of my attempts at poem-making, maybe just to remind myself about how pathetic I/they were. Chock full of late teenhood angst, astonishingly naïve observations, and clumsy as fuck wordsmithery, they are largely only cringe-inducing now. I say 'largely,' because there were some lines that were goddamn good, if I do say so myself—and I do. Even if they were the result of that famous theory that a roomful of monkeys at keyboards will eventually produce *Hamlet*.

I had previously researched my published poet of a prof and didn't think much of his printed work. He snuck one of his crappy poems into the weekly stack of offerings from us. I spotted it and then proceeded to rip the shit out of it.

The mistake I made was looking directly at him while I gleefully tore into his work. He knew what I was doing. So I wasn't overly surprised when, after the first semester, he had given me a D-minus. But I was furious, even though I knew I was a lousy poem-maker. Why not just a D? I know my contribution had been shitty, but D-*minus* shitty? That was way too specific for me.

I went to see him in his office, eager as any first-year student to learn the intricacies of literary criticism.

"What the fuck is that bullshit D-minus about?" I asked to get the conversation started.

"Reading you is like reading Edmund Lear after Shakespeare," he told me, as he glanced around anywhere but at me.

He went on to add that I was a detriment to his class and said that, if I didn't shape up, he would toss me out. On the spot, I threatened to toss him out his fourth-story office window.

Apparently, the head of the English Department to whom he complained saw my threat as being slightly more serious than his, citing an obscure rule in the Code of Conduct that discouraged the murdering of faculty members.

Rather than start the cumbersome process of rustication (I had to look it up), never mind criminal charges, the department head suggested that I might be happier at another school. I agreed. And thus Trent.

The small, mainly liberal arts university in Peterborough was British as hell, divided up into colleges (two in town and three out at the main campus just north that spanned the Otonabee River). Big on Brit tradition, the colleges had masters and principals and dons. Academic gowns were mandatory for lecture attendance until the early 1970s, although caning never caught on except, I assume, of the recreational variety.

This Anglo-loving feature had resulted in Trent's nickname as Oxford on the Otonabee. That is, until the human rights lawsuit lodged a few years before I got there. What a coincidence that up until that complaint, the English department head at the time would only hire Oxford graduates. Its unofficial motto could've been: "Fuck Cambridge and Double-Fuck any Grads from the Colonies!"

I reminded myself that there was a single scene that summed up my three years at Trent. It's the ending of *Fahrenheit 451*, the '66 Truffault version, where the outlawed book people are strolling along a riverbank reciting out loud from memory the one novel they'd chosen to know by heart, in the hope that one day books would be allowed again. A light snow is falling, as they pass each other chanting the lines from the classics. It's one of the most poignant, moving finales in any movie and it could've been filmed at the northern end of Trent's 1500-acre campus, where there's nothing but river with its banks crowded by pine, spruce or whatever the fuck.

Budding slacker that I was, I remember pitying the poor bastard who voluntarily selected or was given *War and Peace* to commit to memory. I would have picked *The Little Prince*, maybe *Animal Farm* if I was feeling ambitious.

In a way, that scene also captured what the learning was like at Trent. Books, books, and more books. At stretches, a novel or a play a day. When you weren't reading them, you were writing about them or arguing about them. Back then, because Trent's student body was about 40% English majors, you could spontaneously go *humano-a-humano* with a lot of people. Picture the final showdown in *The Good, the Bad and the Ugly* — "Hey, Blondie! *Clea* is obviously the weakest book in Durrell's *Alexandria Quartet*, right?" There were few lectures but loads of small seminar groups where you were constantly preparing to give half-hour presentations. Although I'm a card-carrying introvert, I always relished the opportunity to stand up there and tell people What I Believe. Big surprise, huh?

I'm just not a black or white kinda guy about most things. I want to operate in that huge grey area of opinion and subjectivity. That inclination made English Lit the perfect academic pursuit for me, as opposed to, say, mathematics which always struck me as too, I don't know, *arbitrary*. Not a lot of wriggle room there; you're either right or wrong.

Same goes for career choices. Give me a job where what I *think* matters, not my knowledge of what actually *is*.

Put one way: About the last thing you'd ever want is for me to be the air traffic controller for your jam-packed 737 on approach: "Yeah, Delta 5-2-8-something or other, how about you try northwest at, say, 5000-feet, give or take? On the other hand, bud, you might consider east south-east at somewhere around 6 or 7000; that might work."

Put a simpler way: Give me bullshitting over facts any ol' day.

In short, Trent was exactly what I had dreamed of and hoped for in my university career since about grade 10 when I decided irrevocably that I would become an English teacher where I would keep reading and tell kids about what I had read, and they'd tell me what they thought. And in my spare time I would write my own contribution to the growing pile of dead trees.

My pleasing university days at Trent got a real blast of ecstasy when I met Beth towards the end of second year there. In about a minute—maybe a minute and a half—I decided she was the one. Or rather, The One. Boy, was it a good thing when she apparently came to the same conclusion.

I abandoned my standard issue shithole of a university student apartment and she left residence and we moved in together (known primarily as 'shacking up' back then) and finished out our undergraduate careers deliriously happy and in love.

She got her Honours BA and I got mine. Together, we got married.

I nursed the dream of all books all the time. I lived that dream until I was rudely introduced to what had been, so far, an ugly foreign concept, something called reality.

Beth was all in backing my dream. We'd spent a year in Kingston being in love while I pretended to be an academic at Queen's University because Trent didn't have (a) graduate program. After I finished my Master's—self-financed thanks to various Awards Officers who succumbed to my native talent for wheedling, cajoling, and begging—she would've gladly worked while I either went to Teacher's College or onto to a PhD—Mark Twain's was going to be the literary carcass I would pick over.

I had been spoiled at Trent, so much so that I may have sabotaged enjoyment of my MA year at Queen's. One incident in the first week set the tone. Frosh Week back then was just an excuse for all returning students to be drunken dicks towards freshmen (freshpeople?). An upper-class Engineering student spotted me carrying my orientation package and we engaged in the intellectual give and take that is the hallmark of higher learning. He ordered me to roll a peanut with my nose across the quadrangle. In the spirit of academic reciprocity, I suggested he go fuck himself.

But finally, I couldn't handle Beth's selfless generosity in funding me just so that I could do whatever the fuck my little heart desired. No amount of reasoning by her (or me) could justify it. My old man had fucked off for good only a couple of years before. He left to pursue his calling. Unfortunately, that calling wasn't to become a world-leading heart surgeon; it was so he could literally gamble his life away as a professional gambler.

I loved most of my Trent professors back then, when I was trying to be as earnest about literature as they were. It didn't take.

At the very least, I was impressed as hell at how smart they all were even though there's some danger in unqualified admiration. Maybe that's why I have dedicated my life to studiously avoiding doing anything admirable. The fan club obligations alone would drive me nuts.

My professors looked like their field of specialization. For 19th century American lit, we had this big bastard, with an Amish-type beard and round wire-rimmed glasses. In the spring, he could be seen tramping the campus in rubber boots, straw hat, and one-piece denim overalls. And he actually spent his summers on or near Walden Pond.

Professor Sanford was the delightful Pope and Swift guy who always spoke softly and sensibly and always wore a suit with matching tie and socks and spit-polished brogues.

The Irish playwright fanboy was Sean O'Meara. Roly-poly, he accentuated his figure by constantly wearing those thick cable-knit fishermen's sweaters in all weather. Canadian by birth, O'Meara would, I shit you not, lapse into a lilting brogue when he was rhapsodizing about anybody and everybody who was ever born in Ireland and started a blank page by writing ACT ONE. I didn't much care for him as I can't accept that birth on a particular island is an automatic passport to theatrical greatness.

Our Romantic period professor was a fanatic for William Blake. Never mind the shorter "Tiger, tiger, burning bright"–type poems. He was deep into the Blakean universe of mythic creatures with names like Orc, Albion, Tharmas, and Enitharmon, a universe Blake had lavishly illustrated with fantastical engravings. Blake kicked off the English tradition, followed by CS Lewis and Tolkien, of imagining worlds a whole lot more epic than what's available in their tiny country saddled with—for most of them—its stifling class system. (Yeah, I know; there has to be a recent asterisk for American-born George R.R. Martin, but he's from New Jersey). I just couldn't get all that excited about spending a lot of

time deciphering and translating all these characters who basically just represented some pretty simple ideas.

Although I didn't enjoy the long stretches of detailed discussions about the addictions of mediocre Paris-based writers, it was
hard not to feel like an adult in Ted Bromley's seminars. They were
held not in a classroom in daylight, but in the evenings in his ec-
centrically over-decorated living room in town like we were in
some goddamned Parisian salon. A bonus was swilling the cheap
Hungarian red wine he provided by the flagoon. Put it this way: I
remember the wine, mostly for my whanging hangovers, (it was
Szekszardi Voros) but hardly any of the writers.

Ted was as informal as you could get with Bromley's first
name. He was no Teddy in a Roosevelt or even a Ruxpin kinda
a way. And Theodore is one of those names no one ever says out
loud, unless it was his mom when she was pissed at him. Like the
way Mrs. Cleaver would say it when she worried about the Beaver.

My favourite educator at the time was Rob Byford, a big bois-
terous curly blonde bastard who mainly taught early 20th century
British literature with an emphasis on D.H. Laurence. Unlike his
hero, Rob had a great sense of humour and a foul mouth when
he wasn't in a classroom. Oh, and he really liked to drink. Only a
few years older than me, Rob was/is one of those guys who had/
have a zest for life (whereas I have/had a zest for reading about
life). He was a wunderkind literary scholar, played hockey in the
university house league, sang light opera with the local amateur
troupe, and had even spent time as a wandering teenager with
Leonard Cohen on Hydra. He built his own cabin in the woods
(with the press-ganged help of students like me) and would vora-
ciously smoke my cigarettes when we were drinking but not touch
them otherwise. Beth and I had him over for dinner a few times.
Beth really liked him, as most women did.

Now, all my teachers were all either dead or retired or both.

Including Ted Bromley who, until a few months ago, was over

on the Alive side of the ledger.

Rob had been a good if occasional friend since my Trent career ended. We had stayed in touch, sort of. Hand-written letters every couple of years that somehow found each other and then e-mails from time to time, even though I lived in the area, and he taught at Trent until his retirement three years earlier.

Rob had done a swell thing for me about five years ago. Unsolicited, I had sent him huge chunks of the first draft of *On the Rails*, my novel-to-be. He wrote back:

"Stop wasting my fucking time! Get an agent, get it published, get it out there. It's more than good."

I took his encouragement as a sign of his incredible insight and taste, rather than simple politeness towards a friend.

Two years after that, he had invited me to attend his retirement soiree held by the English department. I was deeply honoured. Ex-students normally weren't asked, the same way high school students don't get into the sacrosanct Teachers' Lounge where, it was rumoured, smoking took place! I told him that. He pointed out that he liked drinking with me. I told him I was even more deeply honoured.

When you're away from the literary academic world, as I had been for comin' on forty years, it can be a real jolt to immerse yourself in it again.

Faculty speaker after speaker got up to roast/praise Rob. And every goddamned one of them was funny and astonishingly articulate. And not one of them said "Fuck." Talking to them before and afterwards, I even managed to curb my usually vile tongue, except for brief chat with Professor O'Meara. I went out of my way to convince him that after university I had had a lengthy career as a longshoreman.

Christ, I can be petty.

Rob insisted I stay afterwards and then we did what we used to do when he was a newbie prof and I was a student. We got shit-faced, starting at the faculty lounge and then cabbing it to downtown Peterborough. I hadn't spent much time in Peterborough since I bought the Hovel-by-the-Lake even though it's only a half hour away, mostly because the city was a relatively large collection of humanity. I certainly hadn't done any drinking there as I preferred Carl's predictable company at the Angler Arms within walking/stumbling distance of the Hovel.

"So what'll it be?" Rob asked in the taxi. "Wine bar, gastro-pub or craft brewery?"

"Aw, for fuck's sake. Don't tell me. The Princess?"

"Closed."

"The George?"

"Closed."

"American House?"

"Closed. Sort of."

"What's that mean?"

"It's still a dive bar, been called the Red Dog for years, but there's live rock music every night. So we can sit and drink and yell if you'd like."

I especially lamented the loss of the American House as your strictly sketchy hole-in-the-wall tavern for a drinking evening. In addition to shitty surroundings, really cheap draft, grim but astonishingly efficient service, the AH used to feature two-dollar buffets on Thursdays—a student's dream. Oh, and I met local resident Ronnie Hawkins and Kris Kristofferson there. I say "met" but not really. I said "Hi" walking past their table. Kristofferson said "Hello" and Hawkins gave me a two-fingered salute off his cowboy hat (or maybe it was one-fingered). So perhaps I can't claim a life-long connection to the music legends.

Rob and I passed the Red Dog and, indeed, I could hear the music pounding out into the street.

"You can't go home again. Remember?" Rob said, noticing me staring.

We wound up at a sports bar, replete with jockish decoration, cheerful but useless service and wildly overpriced bottled beer (but no Molson Ex; it was getting increasingly hard to find anywhere as it had plummeted out of fashion). I settled on an ale because all the fucking drafts were Light lagers, which ought to be a criminal offence.

We did what old friends do when they meet up after nearly forty years. We reminisced—something I found hard to do in the e-mails we had sporadically swapped. Such a stroll down a hazy memory lane demands an in-person conversation where you each get to kick in context and little details as they occur to you. We had a very pleasant rest of the evening and Rob invited me to sleep it off at his place which he swore was "just a couple of blocks away." With neither of us in any condition to drive, I agreed. We stumbled west along Hunter, following the street as it petered out from being the town's busiest east-west thoroughfare until it narrowed and trickled into an old established neighbourhood.

I knew this part of town very well and it hadn't changed. Rob turned up a walkway to a house that I knew better than any of the other big, three-story, red brick century homes squatting under giant elms that the insidious Dutch hadn't got at yet. I used to live there.

"What the fuck?" I said as we stood on the familiar front porch and Rob unlocked the front door.

"I always liked this house, so when it came on the market…"

"Cabin didn't work out?"

"Fuck, no. I gave up living there years ago. Got real sick of chopping wood and freezing my nuts off. Plus, it cost me at least one girlfriend and untold wealth in cans of Deep Woods Off!"

"You own this whole house?"

"Yup, took a bit to convert it back to a single-family home from student apartments. That's why I'm glad I kept the cabin. It didn't cost much."

"That's probably true," I noted. "You used slave labour to build it."

"I rent it out—mostly in summer," he continued. "It's good money. Helps me pay the mortgage on this place."

Walking into the foyer was like walking into my personal museum. Nothing much looked like it had changed from the countless times Beth and I had crossed its threshold to our ground floor apartment, except for the fact that the wall between the common foyer and our living room had been taken down. Same dark hardwood floor, intricate deep baseboards and crown molding in a honey maple colour, same stained glass or cut crystal windowpanes.

Even the fucking wallpaper in the living room was the same. A rich tapestry sorta design on a hunter green background filled in the spaces between all the built-in bookshelves. The furniture, of course, was different but not the gold sconces flanking the same wide brick fireplace, elaborate with its heavy carved mantle, the works. Christ, there were, I swear, the same creaks in the same places on the floor.

Maybe all the beer caused it, but I felt my eyes well up as I was overwhelmed by two facts: Beth and I had been happy there and now Beth was dead.

"Night cap?" Rob asked.

I followed him into the familiar kitchen. New appliances, but same old dark wood cabinetry with glassed doors. Above one bank of upper cabinets, the bell system was still there, left over from the days when this was the stately residence of some wealthy doctor or lawyer or lumber baron who wanted to summon a servant or two because he was too fucking lazy to move from any of the five rooms wired to the bells. Through a rear window, I could see the parking lot for the four renters when I lived there had been dug up and replaced by an English courtyard-type garden, with spotlights trained on weeping mulberry and elderberry trees.

Rob fished two Molson Ex from the fridge. I congratulated him on his good taste.

"You did that," he said as we clinked bottles. "Haven't switched since."

We retreated to the living room and wound down the evening/morning quietly as we finished our beer and reverie.

"If you can walk, I'll take you up to a guest room," Rob said.

"Mind if I crash here on the couch…for old time's sake?"

"Maybe you *can* go home again," Rob said, smiling.

He wandered away and I heard his creaking footsteps up the stairs.

Different couch, same location, as I thought back to the last time I saw Rob almost forty goddamned years earlier.

I ran into him just before my final exam. We agreed to mark the end of my Trent sojourn and the conclusion of his teaching year with a night on the town. He'd drop around to collect me at some unspecified time.

The hours rolled by and I fell asleep on the couch, tired of waiting and just tired. I was awakened by rough hands shaking me like a rag doll.

"Get the fuck up, you bloody dilettante!" Rob bellowed.

The wall clock said it was just after eleven. Rob was already wired to the tits and looking for more. (Note to my back-then-self: time to start locking the front door). His one-man commotion had roused Beth who looked alarmed, concerned, and yes, pissed off as I left with Rob.

At least, he let me drive and I deliberately chose the AH because it was only about a half mile straight down Hunter. Many glasses of draft ensued. I had a decent beer hum when we got tossed at closing time but, added to whatever he'd consumed earlier, Rob was well and truly shit-faced as he staggered out to the car. He wanted to go out to his cabin way the fuck and gone in the country. I drove back to my apartment instead, and more or less carried him in. He collapsed his lanky frame onto the couch and was loudly snoring in nanoseconds.

So there I was, some forty years later in the same place. Will the circle be unbroken, indeed?

Sometime during the evening, we had apparently agreed to a home and home series. Rob came up to the lake a couple of weeks later. I gave him the tour. That never takes long. Water, Hovel, pine, spruce, whatever the fuck, aaaand done.

"What do you do all day?" he asked, as we settled into the deck chairs.

"Not a helluva lot. And yet somehow, the hours just roll by. Read a little, write a little, tinker or putter around the joint. Oh, and I drink. In the winter I do the same thing only under palm trees."

"Happy?"

"Endlessly."

"Think you got it nailed?"

"For me? Oh, yeah. But happy's a strange word, isn't it? I run the range between contentment and joy. So, on average: happy."

(Sidebar: Subsequent to this smug bit of self-assessment have been several years where the horrendous crimes and cruel deaths I was around dragged down the fucking average. But also, I fell in love with Alexandra which considerably upped the joy quotient).

"As long as you have your health," he said.

"Not a factor. It all ends horribly tomorrow, I'm good with it."

"Maybe," he said.

CHAPTER FOUR

One of the many reasons I love Alexandra is that she—like Beth—is a whole lot nicer than I am. It wasn't just a matter of the little considerate things she'd do or the kindness in her eyes. She took action.

Like the morning in May when I came back from the community bank of mailboxes with a bundle of mostly junk mail. Among the pointless slaughter of trees was a thick envelope from Allstate Insurance. I was going to toss it because I already was in good hands with a local broker and a policy on the car and the Hovel-by-the-Lake that was almost insultingly cheap, such was the value of my earthly possessions.

Alex stopped me. Puzzled, I opened the envelope. It was a policy and a receipt for over $5000 for complete wind and water damage coverage on 111 16th Ave., Indian Rocks Beach, FL 33785.

"You happen to know anything about this, darling?" I asked.

"You said last winter that "we" were building something there, didn't you? Well, this half of the "we" would rather protect that something if a hurricane hits it."

"Fine, but that's a lot of money."

"I have money."

"And now you have a lot less."

"…Not really."

"Oh…"

In our story so far, Alexandra and I—like most people our age—had avoided talking about our individual financial circumstances. I don't really care about how much anybody makes or has (except maybe some of the absurd contracts awarded to a few back-up NFL quarterbacks). Going by her tasteful house in Framingham, her new Prius, and her clothes, she did more than OK for herself.

I live cheaply, mostly because I have to. And that was strictly my choice because I decided in my mid-fifties that I didn't want to write words for somebody else anymore and I didn't want to see snow again. I consider it a victory in financial planning when, at the end of each fiscal year, I have enough left over for a case of beer and maybe half a carton of smokes.

Pretty obvious that Alexandra didn't want to talk about money either. Our conversation faltered, kinda just hung there. The suspense was killing me.

"Babe, I gotta ask you a question—it's a two-parter," I said. "One: do you have enough money to make me a kept man? And two: If yes, what the hell's been holding you back?"

"I really don't want to insult your pride."

"Trust me, I have zero pride. I'm a Toronto Maple Leafs fan *and* a Raider fan."

"Pride or no pride, I don't want *our* place to be a write-off in the next hurricane."

See; that's the kind of nice I was dealing with.

A few days after she and I had ensconced ourselves in the Hovel, I got an e-mail from Steve Golding, a dear buddy of mine and erstwhile crime reporter for the *Toronto Sun*. Steve and I went waaaay back to another time and another universe, when I actually had a job as a public and investor relations guy for a large publicly traded computer services company and he was a business reporter for the *Globe and Mail*. Our friendship had dwindled after Beth died twelve years ago from cervical cancer, only to be rekindled following the murder of my former boss a couple of years back.

We spent a lot of time together after that as he mined me for the inside scoop on my subsequent half-assed investigation of that murder that led to me stumbling upon a worldwide hacking scheme. He got a successful book and a shit-ton of money out of the deal. I got $250,000 from him as thanks, money that I used to buy a fire engine for the beach town in the Dominican Republic where I was wintering at the time.

I had been expecting his e-mail and was surprised only by the few months that he had allowed to pass since I gained some more media notoriety by finding out about a massive defrauding of American tribal casinos, a scheme that also wound up causing a few less-than-accidental deaths.

He wrote: *Hey, slacker! Are you back yet? We should catch up. Quite the publicity whore you're turning into.*

I wrote back: *Good to hear from you, buddy. Lemme guess, you want to again exploit our friendship for profit from another book. Am I close?*

His reply: *Exactly, you infinitive splitter! When's a good time?*

My first choice would be never, I replied. *Second option: Gimme a month. Alexandra is here until the end of May so I'd rather you weren't.*

May was ending. My month with Alexandra had been full of grace and comfort and fun. Sad but true, few people spend much time describing a run of ceaseless good times and still fewer people want to hear about it. In the utter absence of fucking drama or violence and nasty doings, such wonderful days melted into one another and filled me up.

About the only semi-exciting thing that happened during this blessed period of calm and happiness was the beep-beep-sound of a truck backing up in my long driveway. I was mystified. The only truck around the Hovel was Carl's ancient F-150 that I let him keep there and the only sound it made in reverse was a loud backfire -accompanied by a puff of black smoke.

The driver of the large UPS delivery van stopped, got out and walked towards me with his spiffy electronic whatever the fuck device.

"Jake Lydon?" He asked.

I signed the tiny screen with a shaky forefinger, my signature looking like a standard Rorschach test. He slid the door up and we wrestled a very red, very awkward, and very heavy Adirondack chair to the ground. It was made of some kind of resin or plastic.

"Know anything about the Furniture Fairy?" I asked Alex when she came out to watch.

"It's a gift for Carl since I stole his."

"Well, that's sweet. It really is. But I don't think the ungrateful bastard will appreciate it."

"But it's more durable and less rickety than his. And it'll also last longer than he will," she

Said, pleading her logical case.

"It's also red and not wood. Oh, and not *his*."

Not to my complete surprise, Carl was awkwardly quiet when first presented with his present.

"Um…thank you…but you should have it, Alex. It's better than ours…and it…suits you," the backwoods diplomat offered.

Alex took her new red seat, looked at me, and said: "Not a fucking word."

On the morning of the day before Alex left, the phone rang. She answered it, then handing me the receiver, she said "It's Sergeant Les Macgregor from the Peterborough Police."

Uh-oh, I thought. She had announced the call with the same unnice tone she would've used had she just informed me that the Sexually Transmitted Disease Clinic was on the line confirming that my tests were positive.

"Call you right back, Les," I said.

I followed her out onto the deck.

"What is it, Alex?" I asked, knowing damn well what it was.

"You know damn well what it is," she said. The police want you to look at a case. Probably that dead professor of yours."

"Look. I can't *not* talk to them. These people have radar traps… and *guns*. I'll just see what they want. I swear."

I meant it too.

For years, I had been involved with law enforcement—and perhaps surprisingly, mainly not in a felonious way. The cops would, from time to time, ask me to look at a case that had stumped them. For shit money, they'd give me what they had and send me away to obsess over the case. Drawing on my slightly OCD, Asbergian way of looking at things, I could sometimes come up with an answer. Put it this way, I had a much better track record than the fucking mediums and clairvoyants that are sometimes called in.

I owe a debt to the world of moving pictures for a distinct advantage in these half-assed investigations. I watch a lot of films and TV shows. As a result, I find myself constantly making movies in my wee mind. Everybody does it to recall occasions or moments in their lives. I do it too, but I don't restrict myself to clips of things that have happened. I make detailed, feature-length scenarios recorded by dispassionate cameras of events that *might* happen. I would cast the movie, add a stirring musical score, expertly edit it, and shoot it from all sorts of innovative angles that recall later Scorsese or Friedkin at his best. And I am painstaking in ensuring that the fucking script is plausible.

Over the last few years, I personally and unfortunately have also been around enough murder investigations to know what to ask, to know where the holes might be. Even more unfortunately, these have not been purely academic discussions as people around me have died from literal holes.

The cops had the what, the how, and the when of Bromley's murder. As always, the two big questions—the who and the why—were missing. They wouldn't have called me otherwise.

"Les, old sport, just how the Christ are you?"

"Cut the crap, Jake, you couldn't care less how I am."

"Technically, you're right, but how would it be if I started off with 'What the fuck do you want?'"

"Brass told me to call you. Bring you up to speed on the Bromley case. So that's what I'm doing."

"You don't have to sound so goddamned glum about it. You're doing a great job so far."

Les ignored me, as he should've—hell, as most people should—and we got down to business.

"What do you know about the Bromley murder?" he asked.

"I read a bunch. Pretty much everything's that's out there. Tell me what you got."

"Not much more than that. We're stuck."

"No kidding. Who the fuck ever murders an English professor? Maybe if he taught Victorian literature, he'd have it coming. But Bromley didn't. Any kind of motive yet?"

"We had to look at robbery."

"Who the fuck drives ten miles out of town to lie in wait just to mug and murder an underpaid prof? Wallet?"

"Looks untouched. Twenty-five bucks, one credit card."

"What did he drive?"

"2008 Corolla."

"Who the fuck ever carjacks a 14-year-old Toyota?"

"Any more than there's a widespread car theft ring boosting—what do you own, Jake?—fifteen-year-old Pontiac Vibes."

"Sixteen and that's different. Mine's an American classic, worth a shitload soon," I said to his jab at my automotive choice. "What about his bank records?"

"Nothing sticks out. But geez, they don't pay them much."

"Did he have money from any other source?"

"Not that we can see."

"I remember Bromley as a guy who sniffled a lot. Do you know if he was still sniffling?"

"There might be something there. Autopsy found a trace amount of cocaine in his system. He had a stash in his townhouse."

"How big a stash?"

"Not big. Maybe fifty bucks' worth."

"So you don't suspect him as the major cocaine king of Peterborough and environs?"

"No."

"His snorting fits. He used to make a big deal about coke and opium being part of the decadent Paris scene in the 1900s. But if he was a committed cokehead, he'd be pretty fucked up after fifty or so years of dedicated usage. You could probably drive a truck up his nose, his heart would be messed up, so would all his other organs. You find any of that at the autopsy?"

"No again."

"So let's bet he was still just a dabbler. Did those bank records tell you anything about the debits?"

"Nothing. Cash withdrawal, a hundred bucks a week like clockwork for the last ten years."

"Know who was selling to him?"

"We have an idea."

"Might be worth a chat. Maybe he owed a couple of hundred dollars. No telling what dealers might do for a few bucks these days. But pending your chat with his supplier, I think we can rule out the money angle. What about relationships, although there probably aren't many eighty-year-old English professors involved in murderous love triangles?"

"Lived alone. Wife died five years ago. Dementia. Three kids scattered to hell and gone. None of them came back for his funeral."

"Alrighty then, did his computer or papers tell you anything?"

"Looks like the password died with him. We can't get a court order to crack it open. No grounds. As for his paperwork, you're gonna need a fuckin' army of librarians to go through it all. You want to try?"

"Are you telling me I have to?"

"No, but—"

"—So you're telling me I have to do this?" I cut in.

"Jake, I just said no. We don't have the—"

"—For Christ's sake, Les! Just order me do it, will ya?"

"Fine! Consider yourself ordered."

"Thank you, boss."

"Fuck, you're strange."

"So I can get a key?"

"It'll be at the front desk. But you better hurry. We understand a son, living in Australia, is coming to clear the place out and sell it."

"Got it. Now tell me about the murder. How'd he die?"

"Five stab wounds from behind, four below the rib cage. Killer really moved the blade around, tore up the intestines, liver and a kidney pretty bad."

"Still, that's a slow death."

"Except for the fifth stab. Into the heart."

"From behind?"

"Yes."

"End of March, still pretty cold. So Bromley must've had a coat to get through as well. Jesus, that's a long knife. And, Jesus, that'd take some force."

"At least ten inches we think, probably longer. Thin and narrow. Sharp too."

"What, like a BBQ skewer?"

"Yeah, maybe. But how do you grip one of those?"

"I hear you. Anything on the killer? Height? Gender? Footprints?"

"Nothing. They don't have CCTV on that lot. It was pretty warm, so any snow had melted; sidewalk was dry, just a few puddles in the parking lot. There's a pretty wide arc for the first wound that went straight in. It all depends on how far away from the deceased the guy was standing, so we can't calculate height. We figure that one brought the professor to his knees. The next four had a slight downward entry which meant the killer had to bend over to thrust. No way of knowing how far."

"You said 'guy.' Could a woman have done it?"

"Maybe. Coroner said the blade that sharp would've gone in pretty easy. But that kinda of violence is rare for them."

"Let me have a think, Les. I'll get back to you."

Something occurred to me.

"Wait a minute. Did he have a cellphone on him?" I asked.

"No. He didn't own one."

"Sure?"

"No account we could find. Why'd you ask?"

"I can't understand what the hell was he doing out on campus."

"You might've missed this part, Jake, but he was a university English professor; he was out at the university professing English."

Ol' Les pounced on that one, like I had just served him up a lob ball.

"That's really funny, Les," I said. "Look, and maybe you missed this, but he really hated going out there. Ever. All that concrete and straight lines and standard furniture really bugged the hell out of him. Can't imagine he would've changed his mind over the years with even more of that shit out there now. He used to hold his seminars in his living room in town. Bethune Street, if I re-member. Like I said, maybe you didn't know any of that."

"So what?" was his clever retort after a pause.

"So what? So you know that with no cell phone nobody could've tracked him through GPS, and if it was rare-to-never that he'd hold seminars on main campus, then why was he out there? But more importantly, how did anyone know he was? Bet you someone in his class might have an idea."

"We talked to them all."

"Did you ask them that specifically?"

"No."

"Then maybe you ought to go have another chat."

"OK, Chief. Any fucking thing else you want to tell me to do?" Les said with exaggerated sarcasm.

"Give me a minute; I'll think of something—"

I was going to suggest checking the office coffee supply, but he'd already hung up. I smiled. Pissing off Les was one of my little life pleasures. He was an OK guy, but he really resented me being anywhere near their cases. He took it as an insult to his depart-ment. Which it kinda was.

I grabbed another beer and rejoined Alex on the deck, catch-ing the last bit of sunset.

"Ya know, Alex, I could get used to this sleuthing by phone."

"So could I." she said as we clinked bottle to wine glass. "Let's hope it lasts," she added.

Alexandra had set her work scheduling clock to snooze for one month. June 1 on the nose, she had a Sunday flight back to Boston, to be in her office early Monday.

I was only partially depressed over her departure because my time without her would be limited. Sucker for punishment, she wanted to come back for the month of July. Sucker for a great time, I was elated.

It felt odd driving her to Toronto. Before this, there had always been quick departures, me leaving her or vice versa on the steps of our homes. This was the long good-bye.

She always had a slightly disgusted look whenever she was in the Vibe. Not that I entirely blamed her. It had to be difficult for her to overlook the cigarette stench, burns in the upholstery, and a fine Pompeii-type dusting of ash everywhere. The car—like its owner—rattled. Over the years—like its owner—it had lost what little power it once had. Unless it was heading downhill on a steep incline and had a gale-force wind at its back, the Vibe couldn't pass a tractor pulling an overloaded hay wagon.

Mercifully, Alex was never in it for long. Jaunts to a couple of local antique stores. Dinner at the Buckhorn Lodge ten minutes away. A couple of half-hour trips to Peterborough to raid the Canadian Tire garden centre. But two hours running back to Toronto gave her plenty of time to be disgusted.

"It's making funny noises," she said, like that was somehow my fault.

"It *always* makes funny noises. Just turn the radio up. That's what I do."

"You be careful," was the last thing she said to me standing beside the car in the unloading zone. "And I don't just mean when you're driving this."

"Got it."

Driving back, I didn't regret keeping my police "assignment" from her. What's the worst that could happen to me reading the papers of a dead English professor? Serial paper cuts?

CHAPTER FIVE

But I didn't get to Bromley's archives right away. He wasn't writing anymore, or doing much of anything else for that matter, so the urgency just wasn't there. Plus, I had a bunch of things to do.

First off, I had to deal with Steve Golding. Predictably, he'd respected my wishes and left me the fuck alone for May but, just as predictably, he'd sent a note early on June 1 wanting a get-together.

There was no good way to avoid him. He was a friend and I'd already set precedent by helping him with his first book, filling in the details that no newspaper story or magazine piece had. But I didn't really want to co-operate this time. Yes, the shitshow of the previous winter had many of the same elements: an unexplained death, a widening circle that eventually encompassed large-scale criminality involving gobs of money, a few additional murders, and some very bad people who got caught. Oh, and yours truly was in the mix. This time it was different, way too personal. One of those deaths was my father's and one of the other deaths, I had caused.

Reluctantly, I told him to come up the following weekend.

In the meantime, I had to return to my GP on a call-back after the routine check-up I'd had before Alex left. Usually, Doctor Dan would just phone me after he'd received the results of my blood tests to harangue me about my diabetes control and my general state of disrepair. This time he demanded to see me and there was no hint of fucking around in his voice.

I sat in an examination room picking at the paper shield on the table. Dr. Dan breezed in, file folder in hand, grim expression on face.

"I'm not going to sugarcoat this, Jake."

"Well that's good to hear, Doc. I'm a diabetic, you know."

Normally, that tremendously witty remark would've earned me at least a polite smile. Not this time.

"You are declining quickly," he announced. "Something has to change or you're either going to go blind, have a heart attack or start losing fingers and toes. Or all three."

Nary a trace of sucrose with that diagnosis. My diabetes had worsened as progressive diseases tend to do. I had hurried its progress along by only occasionally taking my meds over the last six months, eating shit food, and resisting any form of exercise until a month ago.

I attempted to explain all the events that had transpired to prevent me from living the good life. He cut me off.

"Jake, this is a doctor's office, not a damn courtroom! You can't argue your way out of this!"

"Alright," I said, suitably chastened. "What next?"

"To start, I'm adding insulin to your metformin. You're going to monitor your glucose levels regularly. And we need to see where we stand with everything else so I'm ordering a series of tests."

"Do I have to study?"

That brought a slight smile that disappeared quickly.

"And Jake, if you don't make it to these appointments, you can find yourself another doctor. I have a waiting list of people needing a doctor whom they just might listen to."

I walked out of there, feeling pretty morose.

But what the fuck did I think was going to happen?

That was the question I asked myself several times sitting and smoking in the Vibe outside Dr. Dan's office.

The pointlessness of repetitive rhetorical questions aside, I had no good answer.

What I did have was a sheaf of referrals to specialists to find out what the hell was going on inside my sack of flesh and bone. I was due to have, in short order—a colonoscopy, a lung cancer screening, an eye exam, and a stress test.

Of course my unhealthy ways had to catch up with me. As I do with most things, I had procrastinated—in this case, for decades. The main issue as I see it is self-perception. In my mind I have been perpetually eighteen since I was about thirteen. Consequently, any damage I did—a pulled muscle, a twisted ankle, a killer hangover—used to heal quickly. And I had never given a second's thought to my internal workings or what I put in there to either fuel or impair them. But now, with about half a century of willful neglect and abuse tacked on, the toll was getting painfully obvious.

The depressing part was, walking into Dr. Dan's clutches, I had been feeling pretty good about myself. I had dropped about ten pounds since my return to Canada a month earlier. Although at the time I thought I'd never forgive her, Alex had roped me into walking more, playing tennis at least once a week and canoeing—once I gave up trying to attach an outboard motor to the pointy stern. It's not like Alex had been a drill sergeant whipping me into shape (she's smart enough to know that ain't gonna work). But I did feel and look better. Yes, I am that vain—although not so vain as to think that song is about me.

She also took over the cooking. There's nothing sexist in this, so relax, people. It was a matter of survival for her. My culinary skills are limited to French toast, grilled cheese, frozen pizza, French fries and gravy, Eggos, and some form of dead cow on the BBQ. I have zero interest in expanding my repertoire. OK, maybe beans n' weenies. I do not count sandwich-making as that's more like IKEA-type assembly than cooking.

Previously, my vegetable intake had been limited to tomatoes, garlic, and onions. And let's not forget potatoes—usually restricted to two kinds: barbeque chips and French fries. But, hey, a vegetable is a vegetable, right? Oh, and what about the eleven different herbs and spices that go into the secret coating on KFC chicken? Health news flash: all eleven are vegetables!

All the other vegetables and I have a hate-hate relationship. Armed with absolutely no expertise in biology or nutrition—or even a rudimentary understanding of either—I have become completely convinced that there is not a thing of value in green things that grow. Rather, we've become increasingly victimized by the powerful vegetable cartel. OK, OK, the rabbit-oriented foods have some value because they take up space in your stomach that otherwise should be occupied by real food—like hamburgers and fries.

The problem with all this focus on self is that it makes you concentrate on the whole package of your physical being, as if it really fucking matters much at my age what I look like. A sideview in the mirror of my beer belly proved beyond any doubt that my six-pack had long ago morphed into a keg.

I don't just have bags under my eyes, I've got a whole goddamned set of American Tourister luggage. Why wasn't I told that smoking, near-constant exposure to the sun, and irregular sleep patterns had a disfiguring effect?

I am dismayed at the lines—crevasses really—around what is fast becoming my turkey neck. They show up most on those rare occasions when I shave. As I pass the razor around my budding wattles, the shaving cream fills the wrinkles like caulking or Bondo on a battered old Chev.

Then you swing into full hypochondriacal mode, imagining all the terrible things going on inside your aging body. That new brown spot on the back of your hand? Cancer! What about that pain in your chest that you've had for twenty minutes? Stroke! And you can't remember the name of Uriah Heep's lead singer or the capitol of South Dakota? Early onset Alzheimer's!

If you want to feel like an old junkie, may I recommend a two-step program: 1) get diabetes and 2) start injecting insulin. First, there's the drawing of the wonder drug from the little glass bottle, then sticking that needle in my guts once a day and another one in my finger twice a day to measure my blood sugar level.

It didn't take me long to get stubborn about the recommended regime. I refused to bend to the will of the single-use syringe cartel. I discovered I could get upwards of thirty shots out of one needle. It did, I admit, get a bit ouchy near the end as the point had dulled trying to pierce my leathery hide.

After my sad bodily inventory, I did the thing I always do: vow to undertake a rigid regime of self-improvement. And as I always do, I ignored it.

CHAPTER SIX

The day after Alex left, I got an e-mail from Rob Byford.

He asked if I wanted to be his Plus One for Clayton Thompson's sold-out second public lecture as Trent's newest writer-in-residence that was to take place four days later.

I was delighted, mostly because Rob had obviously stayed in Peterborough after his retirement party three years earlier which was the last time I saw him.

I accepted. In my reply to him, I also felt compelled to note that Ted Bromley's death was a bitch and that I thought we could talk about it.

I hadn't exactly been keeping tabs on Thompson, Trent's most famous—or notorious—alumnus (Class of 03) who had eclipsed—sadly—even swell novelist Yann Martel and master mystery writer Linwood Barclay in the home-grown fame department. I didn't know much about Thompson beyond the fact that he had been something of a media superstar for a while as the latest in an apparently endless string of pop psychologists who, for a price, will tell you how to live your fucking life.

I knew that it had been quite the coup to land Thompson as writer-in-residence, although this pride may have been somewhat like being pleased as punch with signing the twelfth version of Foreigner to play your county fair. Thompson's star had skyrocketed to the zenith—thanks to the success of his first book and a bunch of swell articles after a few of his lectures at Rutgers had gone viral. But I had also heard that his star had dimmed considerably.

Thompson had joined—and maybe tarnished—a long list of illustrious writers-in-residence at little ol' Trent, chief of whom in my books—see what I just did there?—was Margaret Laurence. She had written what I believe is the finest novel in Canadian literature. *The Stone Angel.*

In that literary star-fucker way I have, I was tickled to meet her briefly several times at faculty gatherings I had been invited to. She had moved to the area in the mid-seventies completing her last novel in the quaint-as-hell little town of Lakefield about ten minutes north of the campus. True to its billing, Lakefield had been built on a field near a lake (actually a bulge in the Otonabee River, the same river that then flowed lazily south through the university).

A couple of years after I left Peterborough, Laurence was elected/appointed Chancellor of Trent, a job she held for three years. I assumed that chancelloring wasn't a full-time gig, but she obviously liked the place—both the university and her home upstream from it. That affection only lasted for a while. At the age of 60, she killed herself in that home—bravely I thought—after a terminal lung cancer diagnosis.

In my MA year at Queens, I saw her again and couldn't resist more or less blurting out that *The Stone Angel* was going to be central to the premise of my thesis but that I didn't want to talk to her about it. She patted my hand and said:

"Thank you, dear boy." (This was back when I was both a boy and dear as fuck).

So let's find out some things about the latest writer-in-residence, shall we? I fucked away a good part of two rainy chilly days burrowing down any number of internet rabbit holes.

As per usual, Wikipedia was my starting point for a few facts. I never question their basics. If his entry had said 'Born 1597 in Genoa,' then, OK, *maybe* it's unreliable, but it read 'Born 1983 in Ottawa.' Ottawa public school system, then Honours BA in Philosophy (my, my, *not* psychology) from Trent, MA from McGill, PhD in Edinburgh. Associate Professor at first, Brown, then Rutgers. 'Single (Divorced). One brother (chemical engineer) and one sister (career public servant'). While obviously educated, nothing stood out until his taped lectures started to get e-passed around like a bong on 4/20.

It was these live performances that first propelled him into the twittersphere. His taped lectures from Rutgers University attracted notice by some people who posted and shared, posted and shared—because that's what everybody fucking does these days instead of having an original goddamned thought or opinion—and soon he was anointed by social media as their next darling. Millions of viewings, hundreds of thousands of 'likes' soon followed.

I watched a couple of Thompson's early videos. Fuck, he was good, a natural-born showman. The Mick Jagger of the philosophy set. And like Jagger in the early years—think Sir Mick circa 1964 (the earliest film of the Stones on a US television show—*The Red Skelton Hour*). Mick's on a small stage crowded by the lads and you could see the camera struggling to contain him. Likewise, Thompson seemed to be forcing himself to stay in one place, within range of the Rutgers single fixed camera. His stage voice was deep, emotional, and he played it loud.

Pretty easy to see that there wouldn't be any students dozing off in his lectures. He was bursting with energy, keen to make his points. With an enthusiasm that bordered on zealotry, he exhorted you, me, everybody in the goddamned developed world to smarten the fuck up and en masse change the way we all lived. He laced his lectures with supporting references from philosophers long dead who echoed what he was talking about, the way we all choose lines from songs or movies that state our point of view, only better than we could say it.

This was not a guy interested in quiet, thoughtful academic discussion; this was a rabble-rousing revivalist preacher intent on putting philosophy into action.

And once internet-famous, the inevitable talk show circuit followed. I e-dug up some of his early interviews. Here, I will belabour the Jagger comparison. Like Mick, he didn't seem at all like the same person that he was on stage. Confident, yes, but quiet, polite, and well-spoken. Thompson seemed almost embarrassed or befuddled by his celebrity.

Then, of course, the big book deal followed. Much fanfare resulted from the seven-figure advance given him by Jameson & Lord, the winning publisher of the bidding war.

Sidebar: I know something of these seven-figure deals. Coincidentally, $6.99 was the moo-la my regional publisher laid out for my diner breakfast (with bacon *and* sausage, I'll have you know) when I signed my deal for *On the Rails*.

Not content to spend his time toiling away at Rutgers over the deeper meaning of Descartes' grocery lists or wading into the fiery "Was Bertram Russell a dick or what?" debates, Clayton Thompson had written a slim volume that was half-fictional parable and half-moral treatise about how we ought to live.

Here's a quick summary of the plot line for *The Returning* and stop me if you've heard this one before: a country boy, intent on escaping both boyhood and the country, confidently heads to the big city in search of fame, money, and excitement. He finds none of those things and, after years of trying, he elects to return to his pastoral origins, thoroughly impoverished, beaten, and humiliated. At the end of each chapter, Thompson inserted an analysis of how and why his fictional hero was fucking up and then later, as he sees the value of country life, more philosophical references to what and how he was learning.

The book followed the well-worn path—hell, it was a superhighway—about the evils of urban living, the trap of hubris and self-delusion leading to an inevitable crash, then finding the strength to recover and start all over again, becoming wiser and more content.

Sidebar: Looks like people are buying these books but not paying attention to them, as big cities continue to get bigger.

I took a chance and next day went to the Buckhorn thrift shop, the kind of place where the works of gurus-du-jour go to die. I bought the book second-hand for a buck and read it in one sitting—enviously I concede—because Thompson had sold millions by this point. It wasn't just the sales figures that were jealousy-inducing. There were passages—sometimes just a sentence or a phrase that—much to my utter surprise—absolutely blew me away. Sparkling metaphors, poetic and evocative similes, astonishing descriptive bits that made the scenes come alive. His writing did what good writing is supposed to do: make you smile, move you, drag you into the story, and make you feel and perhaps actually *be* a better person for having read it.

These narrative sections struck me as completely stand-alone. You could hack out the ten or so pages of simplistic preachy bullshit after every chapter and have a really fine book that would make every point the sermonizing tried to do but without using a fucking sledgehammer. Who knew a philosophy major could write like that?

As much as I wanted to believe that the powerful writing had drawn the crowd in, it was pretty clear that his megaphone messaging held the most appeal. Although more than one reviewer commented that without the great narrative, the message-y bits wouldn't be so effective.

Sales of *The Returning - A Guide to a Simple Rewarding Life and True Freedom*, jet-assisted by a PR push and gushing celebrity endorsements, took off, blasting to the top of best-seller lists and staying in orbit up there for months. There were just under a billion reprintings.

A surprise money generator was Thompson's misplaced adoption by far-right-wing groups. They championed his "values" of family, faith, and country while ignoring Thompson's pleas for kindness, racial tolerance, and his obvious avoidance of identifying the Christian god. Same way the flag-huggers more than thirty-five years ago tried to adopt the chorus of *Born in the USA* as a patriotic anthem while conveniently skipping over the Boss' verses with their tale of a poor, disillusioned, and shattered Viet-Nam vet.

In earlier interviews, Thompson made some attempt to disavow the fan support from the extreme right but later, as the publishing juggernaut revved up, he shrugged it off, skillfully evading the questions.

I could see why. It was a real simple equation: more fans = more book sales + more speaking engagements = more money. He had a direct interest in making that happen. I assumed, at the very least, his publisher and his agent—because they too stood to make out like literary bandits—would be telling him not to piss off the guns, God and flag crowd.

Mercantile motive aside, I bet that Thompson, like every other writer, had another simple goal: he wanted as many people as possible to read what he had written.

The intolerant left took note of the intolerant right's approval. At universities across the north-east US and a few in Canada and Britain, demonstrations were held protesting his appearance at their hallowed halls of learning that ought not to be sullied by a hero of *those* people. Thompson and his publisher fought for the right to be there. Freedom of speech issue? Sure. But freedom of business also figured in. The resulting controversy—fanned by uninformed media sources—goosed sales some more as people bought the book just to see what all the hubbub was about.

It wasn't the first time a good old-fashioned scandal was a business asset. After a Massachusetts library removed *Huckleberry Finn* from its shelves, Mark Twain gleefully wrote to tell his publisher that "they have expelled Huck from their library as 'trash suitable only for the slums.' That will sell 25,000 copies for us for sure."

Thompson took his show on the road like a one-man band touring behind a new album release, playing to bigger and bigger sold-out halls and auditoriums. His speaking fee was rumoured to be in the 100K dollar-a-gig range. His personal take had to be huge because his overhead was so low. He didn't have to pay an army of roadies, sound and light guys, semi-tractor trailers full of equipment and staging. Just him, a microphone, a few spotlights, couple of cameras, and a projection screen behind him.

All that fame, all those riches probably started their decline about a year earlier. Einstein had called the shot decades before: For every action, there is an equal and opposite reaction. The critics had piled on. Scholars decried his betrayal of the "Queen of Sciences," with his simple, nuance-free pronouncements. Both the left- and right-wing commentators grew tired of him, deciding that his position, while admirable, was childish and unrealistic. A second wave—the muckrakers—moved in, unearthing rumours disguised as fact. His dissolved marriage was a nasty affair, they said. He had an opioid addiction, they said. A Rutgers undergraduate asserted that he had been "inappropriate" while declining to give details or be identified. All in all, a media firestorm had engulfed him and badly singed if not burned his career to the ground.

I went back to the joint press release from his publisher and
Trent announcing Thompson's writer-in-residency. It was an odd
mixture of messages. Trent expressed its delight at welcoming a
native son's triumphant return while the publisher claimed that
Thompson was exhausted from his hectic schedule and from
being hounded by outrageous lies. He needed to "re-calibrate,"
while he worked on his long-awaited and sure to be bestselling
follow-up to *The Returning*.

Net-net, it struck me that Thompson was taking his own goddamned advice to slow the fuck down. Trent would be the perfect
place for a layover, although personally I would've chosen a place
bristling with palm trees and tiki-bars.

I was primed for all things Clayton Thompson as I waited for
Rob at the small box office at the Wenjack Theatre.

Rob showed up just before Thompson was supposed to go on.
I was alarmed as Rob walked towards me. Gone was his energet-
ic stride; he was almost shuffling. It looked like he'd lost a lot of
weight and his face was drawn and sallow. Sure, he was pushing
seventy, but this was too big a difference from his appearance just
three years earlier when I saw him last.

"Good to see you, bud," I said. "Are you OK?"

"Yeah, fine. Just getting over a really bad flu; kicked the crap
out of me."

There was no time for chit-chat about Thompson—or Ted
Bromley—as the lobby lights dimmed and we took our seats in
the packed-to-the-rafters auditorium. I had no idea what we were
about to see. I wondered if Thompson would pull a Guns n' Roses
and keep everybody waiting for hours.

But he punctually came out to a warm—actually a red-hot—
welcome. He was resplendent in the now-mandatory black fucking everything—shoes, jeans, T-shirt and jacket—as he took his

position in the single spotlight.

That night at Trent, the wide stage of the auditorium was his—completely his—as he stalked and prowled and shimmied with his every movement projected on a big screen behind him, two cameras alternating between long shots of Thompson moving around, energetically waving his arms, and close-ups, his eyes blazing, his face drenched in sweat, while he played a medley of his greatest hit, with the same phrases, the same delivery I'd seen in at least a half-dozen videos. But no one could miss the fact that the boy was workin.' And the crowd rewarded him with a thunderous standing 'O' that I took to be at least partially as the result of hometown pride.

In show biz parlance, Clayton Thompson killed that night.

I waited a bit as Rob was trying to yank me from seat to go backstage (full-access pass!). I wanted to see if pop philosophers gave encores or if the crowd would start swaying, holding their Bic lighters aloft. FYI: neither happened.

And what did he actually say? Oh, that. For an hour and a half, not much. There was little of the poetry in the book and a lot of the sermonizing about how one *should* live his or her life. There was that trigger word for me again: *should.* So, I kinda tuned out in the same way you don't really give a shit what Celine Dion or Michael Jackson actually sing about; you enjoy the show, mostly for its dazzlingly high production values.

Homilies, bromides, mottos, coherently strung together and decorated by supporting quotes from Thoreau, Emerson, Aristotle, Russell, and Milne. Utterly confident and forcefully persuasive, although—given his plain-as-the-nose-on-your-face material—he didn't have to do much persuading. Arguing against his "Slow the fuck down and live more simply" credo would be like protesting the goddamned fact that the sun rises in the east or that *Jaws 4* really, *really* sucked.

We made our way backstage. No sign of Jack Daniels bottles, silver trays with lines of coke, pretty, young groupies or even bowls of M&Ms with the brown ones picked out. Instead, there were little clutches of academics sipping wine from plastic glasses and munching on crudités, that simplest, cheapest, and most repulsive member of the hors d'oeuvre family. One or two platters of pigs-in-a-blanket could've saved the evening for me.

Flu-bitten, but ever-gregarious, Rob seemed to know everybody, bopping between small groups of what I assumed were mostly Trent faculty members. Rob had told me the Thompson PR machine had comped every English and Philosophy faculty member.

He steered me towards two people that didn't seem to belong to the corduroy and tweed set.

Patricia Morland was Thompson's agent. I knew her, although not so's she'd recognize me. I knew her from the fuck-off letter she'd sent me years ago in reply to my request that she represent me with my first—and so far, only—finished novel.

A tall, very attractive, and sturdy brunette, she was immaculately dressed in an oh-so tailored and crisp dark blue business suit. Her hair and make-up were perfect. She exuded confidence and style.

Next in Rob's unofficial receiving line was Daniel Truscott, the relatively new Chairman of Jameson & Lord Publishing. No rumpled, pipe-ash-sprinkled academic type he. Trim, longish silver hair, and in his late 50s, he wore a classy dark grey suit and looked like he was coming to or had just left a corporate boardroom or annual meeting.

It was a two-for-one kinda evening because I knew Truscott too. He had also told me to fuck off some months after I sent him a query letter and sample chapters of *On the Rails*.

A lesser man would have been stewing in his own bitter bile meeting his rejectors in person.

Turns out, I'm a lesser man.

As I was stewing away, Rob was busy pointing out to them how they had fucked up big time by blowing me off years earlier.

They—predictably—inched away with frozen smiles.

"Thanks for the cheerleading, Rob," I said, "but what the fuck were you doing? Think they were going to fall on their knees and beg my forgiveness? Cut me a big fucking advance cheque on the spot?"

"Remember that shit you used to pull with me?" he asked.

"What shit?"

"Oh, come on. You'd always accost me after every grade that I gave you for a paper or a seminar and, no matter how high the mark, you'd tell me that it deserved a higher one, that I hadn't read or listened to it closely enough."

"Oh, *that* shit."

"Did you send the first book to them?"

"Yup."

"Are you writing another book?"

"Yup again."

"Is it as good as the first?"

"Better."

"Well, maybe that pair will be a little more receptive next time out."

"So that shit I pulled, as you so elegantly put it, worked back then?"

"I didn't think so; it was so obvious. But I went back over the marks I gave you during the year and damned if they didn't go up."

"Don't be hard on yourself for falling for it," I said. "I thought you just got better as a teacher."

"I'm glad to see you're still an arsehole, to quote Chaucer."

"I think I owe you a beer."

"Tough darts, laddie," Rob said. "I checked it out; you get red or white."

"Both, and I'll get it," I said, spying the wine bar.

I asked the bartender for a tray; he declined. I asked for white wine. He told me they were out just as Clayton Thompson with a much younger woman took their place beside me.

"Good show tonight, buddy," I said. "On behalf of all the alumni, let me congratulate you on your personal returning to Trent."

"Ah, thank you. You are…?"

"Jake Lydon," I said, extending my hand. "Class of…class of way the fuck before you went here."

He smiled but our handshake was not consummated as the pretty young woman accompanying him pushed a wine glass into his hand.

"Oh…this is Jan Morris, my…my publicist," he said with the slightest tinge of embarrassment. "Jan, this is Jake Lydon,"

Our introduction was also not completed.

"Come, Clay," Jan Morris said, briefly regarding me like somebody spotting a mouse scurrying into a corner of the kitchen. "That Fraser fellow from the *Globe* wants a one-on-one."

And they were off. I was left with two glasses of cheap red wine and the first impression that Thompson was a decent lad, or, at the very least, a polite one.

That's what I said to Rob as I gave him his glass of Chateau du Plonk.

"He is. I had in my D.H class. But a bit simple."

"How so?"

"He must've been bitten by a nuance when he was a child, because he scrupulously avoided anything like that."

"Good writer though?

"Average writer, so he stood out in my class of fucking terrible writers."

"Whaddja think of the show?"

"Meh," he said, shrugging. "Pretty well the same stuff I heard last time."

"The last time?"

"March. His first lecture after he got here. I just hope the evening goes better this time."

"What do you mean?"

"That's the night Ted was killed."

Fearful of cop stops and wicked tannin hangovers, I wasn't about to get shit-hammered on lousy red wine.

"C'mon, Rob; let's leave the cars here and take a cab downtown. I need beer!"

"Gonna have to pass, sport. I still feel like shit."

I didn't try to persuade him otherwise. He looked like shit too.

"Jake, what you said about your new book being better than the first one...."

"Yeah?"

"Prove it. Send me something."

Driving home, I thought about the evening and about Thompson's success with the crowd. On the whole, I had to hand it to him. If his slick presentation and obvious talent as a performer had caused some people, maybe a lot of people, to slow the fuck down and live more simply, then that was a good thing, right?

As happens, a weird connection in my wee brain kicked in, this from my high school Latin class. After we had progressed past "*Semper ubi sub ubi*," this sentence stuck in my mind: "*Exitus acta probat*"—"The result justifies the deed." Ovid jotted that gem down around the time Christ was being born. Later, it was slightly altered by Machiavelli to "The end justifies the means." That same wee brain noted that the pair of them—separated by a millennium and half—was famous enough to operate with solo names, just like Beyonce or Bono (the Irish one, not the Sonny dude).

Another thing stood out for me. Just one fact from Rob that went a distance in clearing up—and also confounding me about Ted Bromley's murder. Was it too much of a coincidence that he died on the one night Clayton Thompson was packing 'em in? The confounding part: if the two events were connected, how?

And a more logistical question: why was Bromley parked way the fuck and gone on one side of the river when the Thompson Show was going on across the river at the Wenjack Theatre?

CHAPTER SEVEN

I sat in the Vibe furiously smoking in the hospital parking lot while I awaited the results from the lung cancer screening I'd just had, a marvelous program for us long-term smokers who are still alive. I wasn't expecting good news. But then again, I never expect good news. Preparing for the worst was a plus in my former PR biz, but in real life, not so much.

A no-nonsense nurse ushered me into a small conference room, handed me a folder, then left.

The folder had all sorts of literature about what a fucking moron I was being by still smoking—like I needed reminding. One pamphlet broke down the general groups of results that I was about to get. Basically, there were four: 1) You're fuckin' lucky, buddy, 2) Not bad but come back every year for testing, 3) We're worried and you should be too, and 4) What are you doing tomorrow cuz that's when your chemo starts?

The suspense was killing me, well before the cigarettes did.

The nurse came back and opted to prolong the agony of anticipation by making me wait through a verbal lecture about how I was, as Vonnegut put it "slowly committing suicide by cigarette."

At this point, I was dying for a butt.

The envelope, please.

She seemed pissed off to tell me that I was firmly ensconced in Group 1. My breathing bags were completely clear.

Elated, I, more or less, floated out of the hospital and sat in the Vibe to consider my good news. I had two plain choices in front of me. Quit while you're ahead, Jake or, you lucky fuck, maybe you'll always be clean, so why stop? I needed more time to deliberate over my options, I thought, as I lit up and drove away.

In short order, I had an eye exam, the first, Dr. Dan told me, of what better fucking be an annual event. No diabetic retinal damage. Yay!

Up next was a colonoscopy. Gosh, that was less than fun, particularly the cleansing ritual beforehand. But the ass-cam revealed no polyps. Yay again, although I was disappointed the technician wouldn't cut me a copy of the film footage or even a wallet-size still photo to trot out when somebody accused me of being full of shit.

Last up was a stress test. Huffing and puffing, l came away with a renewed loathing of treadmills and a workable theory that hamsters' short lifespans were due to their mass suicides. I was also grateful to be spending half the year in dead-flat Florida where the only inclines I might face would be on the ramps in shopping malls.

Dr. Dan called me with the results. Clear sailing through all veins and arteries. Yay, once more. My sterling results were likely due only to Alexandra's insistence that we spend most of May walking, for Christ sakes, so I was ready for the ever-inclining treadmill.

My joy over my test results was tempered slightly by the cost of all the extra drugs the doc wanted coursing through my veins. That's an out-of-pocket expense until I turn sixty-five at which time the government pays them and also gives you money just for being old. Ironic doncha think, that the two things you really wanted as a teenager—cash and drugs—arrive free when you officially become an old fart.

In between my tour stops of the Canadian medical system, Steve showed up, eager to get my take on the shitstorm of the past winter. He arrived with pages of questions and two cases of beer. He had, I knew, resumed drinking again, "But no high-test," he claimed. Cynical bastard that I am, I also assumed that beyond two friends pounding ales, the beer-y supply was meant to loosen my tongue. Reporters know that an interview subject is more likely to yak away when they're half-cut.

"How do you want to start?" I asked, looking at him looking at his page of notes.

"I begin asking; you begin answering," he said. "That's the way these sorts of things go."

"OK but first, you answer some of my questions."

"Shoot."

"Is this on spec?"

"No. It's a done deal; publisher loved the pitch."

"You get an advance?"

"Yes."

"How much?"

"Why does that matter?"

"Lets me know how keen your publisher is. You made a shit-ton of money for them last time. I'm betting they know you'll do it again."

"Two hundred thousand."

"Wowza! Include a movie?"

"Or maybe a TV series, but that's separate, yet to be negotiated. The option on the book is also a done deal. And I get first crack at writing the treatment."

"What's you're deadline?"

"End of July."

"If I could, I'd be whistling right now. Tight deadline, a lot of dough. I'd say the heat is on, buddy-boy."

"I can handle it. I go on sabbatical first of July."

"I'd also say you got a lot riding on the next couple days. A casual observer might think you really, *really* need me."

"Yeah, except that…"

"Except what?"

"The book's about two-thirds done."

"Oh….How'd you manage that?"

"You'd be amazed how much shit was written about this caper…and you. From the strangest places. Florence, Oregon? Tulsa, Oklahoma? I gather you haven't been following your press clippings."

I hadn't. What could I possibly care about the verbiage piling up as arrests were still being announced across the U.S. as a result of exposing all the moving parts? Why would I spend a second of my ever-dwindling life reading about what I had just lived through?

"So, what do you need me for?" I asked.

"I've got names," And here he rhymed off the people in different places who'd played a role—sometimes a life-saving role—in the way things turned out like they did.

"You've called them?"

"Yup, I've reached out."

"Which means they don't want to talk."

"I've got a cop in Oregon and an FBI agent in Tulsa who both agreed to giving me off the record deep background. That's all. So that's where you'd come in. They don't know me. You could help smooth the way to getting them to talk."

"By telling them you're just half a notch above a celebrity-stalking paparazzi who's out to make a quick buck no matter who you have to hurt with all the shit you make up?"

"I was hoping you'd be a bit more complimentary."

"Sorry. Not gonna do it, bud."

"What?"

"They all would have their reasons for staying quiet. I'm not going to try to change their minds. That's up to you."

I was suddenly seized by the desire to yank Steve's chain a bit.

"You know, bud," I said, "Now that I think about all the shit that just happened, I'm starting to realize that maybe I should write a book."

"What?!"

"To be fair, you know I write pretty well and have a pretty good memory, and, after all, I was the one who was actually *there*. Think another publisher—or, fuck knows, maybe even yours—might be interested in the *only* first-person account?"

"But…but…!" he said in a horrified sputter.

"I mean, last time out, I passed and gave you the story. But a shit-ton of money might come in handy right about now. This hovel needs a new roof, and I got a gut job of renos to do at the southern hovel."

"I'll give you half my advance right now!"

"Half? I had something like 75% in mind."

"Aawwww, Jake…"

It was time to let him off the hook.

"But on the other hand, that's a lot of work," I said, smiling. "And I hate work."

"You fucking monster!" Steve bellowed as he realized I had been fucking with him.

"But funny, right?"

"Seriously, Jake. You know I'll be fair."

"I do. Now getting back to the witnesses, why don't you call them again, say you've spoken to me and let them know that if they want my opinion, they should call me."

"Alright. Fine. Will you at least fill in some gaps? I mean, I think I have a pretty good idea how your strange little mind figured it out, but you could clarify."

"Deal."

"And there's another thing."

"Which is?" I asked, pretty sure of what he was driving at.

"Well, seems to me, the book needs some humanity. Some personal insight. Call it flesh and bone."

"I can see that, given you're a cold-blooded, heartless bastard."

"Particularly about two events," he continued, "that sort of bookend the story. You know what I'm talking about."

"My father's death and the shootout at my home in Florida."

"Yup."

"Steve, let me suggest that we've stayed friends because we're really not that different. Fair enough?"

"Yeah."

"And because that's true, let me further suggest, that any reactions you might have to those two events if they happened to you would be the same as what I had. So, imagine what you'd feel and then write that. I just ain't interested in wallowing around in that shit."

"Alright, pal," Steve said, and I appreciated his obvious sympathy about re-opening wounds that had just started to close. "Let's stick to the facts right now. I've got a lot, but I still need a lot more."

We ran through what had been early clues about what was going on. A whole series of odd company names and corporate registrations, as well as patently fictionalized officers that only a trivia nerd such as myself could likely see the pattern.

"I've got a few big questions," he said.

"Like?"

"Like how'd you get onto the ex-Mafia guy?"

I thought of the vital link to the main bad guy that came from Nick, a friend of mine and ex-biker and ex-New Jersey citizen who'd provided the connection. Nick was living under the radar in the DR, and I knew that he'd face serious threats to his health and safety if his identity came up in any public forum. Particularly amongst people whose last names ended in vowels.

"Can't tell you," I said. "Remember the anonymous hacker who provided the key in your first book?"

"Of course."

"He's still anonymous and he was pretty much the real hero of that book. I bet the lack of identification didn't hurt sales. Same deal here. You're going to have to paint him as guy who knew a guy who knew a guy. What else?"

"Well, about the time you were in Tulsa—"

"How'd you know I was in Tulsa?"

"Pretty easy. The headquarters for the fraud ring was Tulsa. The guy in your house in Florida was from Tulsa. What are the odds?"

"Fuck, you *are* good."

"As I was saying, about the time you were there, up popped a couple of news stories of a gun battle in a cornfield that left four people dead. Later, the paper identified two people—here it is—a Thomas Tanyan and Pietro D'Angelo," he said, shuffling through his notebook. "These guys were the ones who were attacked, but there was a third unnamed person with them. I'm pretty sure that guy was you."

I didn't lie to reporters back when I was a corporate PR slut, and I wasn't about to start with a good friend. I confirmed his guess.

"So tell me what happened that day."

The whole event hadn't taken long but the details of it were—and probably always would be—pretty clear in my mind.

Without even the hint of modesty, I can say that, in addition to smoking, landscaping, and wasting time, another thing I'm really good at is painting word pictures. While he was writing furiously,

I provided the blow-by-blow descriptions of the actual gunplay as well as its prelude and aftermath.

As one of the most thorough journalists I'd ever met, I knew Steve had done his homework. And as an excellent writer, any book he did turn out would be eminently readable. I'd never tell him those things, of course. But they did make me comfortable that he'd write it as it had played.

Through all this social and medical activity, I tried to focus on Ted Bromley's murder.

I figured one way to reinvolve myself was to visit the actual scene of the crime. Odd indeed to take the long and winding road (Fuck, I gotta get off these Beatles' allusions!) through the campus from the highway.

There were a bunch of new buildings on the long drive up to the Lady Eton and Champlain College clusters of classrooms and student residences, not the least of which was an actual sports facility. We didn't have a gym when I attended, the only university in the entire goddamned country so unencumbered. But we did have our very own drumlin, so top that!

The main buildings, all built at the same time, spread out before me. And, as always, they impressed the hell out of me. Trent was a relatively new university, established in the mid-60s (that's 1960s) but the architecture always reminded me of a grey medieval castle and walled town. Concrete was the principal—if not the only building material.

Les Macgregor had told me that the murder took place in the overflow parking lot way north of the main group of buildings. So I drove up West Bank Drive between Lady Eton College and Champlain College, under their connecting footbridge.

I don't usually make a habit of spending time in empty parking lots, so it felt a bit odd pacing the stretch of asphalt until I found the exact spot where Bromley had died using Les' general directions. It wasn't all that hard to find; it was marked by a faint red-brown stain. I turned to see the main buildings in the distance.

That'd be a hike for Bromley, I thought. And he would've had to make his way through those buildings to the nifty bridge spanning the Otonabee River to get over to the Wenjack Theatre on the other side. His obit said that he was 79. By the time I'd turned fifty, I was already screaming for golf cart shuttles to and from everywhere—although I will concede that I may be a poor measuring stick for reasonable physical exertion; I'm still lobbying for a 10-yard dash to be added as an Olympic sport (and not as one of those candy-ass "demonstration" sports either). Maybe Bromley was a strict egalitarian or, more likely, the faculty-only parking spots in the nearer lot were full that night.

There was one light pole illuminating the parking lot, none between that lot and the one adjacent to the university buildings about three football fields away. No cameras that I could see. In other words, a good place for an ambush. So. Did the killer follow him out there? Or was he waiting, hiding somewhere close?

There was a row of mature boxwoods along the length of the parking lot separating it from the river. Crouching behind the shrubbery was possible. But both scenarios presented difficulties. If someone was trailing him, he'd have to close in on him fast because the first thing Bromley would've likely done when he reached his car was dump his papers in the trunk. Police said he didn't even get the chance to do that before he was stabbed. Books were heaped around the rear bumper; papers were strewn about the parking lot when the body was found the next morning. It could be done, but the murderer would've had to have stealthily hauled ass.

With the murderer in hiding behind the boxwoods, the crime was more easily committed—the killer just had to cross maybe thirty feet of asphalt and confront Bromley who would've had his back to him.

But the set-up would've been difficult. How would the killer know Bromley's would be the only car? How would he even have known that Ted would park there? And how would he have known when Bromley would be retrieving his car?

I played both movies in my wee brain. In both, the scene started slowly, the victim unaware, unsuspecting as he strolled his way to the car. The music also built slowly until it became much louder, more frantic, culminating in not quite *Psycho*esque 'Eee! Eee! Eee!' violin sounds as the knife did its work. But the visuals, as they often do, skipped over the logistics.

There occurred to me a third and, yes, obvious possibility. Bromley and the soon-to-be extinguisher of Bromley had walked to his car together. And as soon as Bromley had his back to him (or her) by the trunk, the stabby part began.

On my way back to the car, I came upon another new feature at Trent—or rather he came upon me. The security guard was officious as hell when he challenged me—which I guess he pretty well had to be, it being part of his job and all.

I told him I used to go there, back when we didn't have rent-a-cops patrolling the joint.

Dubious springs to mind to describe his expression as he studied my straggly long hair, worn Hawaiian shirt (I'll admit it wasn't my spiffiest), and torn shorts. I presumed he was questioning the value of a university degree.

He asked for my alumni card; I didn't have one and instead rhymed off the names of my profs at the time. That worked.

"Any chance you were on duty the night in March when Clayton Thompson spoke here?" I asked.

"Yeah, we all were."

"I hear this lot was full."

"Yup. Almost."

"But why, if he was across the river at Wenjack?"

"That was just the other night. That first time in March, he was in the Great Hall at Champlain College on this side."

One mystery cleared up.

"Can I suggest you get an alumni card for when you're here?" he asked.

"I will." I promised.

"Can I suggest that I go with you right now to the Alumni Office to make sure you get that card?"

"You silver-tongued devil," I said. "Lead the way."

It was a quick, easy process to get the card. But it turns out I wasn't anywhere near ready for my close-up. With no time for coiffing, I wasn't a bit surprised that my photo on the laminated card looked like an older version of Nick Nolte's famous mug shot. The fund-raising pitch took longer. I actually felt bad that my disposable income was touching zero. Trent had been more than excellent to and for me.

I got home just as the phone rang.

"Bromley's keys are still at the front desk," Les Macgregor said. "What the fuck, Jake?" And he hung up. Score one for Macgregor.

CHAPTER EIGHT

When I was actually working at a high-paying but demand-ing job that consumed sixty to eighty hours of my life a week, I just couldn't get to everything I'd planned each day, either in the office or at home. Tasks slipped off the schedule, rolled over into the next day or the next. Funnily, the same thing has hap-pened now even though technically I'm doing fuck-all. Take that month of June. Writing a bit, the medical appointments, outdoor shit I have to do around the place, Steve's visit. Tough to fit every-thing in and still regularly drink with Carl and work on helping to solve a murder. Where, o where does the time go?

Get off your arse, Jake, collect the key and go to Bromley's place.

Alright, Jake. Get off my fuckin' back, will ya? Sheesh!

After getting the key, I drove to Bromley's place by memo-ry. Same neat red brick townhouse—one of six in a block. Same gingerbread detail on the gable ends. About the only thing differ-ent was the size of the maple trees lining the sidewalk. They had grown a lot—as trees tend to do after forty years.

Near as I could tell, the living/dining area where we spent our time as students was exactly as I remembered.

Like a lot of educated people, Bromley had travelled extensively, particularly when he was younger in his post-graduate days. Instead of boring the shit out of us with slideshows, he'd bore the shit out of us in person by lovingly describing the many exotic items he'd collected from around the world that eclectically cluttered his living room. We just had to learn what each was and how he bought them and got them to Canada. Today, he'd likely be known as an archaeological tomb raider.

Still taking up one wall was the giant 18th-century black-lacquered Oriental armoire with a three-tiered roof shaped like a pagoda and made from mahogany. He had convinced a steamer captain in Wenzhou on the strength of a handshake to carry it to Vancouver.

Sidebar: Wenzhou? Why do I remember shit like that?

On another wall was a huge French tapestry, perhaps illegally removed from a Burgundy chateau and depicting some Catholic martyr or other in the act of bloodily achieving his martyrdom. There were a couple of dark, cracked, and flattering portraits of vain and prosperous Flemish merchants, done, I presumed, when there was a Flemland. On another wall was mounted a cribbage board painstakingly carved out of a walrus tusk by Inuit artisans and presented to 19th century English whalers plying the Arctic Ocean who had a whole lot of time on their hands for card games as they waited around to freeze death. Ornate German beer mugs from 17th-century Oktoberfests congregated inside a glass curio, itself leftover from some Mayfair drawing room. He still had the Persian divan from when there was a Persia. I and a couple of others used to recline against it as we were plied with literary ideas and wine.

Dominating Ted's living room/seminar hall was an impressive display of Viking stuff over the fireplace. Bromley was a gentleman and a gentle man, so the war-like exhibition was out of character. Fearsome-looking helmets, long and short battle axes and swords. Centre stage in this shrine to plundering and pillaging was a painted round wooden shield. Arrayed around the top half of the shield were knightly-looking pewter figures.

Discounting the possibility that Lars the Larcenous had ripped him off in the back streets of Oslo, Ted had sworn that the Norse paraphernalia was authentic, except for the wooden shield, as they'd only found two intact after a millennium spent rotting in the ground. I remembered he had removed the shield to show us the complete figures.

Each figure was actually the handle of a long meat skewer.

Fuck me! A meat skewer! A long thin steel blade, sturdy as hell because, as Bromley had wagered, the Vikings did not impale polite little fondue cubes of sirloin, but rather gnawable slabs of all kinds of dead animals. They came with a handle for gripping because, as Ted had explained mischievously, it could double as a weapon to be used for settling après-dinner disagreements.

I stared at the array. *C'mon, Jake, Think! How many were there?* I cursed my goddamned faulty memory. *Think, Jake, think.* I cast my mind back there, could picture me sprawled on the Persian divan, by the end of every seminar, gazing around through a red wine haze. The decades since hadn't made my memory any clearer. I just couldn't be sure. The five figures stared at me. There had been six. Or maybe seven. I was sure. Sort of.

Having no cell phone, I drove back to the police station, excited with my discovery. The papers would have to wait.

When Les finally ambled out to the front desk, he did not share my enthusiasm over the discovery after I explained it to him.

"Gee, Jake, you found something long and pointy. Well done."

"For fuck's sake, Les! Go to his place and get one. You guys can test it. Maybe exhume the body?"

"He was cremated."

"But…but you have the autopsy photos. There must be colour

close-ups of the washed wounds."

"Jake, it might get us a weapon but we're not any closer to finding out who used it or why. That was your job, remember?"

"Yeah, but if it matches, it also eliminates any theory about a stranger being the murderer. Whoever did the nasty was familiar enough with him to have visited his house and stolen the skewer."

"So now we're supposed to find out everybody who ever came to see him?"

"Gee, Les, you're right; that *is* a big job. Maybe you could ask someone to help. Perhaps the police…oh, wait…"

"Funny."

"If you do call them, maybe the police could talk to all the seminar groups who came through the house over the last few months. Maybe that'd be a good place to start. Or maybe you could dust all the Viking shit for fingerprints. You'll find mine on the bottom left and top right of the shield. But that's it. I didn't touch anything else."

"Alright, alright."

"Oh, and I'll need to keep the key; I'm not finished."

"Fine; we've got another one."

I drove back to Bromley's place. On the second floor overlooking the now-untended backyard was Ted's office. Floor to ceiling bookshelves—all full. Two grey government surplus-type filing cabinets with unlocked drawers. Sitting on top of one was a relic from a bygone era: a very old, very heavy Underwood manual typewriter. I typed a few words; the keys clacked away and the black- and red-stripped ribbon bobbed along.

Against one wall were stacks of different coloured plastic milk crates, dozens of them. It looked like a side of a giant unfinished Rubik's cube. Each one of them had a label with a month and year hyphenated with another month and year.

I pulled one of the crates down, marked 'February 2020 - April 2021.' Inside were about fifteen journals, all leather-bound. Supersleuth that I am, I instantly surmised that they were journals, mostly because each one was embossed with the word 'Journal' on the front cover.

I flipped through a few pages of one. Neat, completely legible handwriting dated each entry of Ted's recorded thoughts. Some were extended rants (such as the one from May 17 on the evils of grocery store self-checkouts—which he was dead right about; another from June 5 on the shameful misreading of the anti-capitalism theme in *Les Miserables*). There was a bit of snark in an entry or two. Like the one from February 8, 2021, wherein he referred to his second-year class on Utopian Literature as "as a wholly unpleasant collection of privileged turnips." Or another one that characterized a certain 'PH' as "that decrepit libertine manifestly unqualified to toil in the kitchen of Champlain College, let alone strut the campus as a full professor."

Ouch. Professor Bromley in the study with the poison pen.

In the main, however, his literate writing was definitely not at the diary level of "Bought a 3-pack of mustard today at Costco. U should 2. So much cheaper!!!"

Starting with the dates on the crate at the bottom right of the wall o' crates, I estimated I was staring at about forty-five years of daily journals. Ol' Ted had been meticulous in chronicling and archiving the fuck out of himself.

I gotta admit I felt a bit creepy going through the diaries of a dead guy. But that didn't mean I was going to stop; after all, I had been 'ordered' to help the investigation by the police, for Christ's sake.

Surveying the office, I reckoned I'd need to rent a U-Haul—a big one—to get all this stuff up to the Hovel. Shipping costs alone might've been the main reason Ted never took a teaching job anywhere else. For the meantime, I grabbed the most recent crate, half-filled with the volumes and lugged it out to the Vibe.

Somewhere in there, I guessed, may very well lie a clue or two

as to what got Ted Bromley killed.
    And by someone he knew.

CHAPTER NINE

Maybe it's just an indication of how blissfully boring my fucking life had become, but I was completely mesmerized by the eight journals I had purloined (sounds so much classier than stolen or ripped-off, doesn't it?). The following entry from November last year really caught my attention:

Have not encountered a student so completely full of himself as TC since JL a very long time ago. Is he smart? Yes. One need only ask him - or JL - for confirmation.

JL? JL? Hmmm. Why, whomever could he mean? Oh, let's bet I had made an impression on Professor Bromley. I always view that as a positive.

But [Bromley continued] *the difference between JL and TC is the tone and intent. JL was light-hearted, almost frivolous. TC is grim. Deadly serious. One always sees the heart in one's writing. TC showed me some short stories he'd written (I was not aware of JL writing anything beyond that which he had been assigned). All four of his sordid tales began bleakly and progressed through to utter despair, punctuated by callousness and grotesque violence. He did*

not care for my observations. At all. There is menace in his darkness.
Perhaps I know why. He needs help. And I shall ensure he gets it. I
will stop abetting him and I will contact the authorities if I must. I
must preserve his unique genius. Despite his dingy vision, TC has
done nothing but exceptional work for me. If my annual gift-giving
is to have any integrity I must set aside his issues and reward him.

I remembered Bromley had this rumoured ritual. During every academic year, he would secretly bestow a gift to the student
whom he judged was being the most productive, insightful, and
intelligent. I never paid much attention to the private award ceremony as I was pretty sure I was never in the running.

At least in the fairly recent journals I had, there was no particular threat or worry about his health at the hands of any kind
of enemy that I could see but I'll admit, I pretty much skimmed
them.

I also saw that the last journal I had ended in December. That
meant there must've been one missing from my collection that
covered the first three months of this year.

I did want to get a sense of Clayton Thompson—beyond my
usual snap judgments. I figured his former hang-out at Trent
would be a good place to start. Trent was not only a pleasant place
for students to be, teachers tended to stay put too. The summer-
time campus was void of students but there was usually a prof
or two lying around. I found one in the Philosophy Department
offices.

"So what are you working on, professor?" I said as a way to
interrupt the guy playing solitaire on his computer.

Late middle-aged, balding but with an almost laugh-out-loud
bad comb-over. Full beard wreathing his fleshy face. He quickly
exited the computer screen and rose to meet me. He wore a light
blue golf shirt sized small enough to look like it had been painted
on to his corpulence and plaid Bermuda shorts.

"Philip Harder," he said, extending his hand. "And you are...?"

I froze for a nanosecond. Philip Harder, I thought. 'The decrepit libertine' and unqualified full professor 'PH' in Bromley's journal? This should be interesting.

"Jake Lydon, Class of...a long time ago."

"Thinking of enrolling as a very, very mature student?" he said, with a chortle.

"Not exactly."

"Pity. We're involved in some very exciting projects right now."

"Such as?"

"For example, we're developing AI here."

"At Trent?"

That is correct. [Long sidebar, your Honour: I don't have just one pet peeve; I've got a whole fucking menagerie. One of them is being told I was *correct*—instead of just saying 'yes', 'yeah', 'yup'. It's so goddamned annoyingly condescending. What's next? Tousling my hair and being told "Well done, Little Jakey!"?]

"Oh my, yes," Harder said, "The fact is right here in the philosophy department, we've always had AI...Ancient Intelligence."

And then he gave off another of those self-amused chortles that some academics use. A kind of polite guffaw you'd expect to hear around Victorian parlours after an oh so witty as fuck remark. "Good one, Oscar."

"You understand, such as Plato, Aristotle, Socrates..."

There went another pet peeve—the need to explain an oh so witty as fuck remark that the remarker assumes has been wasted on a complete fucking moron.

"Now what can I do for you?" he asked.

I tossed out a bullshit story that I was writing a piece for the university's fall magazine from the viewpoint of one alumnus (I showed him my card) to another. In this case, I wanted to talk about Clayton Thompson.

He didn't.

"I'm sorry but I can't really help you. He was never in a class of mine."

"Come on, professor. He must have been the topic of some conversation around the ol' department water cooler since he returned."

"Well, if you must know, colleagues who did try to teach him, were, to a person, singularly unimpressed with the depth of his scholarship. And now—unfortunately—millions of people believe that what he spouts is philosophy." Professor Harder caught himself as he was getting amped up. "But you cannot, under any circumstance, quote me."

I had to smile. I learned the hard way long ago with the media, you don't get to claim to be off the record *after* you've said something incredibly fucking dumb. If you don't establish the ground rules before you start, then the toughest of bananas to you; you're quotable. I wished I actually was writing an article for the alumni mag, just to use his comment.

He misread my 'Gotcha' smile. His semi-jovial mood clouded over real quick.

"In fact, may I add," he said, "Using that quote would be terribly ill-advised."

I didn't exactly feel threatened by the aging philosopher, but I was unsettled by the dramatic change of demeanour and the depth of his glare.

"I'll put you down as 'no comment,' professor. Thanks for your time."

I couldn't find any other philosophers hanging around, so I left.

Driving home, I considered perhaps the oldest of old boys' networks—the Greek philosophers who hung out together. You've got Socrates who had a younger bro in Plato who mentored that whippersnapper Aristotle. Not sure if Aristotle was all that much of a teacher as his star pupil was Alexander the Great (presumably, he was just Alexander the So-So at the time). Any lessons Ari gave the kid about virtue or ethics didn't sink in as young Alex went on his revenge campaign to fuck up Persia and then, apparently for shits and giggles, conquer most of the known world, slaughtering millions in the bargain.

Then there was Socrates. For his innocuous teachings, he got himself condemned to death. That was bad enough but worse still, he was expected to carry the sentence out on himself. And worst of all, he actually did kill himself—by drinking hemlock. I couldn't see the honour in caving to the wish of a government or a religion that had a hard-on for you. Me, I'd make the bastards do it themselves and I'd be kicking and screaming and biting the entire time.

Plato had recently become my favourite of the trio, not because of his brilliant insight into the nature of humanity and the universe, but because, I discovered, he was a big fan of getting shit-faced. Those crazy ol' Greeks liked to party down, and Plato came up with a sturdy rationale for doing exactly that.

I have lifted the following summary from Mark Forsyth's wonderful book, *A Short History of Drunkenness*.

Basically, Plato believed that if you can drink a lot and still behave yourself, then you are an ideal man. If you can do this in company, then you can show the world that you are an ideal man, because you are displaying the great virtue of self-control.

He also said that getting drunk is like going to the gym: the first time you do it you'll be really bad at it and end up in pain. But practice makes perfect.

Self-control, said Plato, is like bravery. A man can only display bravery when he's in danger. A man can only display self-control when he's drunk a lot of wine. A guy who spends his days fighting battles can train himself to be brave. A man who spends his evenings getting drunk can train himself to higher levels of self-control.

Isn't logic fucking swell?

Plato thought that if you can rely on a guy when he's drunk, you can trust him sober. Plus, the drinking test has no real downside. If you get into a business deal with a man and then find out that he's a crook, you lose money and have to spend time in court and/or being pissed off. But if you get drunk with him first, you get to see his true character and all you're risking beyond one night of your life was maybe a hefty bar bill and a hangover.

My joy at finding this classical piece of self-justification aside, there's another important point: you can never fully trust a proud teetotaler. And I never have.

CHAPTER TEN

I was surprised as hell at what I found in my Junk mail folder one morning. The subject line was *May I visit?* The author was Clayton Thompson.

My landlord Rob Byford suggested I get in touch with you. I think we met briefly at my last lecture.

At any rate, Rob believes I would do well to have a chat with you in preparation for my second book which, more or less, deals with how to acquire and sustain a simple and harmonious life—without the cataclysmic drama attendant my protagonist of The Returning. *He also recommended that I do so in what he described as your "natural habitat." I hope you are agreeable.*

Sincerely,

Clayton Thompson

I called Rob. He answered in weak voice.

"Your tenant wants to see me, Rob. Said it was his landlord's idea."

"He's been at the cabin since March. He's set up house with his publicist. Apparently, she has the wood and the food brought in while he…thinks."

"Christ, that's interesting. Didn't think to mention it after the show?"

"Both his agent and publisher swore me to secrecy. Terrible things would visit me if I let it leak and all his apostles started turning up to worship him while he was trying to write his book. But I've thought about it, and I realized they can't do much to me now."

"What the hell does that mean?"

"I'm not doing so well."

"What's up, bud?"

"Pancreatic cancer is up," he said.

"Fuck!" I said, stunned. "What are they doing about it?" I demanded.

"Nothing. They're done. I'm done."

"Prognosis?"

"I think the correct medical term is 'I'm fucked.'"

"How fucked?"

"A few weeks maybe."

"Jesus, Rob. Look, can I drop by?"

"No, Jake. I'd love you to come over, but I won't have anybody see me this way. *Anybody*. I would not tolerate an obituary with awful clichés like "after a valiant fight" and "surrounded by his family and loved ones." Can you understand that?"

"I can," I said, and I meant it.

"I'm able to write for a while longer, I suspect, so we can do that."

"Deal…Hey, maybe we can become Facebook friends! You know, share recipes and shit."

He tried to laugh; it turned into a dry coughing fit.

"And maybe you can fuck off," he said when he'd recovered.

There was a pause.

"Good-bye, Jake."

"Good-bye, buddy."

I had been around death a lot in the last few years. Directly and indirectly, I had caused a couple of them myself. But they were sudden and violent deaths, overwhelmingly happening to people who, in one way or other by any measure, had it coming. This was different. This was a friend being trampled by the inexorable march of time and the randomness of disease. A friend only a few years older than me. How do you not get dark and turn inwards, fitting yourself into the same arc?

It's not like I contemplated my place in the fucking universe or any other such lofty bullshit. Just the end of the swell time I had had most of my life.

As sad-struck as I was, how could I not honour his wishes? I knew what he intended. Rob's death would leave a huge and sad hole in the lives of the people he touched. But it would be a hole not made deeper and darker by final images of him diminished and either incoherently drugged or in terrible pain. It wasn't anything like vanity or a desire to escape pity that caused Rob to decide to basically die alone. I understood that it was his gift to everybody who had been affected by his energy, his brilliance, his forceful presence.

A couple of days later, I got an e-mail from Rob. I marveled at the wit and grace with which he pecked out the note, imagined the pain he was in while doing so.

He told me that he was giving me first right of refusal on buying his house, the house I'd lived in as a student forty some years earlier, but that I'd have to act fast as "*The offer expires when I do.*" He commented on his pain relief measures, noting that he was currently "*taking far more wonderful drugs than I ever took voluntarily.*"

Near the end he wrote this:

You should know that Ted Bromley and I were corresponding a bit before he died. No detail but lots of invective directed towards

Clayton for some reason. Said he even wrote to Thompson to tell him off. Whatever the fuck that means.

He then ended with this:

Hope you don't mind, but I sent along the first chapter of your new book to both Patricia Morland and Daniel Truscott. I may have stretched the truth a bit, but I said you were too modest and unconfident to do it yourself. Commissions will apply if it's accepted. Keep writing, amigo.

I got myself a little overwhelmed and felt my eyes watering. This was Rob's sign-off to me. I wrote back right away:

I promise I will, my friend. Thank you for everything. Except the last fucking bar bill you stuck me with.

The only thing I could do after that was open a beer and sit on the deck and think: What a shitty, shitty day.

CHAPTER ELEVEN

Going by the obit in the *Examiner,* Rob died a week or so later. His funeral was to be held in Toronto where the bulk of his immediate and extended family was. He'd once told me that he had been effectively excommunicated at age seventeen by that family whose membership numbered enough accountants to start a sizeable bean-counting firm. "English Literature, Robert? You cannot be serious!" Now the black sheep was returning to the fold, too late to make a difference to anyone, least of all him. I didn't plan to go the service because why would I? I'd pay my respects every time I thought of him.

I did sit down and re-read every e-mail exchange we'd had over the years. I was chuckling and misty-eyed, picturing the man I'd known.

I stopped at the last part of our final exchange.

You should know that Ted Bromley and I were corresponding a bit before he died. No detail but lots of invective directed towards Clayton for some reason. Said he even wrote to Thompson to tell him off. Whatever the fuck that means.

Well, wasn't that fascinating?

Would Bromley have handwritten or typed and printed out a note, then mailed it to Thompson? Maybe. But Bromley obviously used e-mail and that'd be the quickest way to get something off your chest.

Needing to look for the missing partially completed journal anyway, I went back to Bromley's place and stared at his laptop on the desk. There had to be a way in. More than likely, Bromley would've written down his password somewhere. Old farts—such as myself—genuinely dread forgetting passwords more than we fear a stranger reading our innocuous e-mails. Nothing on or in the desk suggested that it might be a scrawled password, nothing taped to the underside of the laptop. But there was a serial number that gave me an idea. I did me some purloining of the laptop and left, after combing his house for the AWOL journal. No sign of it.

Back at the Hovel, I rehearsed my story. In person—owing to the severe limitation of humans to see beyond physical appearances, oh, and fact that I generally look like a bum—I would never be mistaken for an official of anything—except for maybe the past president of The Over the Hill Jimmy Buffet Fan Club.

But on the phone, *if* I can stifle my tendency to say 'fuck' every second word, I can sound official as hell. I called HP, saying I was the executor of the recently-deceased Ted Bromley's estate. Wherever she was, the Help Desk lady refused to give up the password, told me I just had to enter Ted's e-mail while on his computer and they'd send me a new one.

To my credit, I didn't lose my shit at the obviousness of this Catch-22.

"But it seems to me that's the problem, madam. I can't get on the gosh-darned thing to send the request."

She was deeply sorry for my predicament but less than deeply sorry she couldn't do anything else. So I gave her the serial number and asked when the gosh-darned thing was made and if a warranty had ever been registered. It had. After I was informed that there was no goddamned way in the world any portion of that warranty was still in effect, so don't even think about it, mister (or words to that effect), I was told that Ted mailed it in sometime in late October of 2019.

I drove back to Ted's house, convinced that he would've written down the password somewhere at about the time he was registering it.

Along the way, I worried about the extra miles I was putting on the Vibe and the sounds it was making in response. (Thanks, Alex, for pointing them out.) My trusty chariot could ill-afford to have those extra miles tacked onto the 200,000 (I think that's a bazillion in kilometres) it had already run up.

There was a car in Ted's driveway. No time for one of my intricate, complex, stunningly ingenious plans. I switched to Spontaneous Bullshit mode.

After I had established with Doug the Real Estate Agent that I wasn't interested in buying "this rare gem" even though it wasn't listed yet, I told him that Trent wanted Bromley's papers, all of them.

"He was a world-famous scholar," I said.

"No shit?" the agent said.

I then explained that I already had his laptop to start finding and copying his e-mails but that I needed his printed material. I flashed the house key and my alumni card, detailing how I was a volunteer on the project that would probably take years and might result in several volumes of collected works and that I'd be long dead before the project was completed.

There are times when I scare myself that I can pour out a torrent of plausible interconnected lies without even really thinking about it.

"Fill yer boots," the agent said. "His kids don't want any of it. So I was just going to have to haul it all away to the dump."

He seemed relieved that I would be sparing him the ordeal dealing with the paper tonnage. Funny, huh? A person getting real happy about doing less work for the same pay. Who'd've thunk? I was happy to be retrieving it because a municipal landfill seemed such an ignoble end to all that writing by a smart guy.

Doug gave me a week to get rid of it all before the public listing and open houses.

Up in the office, I pulled out the plastic crate labeled Feb 2019-Jan 2020. I had noticed that Ted very rarely wrote anything in the margins of his journals. So that's why this circled word alongside his entry for October 21 jumped out at me. DeQuincey#1. It had to be a password. Upper and lower cases, special character and numeral, all one word. Bromley would never have written De Quincey as one word. Nor would he likely forget one of his heroes, Thomas De Quincey, the early 18th century author of *Confessions of an English Opium-Eater*, regarded as the pioneering work in the field of addiction literature. (Sidebar: you really could argue that every writer is seriously addicted to something—more often than not, writing).

I skedaddled out of there with another randomly selected crate of journals.

Some keystrokes back at the lake and just like that, I was in. I had to smile at the background photo on his desktop page. There he was in a park setting, looking professorly as hell. I remembered him as a short, slight man but, the picture showed, he had compensated for that by growing a massive flowing white beard. Think Karl Marx, Tolstoy, Walt Whitman or two-thirds of ZZ Top.

For contrast in the photo, he was almost dwarfed by a giant dog, a black, long-haired behemoth of a beast, maybe a descendant of the Hound of the Baskerville. It couldn't be the same one, but Ted had had a similar looking dog when I was showing up to his home as a student. It was hard not to be scared shitless when you meet an animal like that on his home turf, but I soon discovered the only threat from the endlessly playful Dumas was possible death by slobbering.

Except if one thing happened. Ted picked me to demonstrate. I was to approach him in "a threatening manner." Instantly, Dumas transformed from a huge furry floor ornament into about one hundred and fifty pounds of snarling menace. He was on his feet and charging, looking like he was about to rip my lungs out, Jim, when Ted called him off.

The home page photo and canine remembrances were as far as I got when the phone rang. Caller ID said 'P'tboro Polic.'

"Les Macgregor, you old enema bag. Glad you called. Wanna play tradesies?" I asked.

"Whattya got?" he wanted to know.

"You first."

"You were right—"

"Oh, *doooo* go on."

"One of those Viking skewers was the murder weapon."

"What a surprise, eh? Now. Did you interview the students in his class that night?"

"Yes. Did it myself."

"…and?"

"You were right—"

"I'm sorry, must be a bad connection. What was that again?"

"I'm not going to fuckin' say it again, Jake! They all grumbled about being out there that evening. They all said they liked being at the professor's house better. Said Bromley was even more pissed off because he had to go to the lecture that Thompson fella was giving and that he had to park in that far lot to make room for the paying customers. Had just enough time to do the class and then get to the speech on time."

"How'd they seem?"

"As a matter of fact, they were all polite and helpful as hell, except one guy.

"Any ol' chance that guy's initials were TC?"

"I'm not even going to guess how you know that. Terrence Childers. Real smartass. Almost got aggressive about me wasting his time again and didn't I have something better to do. Big lad, too. I put the colours in his paint box, but he was a real dick. Now that I think about it, you two might be related. You find anything?"

"Sorry. Nothing yet. Gotta go. Bye!" I quickly blurted out.

"Hey! Wait a min—"

But I had hung up.

CHAPTER TWELVE

Would an aspiring, self-possessed writer like TC become outraged enough at some literary criticism of his work to actually murder a professor? (Just to be clear: I wasn't really going to toss my U of T poetry prof out his office window; call it an ill-advised ad-lib).

I fucking hate any negative commentary on my scribbling. But my reactions to it do not include homicidal impulses. More often than not, I feel pity for the complete lack of taste and insight on display by the alleged critic.

But this Childers sounded touchy enough for me to find out if he had taken his retaliation to a whole new level. He could've easily swiped the skewer; he definitely had the opportunity to do some skewering himself by walking with Bromley to his car after his class and the lecture that night to bum a ride into town. And as twisted as it might be, he could very well have had what he felt was a darn good motive. Time for a chat with Testy Terrence.

That new alumni card of mine was turning into a goddamned golden passport. My registration number got me onto the Alumni portal on the university website which got me on to the current student directory which got me Terrence Childers' phone number, e-mail, and off-campus house address.

A lot of students stay in Peterborough during the summer, get jobs, and generally hang out, like I had done. Hoping that Childers was one of them, I called the phone number. No answer, but at least the line hadn't been disconnected.

I waited outside his place off Charlotte Street, figuring he would come home after work. Les Macgregor had been right. He was a big bastard. Taller than my six feet, he also had the kind of swagger from someone who was comfortable with his physicality. He walked like an athlete, which, I gotta say, was somewhat rare for an English Lit major.

"Terry Childers?" I asked.

"Terrence."

"Sorry. I'll try again. Terrence Childers?"

"Yes?"

Maybe it was because I was dressed in a summer-destitute ensemble, but I got the sense that my stopping him was about the same way he would view being accosted by an aggressive beggar on Yonge Street. A near-scowl decorated his rugged, sharp-featured face. He was a good-looking man, his appearance slightly marred by a noticeably mangled earlobe. Up close, I saw that not only was he bigger than most English lit students, he was also considerably older—by at least ten years, maybe more—than the bulk of university students who graduate from high school at seventeen or eighteen then head off to get them some of that thar higher larnin.'

"A while back, Professor Bromley suggested I look you up," I said. "Terrible thing that."

"Yeah, terrible. What did Bromley say?" he asked, getting past the mourning part real quick.

"He said you were a good writer and that I might be able to

help."

"How?"

"I know some people."

"Who?"

"Publishing people. I have a book out."

"Name?"

"Jake Lydon."

"I meant the book."

"On the Rails."

"Never heard of it."

"Well, I guess it doesn't fuckin' exist if his Lordship hasn't heard of it," I snapped, doing my bit to raise the temperature. But it stopped him and his bulldozing.

"Look, Terrence, why don't you send me a couple of stories? Or not. I might look at them. Or not. And then we'll see. OK?"

"I don't know you, so I don't trust you—or any stranger. So I won't e-mail them, but I can give you a few and part of a novel I'm working on right now. My name's on every page and I sent copies to myself by registered mail so there can be no doubt who wrote them and when."

"Fine."

"Bromley thought it was a good idea," he continued.

"Makes sense."

"Wait here."

He returned with a big bunch of loose pages. Maybe fifty in all.

"I'll get back to you," I said.

"Oh, wouldn't that make my life complete?"

"Ted said you were a good writer," I replied, "but, gosh, I wish he'd also told me what an arrogant, insufferable little prick you are."

For a second, I thought he might spring at me. He was tensed up. But so was I. And he knew it. I was sure he wasn't afraid of a beat-down. Despite my half-assed boxing training, his size, age,

and good physical shape, not to mention our thirty-year age difference made me far less certain of an outcome where I didn't
end up with a bunch of ouchies. But he relaxed. Maybe he'd been
struck by the incongruity of a spontaneous knock-down, drag 'em
out slugfest in the middle of a leafy genteel residential neighbourhood.

Boy, that was some kind of unpleasant, I thought, walking
away.

My first reaction to the notion that Childers was Bromley's
killer was now somewhat suspect. It would've taken planning and
deliberation—to rip-off the skewer for use at a later date, plot to be
alone with Bromley that night, do the deed, and then successfully
escape. Childers' reaction to me had been instant and visceral.

Reading young Terrence's stories I could see that Bromley had
been dead-on. Childers was good. Really good. Clean style, powerful imagery, hypnotic cadence.

But, Jesus, what a dingy way of looking at things. Here's the
subject matter for the first three stories I read: a drug deal gone
horribly wrong, a promising athlete spiraling into drug addiction
and suicide, and a prostitute murdered over a drug deal. See a
pattern?

It was as if he had painted masterpieces of the same open running sewer from different angles.

I skipped the last story and the beginnings of his novel pending a shower.

It took some real effort to see beyond his personal assholiness
and the unrelenting grimness of his stories to consider what he
had actually accomplished. Yes, I wouldn't write something like
that, but so fucking what? He was a very good writer and people
should always see very good writing. Let them make up their own
goddamned minds, but at least give them the opportunity to see
it.

What kind of person writes these stories, I wondered.

The perhaps great, perhaps crappy thing about today is that you don't have to sit around with your finger up your nose or elsewhere just wondering. You can find out about most people.

Most people but not Terrence Childers. The vast majority of young'uns leave a trail of clues about themselves on social media. Facebook, Twitter, and Instagram—plus a host of burgeoning platforms that I don't even know about, let alone understand and use—can provide pieces of puzzle. You have to trust your judgment that you can assemble these pieces to form an accurate, albeit superficial portrait. Favourite TV shows and movies, political opinions, sense of humour, number of friends and what you see he or she likes to do with them in photos, groups they belong to, and on and on. Oh, and how many goddamned selfies of themselves that they post. That alone tells you a bunch.

But no e-sign of Terrence Childers anywhere. As expected, there also wasn't any evidence of him on LinkedIn which tended to be populated by professionals either looking for a job or hoping you'll buy from them or just jerking themselves off with all their accomplishments.

I moved my search to Google news. Up popped just one entry with the right name before the list descended into a bunch of unrelated Childers—a NASCAR crew chief, a country singer, a board of education trustee in Tacoma, and a recently deceased Korean War vet—followed by a lengthy list of near-sounding names like Perry Childs, Mary Binder, Santiago, Chile, and so on.

His first and only mention was in a wedding announcement in the *Montreal Gazette* from seven years ago. 'Childers – Georgiou' was the header. A picture of the couple followed. Eleni Georgiou, the bride, was a gorgeous, dark, and delicate-looking brunette. Notched earlobe aside, Terrence was equally impressive looking in a dress military uniform.

He had a couple of military medals, but no regimental shoulder flashes, no sign of his rank, just the Canadian flag patch on his shoulder. I knew squat about army wardrobe, but I found that odd. At least the uniform explained Childers' late arrival to university. He was busy soldiering while kids his age were less than busy trying to get up before noon.

The nuptials were held in a Greek Orthodox church in Montreal and the parents, Doctor and Mrs. Constantinos Georgiou, were apparently delighted. If Childers' parents had any opinion, it was not evident. There was no mention of them in the notice.

I did some math then some research. Childers very easily could've been posted overseas. The country still maintained bases in Germany, France and, until 2014, in Afghanistan but no presence in Greece or even Cyprus where I knew we once had a military presence as peacekeepers trying to separate the Greek and Turkish Cypriots from their shooting squabbles.

Could I find out what Captain Childers did in the army and where he did it? Not easily. From 2008 on, military records were heavily protected. I was told I could fill out an Access to Information request to the government. I didn't bother filling it out; no bureaucrat had any incentive to answer that request in under a period of months or maybe years. And what I couldn't do is prove that I was either next-of-kin or immediate family.

I called Les Macgregor and asked him if the cops could get their e-hands on Canadian military records.

"Sure. We need them for criminal checks and such."

"Can you look up Terrence Childers for me—for *us*? I know he served."

"Really? When?"

"That I don't know. Maybe around 2009-10."

"What branch?"

"Army, I think."

"On it."

"Les, what the fuck is going on? You being co-operative and all is scaring me."

"I figured that'd mess you up."

"Well, it has!"

It was then that I heard him laugh, I think for the first time, just before the line went dead.

"You prick!" I said to the disconnected phone. "But," I added to myself. "Well-played, sir."

At the best of times, I may be the world's least patient man. It was one of many reasons I wouldn't dare take up golf. If you wanted to spot me in one of those interminable line-ups in the people chutes at an airport, just look for the most fidgety guy with the most agonized expression. I was on one of my monomaniacal hunts and I just couldn't wait for anything Les Macgregor might eventually tell me.

If I couldn't find out anything about Terrence Childers, maybe his wife might help. Back to Google. Eleni Childers was nowhere to be found either. What about Eleni Constantinos?

Let's hear a bingo! Sort of. Eleni Constantinos graduated from John Abbott College in Montreal in 2018 with a diploma in dental hygiene. Then she, like Terrence, seemed to disappear.

Back to Google and the pages of suggested possible links. And another bingo. There was an Ellen Constantine working in a dental clinic in Oakville, a satellite city just west of Toronto. The clinic's website had photos and brief bios for all their employees. And there she was. Slightly older but still as beautiful as her wedding day picture.

Ellen Constantine wasn't invisible on social media either. Her Facebook page was full of recent travel pictures of her and a guy not Terrence in the Bahamas, Jamaica, and Mexico. Six months earlier, she had gushed about her engagement to the un-Terrence.

Some prime-time bullshit was in order if I was going to shed some light on young and excitable Terrence. I was in the process of designing a great big fat lie to unfold on her when Les called back.

"Damnedest thing about Childers," he said. "Records search turned up squat, except to confirm he was in the army from 2008 to 2014. No rank, no unit, no postings listed, no reason for leaving the Forces."

"What's that mean?"

"No idea; I've never seen that before."

Curiouser and curiouser, I thought after I got off the phone. The blank records could mean one of two things: either it was a massive clerical fuck-up or the military didn't want me or anyone else to know what Childers did while he served.

Not ruling out the former, I started looking into the latter possibility. It seemed to me there was a blandly benign-sounding answer: covert operations. I was vaguely aware of only one outfit within our military that undertook such things. It was called Joint Task Force 2 or JTF2, which had always struck me as a quint-essentially Canadian name, lacking the instant panache of the American Seal Team 6 and Delta Force or even Britain's SAS. But, as I learned one rainy afternoon down the internet rabbit hole, the outfit was classed, by a group who apparently classifies such things, as a Tier 1, meaning that it stood equal to those other forc-es, every bit as highly trained and expert at doing secret and nasty things in foreign lands as the other three.

In this all info/all the time world we live in, I was able to find pages and pages about the shadowy arm of the country's military. How they were recruited and trained, what they were looking for and so on. I also came upon all manner of speculation as to what their specific jobs in the Mid-East might have entailed. Building schools wasn't on the list, but joint covert operations, active com-bat, and counter insurgency were. The sites I visited were all mak-ing educated guesses (or wild hunches) and should've come with a warning that may as well have read: "We know fuck-all for a fact and nobody's talking."

This secrecy also might explain why Childers' uniform at his wedding bore no regimental markings.

I modified my original scheme, made notes and called the dental clinic, asking for Ellen Constantine.

"Ellen Constantine?" I asked when she was transferred to me.

"Yes."

"Do you know Mr. Terrence Childers?"

There was a pause.

"Oh, my God. What's he done?"

"No, no it's nothing like that. I assure you."

"Who is calling please?"

"My name is Jeffrey Eaton. I work for the McAllister Freeman Foundation. Perhaps you've heard of us…"

"No."

"At any rate, Terrence Childers applied to us for a scholarship. The Anglo-Sorbonne Scholarship. Perhaps you've heard of it."

"No. Sorry."

"As I was saying, Mr. Childers applied for this scholarship, and he put your name down as a character reference."

"He did?" she asked in surprise.

"Yes. We at the McAllister Freeman Foundation pride ourselves in awarding only the finest possible candidates with this prestigious scholarship. We consider more than scholastic achievement in our selection process as the recipient will be representing this country abroad. Now Mr. Childers more than meets our academic criteria but there are, shall we say, some questions about his character which I hope you can answer. Is now a good time?"

"Yes…I have a few minutes."

"Excellent! That's all we require. Now, to begin with, what is your relationship to Mr. Childers?"

"We were once married."

"Oh, I see. When was the last time you spoke with him?"

"I'd say about three, almost four years ago."

"What kind of person is he?"

There was a much longer pause as she gathered her thoughts. She answered slowly and I started to feel like a real shitheel for reviving the subject of Terrence.

"Terry is a passionate man…he's forceful…he does not suffer fools."

"Good. Good. I must tell you that we at the foundation were somewhat surprised by what's missing from his application. Although he lists some years in the Canadian Armed Forces in his curriculum vitae, there is no character reference from any current or past colleague or superior officer. Can you account for that?"

"I'm sorry, I can't. I know he became soured on the Forces. Disillusioned is maybe a better word."

"Why was that?"

My question obviously upset her. Her voice became tremulous, her words halting.

"His service overseas had a tremendous…a bad…effect on him."

"He was in a war zone?"

"Yes. Afghanistan."

"Oh my. Do you have an idea what his role over there was?"

"I can't say."

"We are under the impression he may have been a member of JTF2."

"….I really am not supposed to say."

"I won't press you any further, Ms. Constantine. I'm sorry if I upset you. That was not my intention."

I was about to end the conversation when she began talking, sounding more confident, more forthcoming.

"You must understand, Mr. Eaton, Terry is a wonderful man. I met him in Cyprus. I was a nurse at a…a facility in Nicosia where soldiers were sent after active duty, before they were shipped home. We fell in love. He was controlling his emotions about the fighting. He returned to Canada, and I went with him. As hard as he tried, there'd be bouts of deep depression, bad dreams…lots of bad dreams. Then he became obsessed with writing and books. There was no room for me, and I couldn't help him. I don't think anybody could. But he willed himself to study and learn and write, until that's all that mattered to him. That's the kind of person you want, right?"

"It is indeed. You've been very helpful Ms. Constantine. I thank you and, again, I apologize for upsetting you."

So, Jake, you nosy little fucker, what did you learn at the expense of someone's else emotional state?

She more or less had confirmed that Childers was JTF2, that he likely suffered—and may still be suffering from Post-Traumatic Stress Disorder, and that he had a monomaniacal obsession with writing—his own or somebody else's.

It got me thinking about what Childers had gone through in Afghanistan. My opening premise: we don't know shit about experiences like that. We can read books or newspaper accounts of war, or we can watch gripping movies like *Hamburger Hill* or *Deer Hunter* or the first twenty minutes of *Saving Private Ryan* so we can be devastated or moved for a few hours. But we still don't know shit about what it's actually like to be in that situation day after day for months on end, what cumulative impact it had on the men and women who fought. And we can get all cynical about the questionable justification for a lot of wars, but it doesn't change or lessen that mental and physical toll on the real human beings who get sent to fight them.

However ultimately futile the effort to understand, I dove back into the coverage of our country's sortie into the Middle East. The "embedded" journalists were pretty well unanimous in their sense that the whole affair was made up of long periods of boredom and inactivity punctuated by short, terrifying, and deadly encounters with IEDs, with unidentifiable combatants and with sudden death and horrible injuries.

A story caught my eye. This from seven or eight years ago by a *Toronto Star* reporter and photographer who had been booted out of the country for unauthorized interviews of Canadian troops. That intrigued me because she was, no doubt, getting the straight goods about just what the fuck was going on over there, and not the PR-sanitized version the military brass would rather see published.

I found the offending article. It was about the thoughts of one unidentified soldier who admitted he was a member of JTF2. I knew that anybody in JFT2 speaking to the media about anything was the tabooest of taboos. In general, the anonymous soldier described the sort of war he was fighting. Clandestine, often with no clear objective and an even muddier result where maybe they were fighters, maybe they were civilians who had been killed. He corrected himself and said: "that I killed."

The accompanying photo meant something to me. Back to the camera, almost in silhouette, he was a big lad. And he clearly had a mangled right ear lobe. Odds were non-existent that this wasn't Terrence Childers. Odds are also pretty slim that Terrence Childers didn't find himself neck-deep in shit for giving that interview.

CHAPTER THIRTEEN

From the deck, I watched an unfamiliar car pull up my driveway. Clayton Thompson got out and briefly surveyed the scene. "Back here!" I yelled.

He was aloof but polite, almost formal. All in all, he was awkward as hell, and I suppose I was too. This was, more or less, a very odd blind date.

"Where do you want to do this—right here or down at the dock?" I asked as we limply shook hands.

He picked my dinky dock because he liked the way it "protruded into the water."

I regarded him as I followed him down the rickety stairs to water level. He was smaller than I imagined, even when I was standing beside him at the reception after his performance. Like Jagger (oh, for fuck's sake, Jake, are you still on that comparison?), maybe five foot eight. His slightly curly dark hair was stylishly cut. He wore neatly pressed slacks, a designer golf shirt and expensive-looking slip-ons.

We settled into the cheap plastic Adirondack chairs I'd screwed into the wooden planks to keep them from blowing into the lake at the slightest puff of a breeze.

He stared down the lake for a while just as a couple of loons started yakking at each other, but he seemed nothing but uncomfortable when he looked at me.

Even the beer I offered him from a mini-cooler (which he turned down) didn't seem to melt the ice. Nor did my weak-ass attempts at jocularity.

"I filed a noise complaint against those goddamned birds."

"So, how shall we do this?" he asked, cutting the chit-chat short after a perfunctory mention of Rob's death.

"He was a good man," he said. "I enjoyed him when I was a student."

"That he was…About your interview. Just start, I guess."

At my age—well at any other age I've ever been—I don't spend much time explaining or defending the way I live but that's what I was about to do.

"So. How would you describe your current circumstance?" he asked.

"I don't have much and I don't want much."

"Why is that so?"

"I have no fucking idea. I've never thought about it much. Facts are facts. I haven't had a regular well-paying job in almost twenty-five years so limited money is just my reality because I've got zero fucking interest in going out and getting more."

"Honestly?"

"Honestly."

"And you're satisfied with that?"

"Overwhelmingly so."

"You know that John Stuart Mill wrote: "It is better to be a human being dissatisfied than a pig satisfied; better to be Socrates dissatisfied than a fool satisfied.""

"So tell me, how'd that work out for Socrates?"

"That's not the point, is it?" he said, calling bullshit on my attempt at evasion.

Oh well, Jake, better plough in there.

"Ol' JS was full of shit," I said. "I mean I get his point: learning's probably a good thing. Some level of dissatisfaction gets things done. Stuff gets invented or discovered, policies change, and life gets better for a lot of people. But, for tens of millions of others, another kind of dissatisfaction didn't get them a better life; it got them dead in stupid wars run by greedy rich bastards, insane leaders or preventable famines, or imported diseases or new and improved ways of killing each other."

"But the notion of progress is innate in mankind, older than recorded history, brought to its first apex by the Greeks, Chinese, and Egyptians," he pointed out. "But before any can occur, one first must have thought."

"All those thinkers were as privileged as I am, as you are. Socrates and the rest of the lads were lucky enough to have lots of time to sit around and think because they didn't have to spend their days hauling giant stones for the Parthenon from dawn to dusk until they died at the age of twenty-seven or being in the front rank of a Roman infantry march in yet another stupid effort to civilize barbarians into oblivion."

"Luxury time and knowledge and ideas put into action form the only activities that create wealth that, in turn, creates opportunity."

"Let's try to keep this personal. You've made some millions of dollars over the last few years. Any better off?"

Here he paused. He came to dissect my life, not his own.

"Not really, if you must know," he answered in a soft voice.

"Why not?"

"The...the stress doesn't stop. People depend on me, expect things from me. I expect things from myself."

"But here you are, in a remote cabin for months, writing on

your own schedule. Kinda a sweet set-up."

"You don't understand!" he said, becoming agitated by either my ignorance or his own life. There's a tempest in my head. I never stop thinking. Ever. About what I have to deliver, when, and to whom. About preserving what I've made and building on it. I'm… exhausted. There's no other word for it."

"I *do* understand. I got a head full of bees most of the time, most people do. The trick is to set the majority of them aside as idle musings, not life or death. That stress shit'll kill ya. And fifty years from now, nobody will give a flying fuck anyway."

"So nothing lasts?"

"Lots of things last. You wrote a book; I wrote one. There they are, maybe for all time."

"So it matters."

"Maybe only to us. And we'll be dead."

"This is a major inconsistency."

"Gotta love Whitman. "Do I contradict myself? Very well then, I contradict myself."

"But might this inconsistency be fixed?"

"Why does it have to be fixed?"

"So things matter but there is no value to them beyond to the maker of the thing?"

"There might be temporary value to some. Tell me then—why the fuck did you write your book?"

"To say something, to give value. People have told me it's had a profound effect on them."

"I've always been suspicious of people who claim a book changed their lives. Amplified maybe, gave comfort, but changed? I doubt it."

"They can also fill a void for people searching for meaning."

"I do understand existential crises and the quest for meaning. I just haven't been troubled by them since my mid-teens. After wrasslin' with these bigger themes for some weeks, well, maybe days, OK, a good few hours back then, I convinced myself that there is no exterior sentient force, no deeper meaning but what individuals voluntarily create for themselves. A freeing moment, for sure. It strikes me as even more fucking arrogant than I usually am to believe that "I was put here to do this," whatever the fuck "this" is. "Joe Schmoe, we, the Lords of the Universe, doth anoint and compel thee to open an organic vegetable store in Wilmington, Delaware!""

"There is nothing wrong about thinking you have a higher purpose."

"No, but as soon as you realize you're just kidding yourself, you can't un-kid yourself. What is wrong with just saying "I really want to do this, and I hope to make enough money so that I don't starve."? Instead of imbuing your "journey"—because everybody's on a fucking journey these days—with divine significance, as if the universe gives a shit what you do. Now I concede that I may have just been a shallow selfish prick for about the last half-century but if pressed to answer the age-old question: 'What's it all for?' 'A while' is the only answer I can come up with."

"So what do you focus on in this 'while'?"

"My comfort and happiness. And not at someone else's expense."

"That's it?"

"That's it. Simple tastes, tastes that even a pig might understand."

"Anything you were reading that had an influence?"

"Re-reading actually."

"What was it?"

"The obituary I wrote for my wife twelve years ago."

"…Oh."

He didn't say "sorry" as a lot of people would have. I was grateful because, unless he had actually contributed to Beth's death, he had no reason to apologize. And he wasn't about to let that bit of old news throw him off his interview. But it did supply him with another line of questioning.

"So you regret not spending more time with her."

"No."

"No?"

"You don't gain anything from regret. You can't hop into your time machine and go back to fix things, and you just feel shitty."

"You've thought about this."

"Briefly and about forty years ago."

"Anything you'd like to ask me?"

"Yeah, there is. Do you mind me asking how you became such a good writer?"

"Excuse me?"

"With all due respect, I understand that you were—how can I put this?—that you had displayed none of the virtuosity that's in *The Returning*."

This took him aback. He tried to look unperturbed, but he was thinking.

"So you read my book?" he asked.

"Yes, sir. All of it."

"So you know I place a great deal of emphasis on self-discipline."

"OK…and?"

"I taught myself to be better."

"Seriously?"

"I know all the words used today. But their selection and order are obviously important. So I went back and studied those novels that have been judged to be great. I analyzed the texts, saw what the writers were doing, and simply replicated it. Discipline."

The guy was a first-time guest, so I didn't lay into him about his pseudo-scientific approach to creativity.

"Really? I've never heard of that working," was the most argumentative I got.

"Rob Byford said you were a good writer," he said.

"I am."

"What did you do to become one?"

"Nothing. I mean, I spent thirty years writing millions of words for other people, so I must've learned something technically, but that doesn't matter shit unless you've got a point, a meaning, and a feeling for your characters. Otherwise, you get fucking Henry James or fucking Jane Austen. And for me, shit either comes to me or it doesn't."

My answer signaled the end of the interview.

He thanked me for my time, but his gratitude wasn't exactly oozing with sincerity. It was more like the forced thank-you you had to make to an aunt for her Christmas present to you, a pair of shitty hand-knitted mittens that would shrink and fall off when they got wet.

I didn't feel any better or worse after he left. Really, all we had been doing was just bantering. Speaking for me—the guy for whom I do all my speaking—it wasn't a matter of our little tete-a-tete changing anything at all. I have neither the time nor the inclination to alter a fucking thing about how I live, and I don't view these kinds of chats as a feel-good way to re-enforce how I regard the life I designed—or lucked into.

Nor did I get the sense that anything I said had any kind of impact on my guest—and I'd have been disappointed if it had. He wasn't a kid listening to a wise, old fuck. He had all the info and experience he already needed to make the choices he had. From the sounds of it, he was grappling with a way to get off the 100 mile-per-hour merry-go-round he had elected to climb onto. I thought: good luck with that, bud, but if you do manage to disembark from that carousel as it whips around, remember to drop and roll, drop and roll.

CHAPTER FOURTEEN

Because I needed a mental palette cleansing after all that pseu-do philosophizing with Thompson and, mostly because I enjoy it immensely anytime, I was delighted to be back on the deck of the Angler Arms with Carl. It was a gorgeous late June afternoon. The surrounding trees were as full of leaves as they were going to be, and the lake was blue as hell. Yeah, it's the same view I had a little ways down the shore at my place where the beer was a helluva lot cheaper, but there was always a feeling of expan-siveness lounging around shooting the shit and being served by the ever-feisty Carla.

"Couldn't help but notice you chattin' away with that fella on the dock," Carl said. "You never sit out there."

"The guy wanted to sit there."

"And you went along? That ain't like you."

"I had to be polite. I'm interviewing for new friends."

"Arsehole."

I told him about Clayton's visit. Asked Carl if he'd ever heard of him.

"Nope. Should I?"

"Can't see a reason," I said.

Among all the people I have ever known, Carl was the least in need of either self-help or instruction on how he should simplify his life. He moved through the world completely comfortable in his own skin, perfectly attuned to the natural rhythms around him, a physical specimen at his age, kind, steady and above all, with absolutely no bullshit about him. Oh, and a helluva drinking and football-watching companion.

Now that I think about, Clayton should've been talking to him.

I was enjoying our day-drinking for itself, but I did have a purpose too.

"I'm picking up the check." I announced.

Carl became instantly suspicious.

"What the fuck's up with you? It's my turn."

"Does that F-150 of yours cluttering my yard still run?"

"Sure."

"Really? I mean, after all, it *is* a Ford."

"I'm sure. And I'm also sure you're an arsehole. What's up?"

"Mind doing a junk hauling drive?"

"Lemme get this straight. You call my truck a piece of shit and then ask to borrow it?"

"Yeah, that about sums it up."

"You *are* an arsehole."

"I also need to borrow you as the driver cuz I'll be driving the Vibe."

"OK, now you're picking up the next tab…and the one after that."

"Ever hear that song *With a Little Help from My Friends*?"

"Nope."

"That's what I thought."

I'm pretty sure we could've been mistaken for the beginnings of a vintage car exhibition, except their vintage owners had not lovingly restored their vehicles. A tip-off might've been the clouds of black smoke that trailed us as we triumphantly rattled and rolled into Peterborough.

We pretty well cleaned out Bromley's office. It didn't take long, except for the filing cabinets which we had to empty first. I marveled at my older and more powerful neighbour casually carrying three milk crates full of journals while I struggled with two.

I debated taking the old Underwood typewriter, if for no other reason than to confuse the fuck out of any millennials—should I ever have one of them in my house.

As we were finishing, a cop car pulled up and blocked the driveway. Goddamned neighbourhood watch. Although I suppose I couldn't really blame the local Gladys Kravitz for bringing the heat down on the two sketchy strangers, one dressed like a down-on-his-luck clown, the other like an extra in *The Grapes of Wrath,* who were emptying a vacant house into vehicles that resembled the 'After' pictures at a demolition derby.

"Can I help you, officer?" I pleasantly asked as I walked down the driveway to meet him.

"You can help me by staying where you are and putting your hands up!" he barked.

I suppose I couldn't really blame him for his jumpiness as he confronted two questionable strangers [Please see description above].

"Seriously?" I rather pointlessly asked as I continued to approach him.

I guess I was a tad slow in responding to his request because his hand went to his holster as he, more or less, yelled: "Now!"

I did as I was told.

"Is this your house?" he demanded.

"No, but—"

"And you're taking stuff out of it?"

"Yes but... Just call Les Macgregor. He can explain. I'm Jake

Lydon. That big old bastard is Carl."

He relaxed but told us to "stay the fuck where we were."

I was a little pissed at this point which might explain my response.

"Well, officer, seeing how you got the driveway blocked, can you honestly picture the two of us old fucks trying to escape by running through the backyards of Peterborough, scrambling over fences and shit while you call in a helicopter to track us, all the while singing "Bad boys, bad boys, whatcha gonna do"?"

He backed up to his car then reached in to grab his radio. I heard loud static and indistinguishable words.

When he was done, he returned to us with his hand still resting on his holster.

"Well?" I asked.

"He said I should let the big bastard go, his words," he deadpanned. "But to shoot you. Also his words."

"What?!" Carl said somewhat excitedly.

"Whoa, easy," the officer said. "Not, like, fatally or anything. I'm supposed to just sorta wing you."

"That prick!" I said, playing along with the gag.

"Have a good day, gentlemen," he said with a shit-eating grin on his face.

"I swear to Christ you're going to get us killed one of these days," Carl said as we watched the patrol car leave.

"You gotta admit, that was pretty funny."

The trip home was uneventful, if you don't count our overloaded vehicles swaying back and forth over the road like we were competing in a grand slalom ski event.

I wanted a beer; Carl wanted to git'r done. So that's what we did.

We re-stacked all the milk crates four feet high in my seldom-used dining room. They formed a colourful low wall taking up two and half sides of the room. I sighed at the reading ahead of me. Digging into Ted Bromley's verbose life's work looked like it could turn into my life's work.

My only consolation was that at least the dead professor could write well.

CHAPTER FIFTEEN

You can't be back again in an intellectual environment like a university and not think about its cultural impact. Their professors make you think harder, Homer, about what artists are trying to say and how they say it. They train you to analyze and discuss what you've read, seen or heard. And then you go forth and pass it on or make your own.

Because I can't build anything more complicated than a wooden deck or sing anything beyond a tuneless version of *Happy Birthday* or draw anything more detailed than stick figures, I committed to literature. God damn, I can read a book.

Imagine if those schools like Trent didn't exist, how impoverished our world would be. Except for opera; we could've done without opera. Chances are, the producers of our great books, works of music and art, wondrous buildings, all learned or perfected their art at a school.

So it's not too difficult to see universities as some kind of bastion against the barbarians at the gates. But the walls are coming down. Enrollment in the humanities has fallen off a cliff as knowledge seekers have become job seekers, signing up for computer science, business management, math and engineering.

If that trend continues, all we're going to have left is mass entertainment and popular culture. There has always been popular culture, mass entertainment that amuses, distracts, and make you temporarily feel good. It has value but, thank Christ, there's more.

Now don't get me wrong. I like wasting my life away watching videos of waterskiing squirrels, drunken Russian drivers, rampaging monkeys, and guys getting punched in the nuts by their kids as much as the next person, but, Jesus, there has to be a limit on the number of them and, for that matter, the number of people who will do dumb shit for a camera. But apparently there isn't. I'll read books from the infinite pile of mysteries, enjoy some blockbuster, and watch disposal TV shows—although I do draw the line at anything Kardashian; that way lies madness.

But there *has* to be something deeper, more original, more moving.

That 'more' lies in the books, songs, and movies we love.

We all spend some time looking for arguments and opinions that support things we already believe. Polls, scientific studies, and above all, music, movies and books give us a shorthand to having a point while revealing a lot about character.

Put another way, you can't tell me you absolutely love Ayn Rand above all writers and not already be a selfish, arrogant crypto-fascist dickwad.

Call me a snob. Call me an antiquated, out of touch, cranky, close-minded snob if you want to be more specific (and accurate). We are told that every generation creates its own identifiers, its own cultural touchstones. And that's probably true, but only recently and in developed nations. And only for the last hundred years or so has the technology even existed that allowed each generation to create and cast out on the waters to be consumed, and then to be scorned and replaced within fifteen or twenty years by the next generation's take on things.

Does that mean that every generation's books, movies, and songs are as good as the generation's before or after that? No, it just means every generation really likes its emblems. Surely to Christ there are standards.

All the kinds of music and movies us old farts like still exist. But they're not popular and you have to be a fucking detective to find them. It's a whole lot easier to just hear or watch the originals over and over again as we sink into drooling dotage.

And that's my point.

Other than technical wizardry, there's a pretty straight line from the current endless string of comic book movies back to the Busby Berkley musicals of the 1930s. Gaudy, mindless big-scale confections designed to distract, amuse, visually delight, while signifying absolutely nothing.

But there was a time, a glorious ten-year period starting in 1967 and ending in 1977, when really great films were also among the most popular. In 1967, the top-grossing movie was *The Graduate*, a film that also had a goddamn point and some pretty nifty social commentary. Flip ahead forty years to 2007, the most watched message-y movie was *Children of Men*, coming in at #75. In 2018, the Academy Award's Best Picture was *The Shape of Water*, not quite dominating the box office at #63. Back in 1969, the Oscar went to the X-rated *Midnight Cowboy* which was also the third-highest grossing film that year—edging out *Easy Rider*.

I look this kinda shit up all the time.

Now we're down to arguing which comic book superhero movie is the best and whether the Marvel or DC universe is superior, for fuck's sake. Why, the same arguments we used to have when we were *children*. A while back, there was unanimous agreement that *Black Panther* was the best of breed. And it may very well be. But that's a whole lot like saying that this guy or that guy is the best ice hockey player in Trinidad. Imagine the lowest limbo bar there ever was. Well, lower than that.

Same goes for which auto-tuned formulaic pop song is better. They're all shit.

But there was a time when musicians wrote and recorded songs that were wildly inventive and, the better ones didn't sound like anything else you'd ever heard or seen. Nobody sounds like Stevie Nicks or Dylan or Mellencamp or Joplin or Jagger or Jim Morrison (or Van for that matter) and a host of others. And nobody at the time played guitar like Hendrix or Robbie Krieger or Carlos Santana, Jeff Beck, and on and on. Again, the same kind of talent exists today, but it's not popular beyond 20-second Tik-tok clips.

Today, it's as if the whole point is to be like everyone else. Nowhere is that more evident than the raft of glitzy talent shows that are little more than gussied up karaoke.

One of the scariest things is thinking how the children growing up will be affected by this disheartening lack of originality.

I worry about the little darlins because they're being given permission to fuck around with original creations. I stumbled across The Disney channel, for fuck's sake, where a baby frog is trying to direct a theatrical version of *The Three Little Pigs*—notwithstanding the fact that baby frogs have a notoriously poor record helming Broadway, or even off-Broadway productions. His actors don't want to play it as written, insisting on a spaghetti house instead of a brick one. He complains to a faceless adult shot from the waist down and is admonished—in song no less—that everybody can change any story they want. What horseshit! It's not your goddamned story! Don't like it? Fine. Make your own up but don't fuck with something that's already been created. Never mind that the point of original is that planning, common sense, and hard work can save lives (tell me, kid, which civil engineering course taught you that spaghetti is as structurally sturdy as brick!).

So what's the goal of all this mimicry? Gotta be the money.

Nothing new here; every artist since forever wants to sell their art. Now though, it's an industry, joining a host of other industries who want to "monetize" the fuck out of everything. Look no further than the insidious influence of the Internet.

Made possible by the web, there's actually a job called Social Influencer, which I suppose is less clumsy and stupid than admitting you're a whore for this new line of purses that, coincidentally, had been given to you by the manufacturer and that, just as coincidentally, you happen to love and happen to just have to tell people about.

I'm convinced there's a guy at Facebook whose only job is to replace the useless ads and posts that were "suggested" for me with lamer still offerings. Although, how can the algorithms be wrong? Maybe they know something about me that I don't. Even though my year-round wardrobe consists mainly of shorts, Hawaiian or Tee shirts and flip-flops, just maybe I have a secret hankering for Italian suits, tailored shirts and leather dress shoes. That must be it! In my heart of hearts, known only to a computer program, I must want to be a sharp-dressed man!

My Junk Mail folder is a goldmine of online hucksterism, lies, and attempted fraud. Some of them are really quite inventive about why you should contact them or send them money. But some of them are astonishingly illiterate. Like this one, and I'm quoting here: *It give notice moreover potentially out and away them as trans in a linguistic context.*

And you wanna feel bad about yourself? Read the subject lines of about half of them dealing with health issues they're convinced you have. It's wondrous to me that all widely taught, practiced, and available medical knowledge is complete crap but that some Internet denizens hold the secrets to health and longevity. They have everything. A cure for toenail fungus. That's a biggie. So is tinnitus, the evils of metformin, nerve damage, thyroid damage, boner cures, as well as diet secrets nobody else knows. Strangers want to shrink my prostrate while supersizing my sausage. My two favourite subject lines: *Five signs your heart is in trouble (and death is near)* and *Clogged bowels?*

Wanna feel old? There are a lot of e-people out there that want to sell me walk-in showers, baldness cures, and bladder control. Feeling vulnerable? Get equipped with tactical knives, tactical sunglasses, even fucking tactical pens, for Christ's sakes. And don't forget to pick up your assault backpack, FREE stun gun, and a military flashlight that's presumably tactical as fuck. Top it off with an open carry gun permit, the best shoulder holster, and then, just a click away, contact the ex-black ops squad member who wants to share 'elite shooting techniques that will let me hit a 'dime-sized target at 50 yards,' although I've rarely felt threatened by ten-cent pieces—from that distance anyway. Wanna feel poor? Apparently, I've been pre-approved for loans from stalwart institutions like Fast Eddie's Bank totaling on any given day about 165K.

This is addition to the old standbys: Nigerian Princes, Togo lawyers, and dying widows from Burundi, all of whom want to give me at least 10 million bucks just for me being me. Secretary of State at the time Mike Pompeo even sent me one with the ten million buck notification, as did Fed chairman Powell and Warren Buffet who said he was a "business magnate." But I must say, I'm a little disappointed about their vetting process; I'm convinced they'd have the resources to find out that my name is different from my e-mail address.

Because I'm a little wary of these big money promises, I'm thinking about playing small ball by collecting on all the loyalty rewards offers from the "associates" of chain stores. CVS, Walmart, Costco, Sam's Club, Best Buy, Kohl's, Beall's, McDonald's, all want to thank me for shopping with them even though I've never set foot in their stores. They seem to be a little embarrassed about their generosity because they refuse to use their corporate web addresses and instead opt for easily-memorable addresses like: FWqBq-UKa@MRfADfa6E.MRfADfa6E.com. And if these freebies aren't enough to survive on, I can go to work for that Japanese steel company that's been head-hunting me like crazy. Six-figure income for part-time work from home as their North America Accounts Payable officer? I could do that.

It's hard not to despair about the current state of things, the dumbing down of so many institutions, and the constant sales jobs.

So it was easy for me, despite the nasty doings that brought me there, to enjoy the setting of my old university where everybody was pretty goddamned smart and nobody tried to sell me anything.

Except maybe a killer.

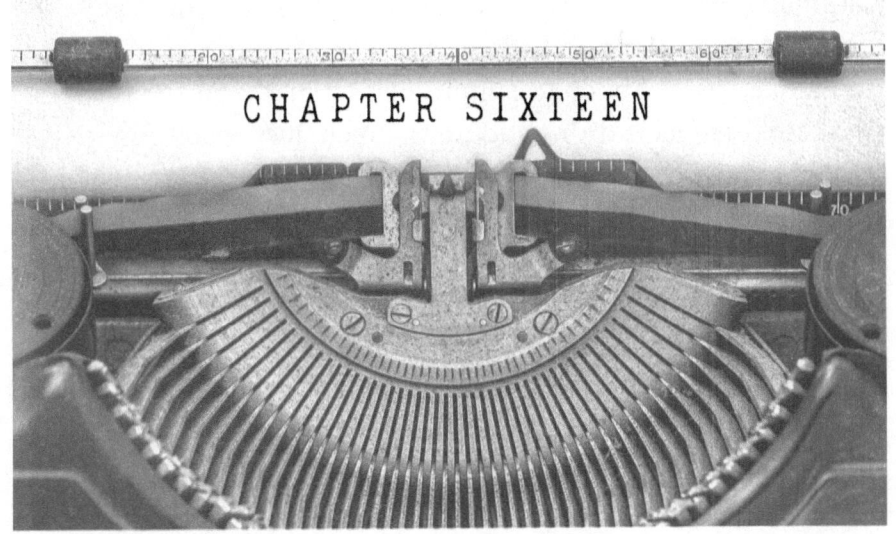

CHAPTER SIXTEEN

Every morning, before I do anything—except make coffee—I perform a news scan to find out what I've missed in the world while I was wasting my time sleeping. Local, regional, national, and international sources in a widening circle. I don't have a fucking clue why I feel I have to do this, but I do. I justify this routine as at least being informative, as opposed to many of my other habits that can only be classed as costly, mindless, and unhealthy.

This headline in the *Toronto Sun* caught my eye:

"Book Editor Murdered in Distillery District Condo"

The victim was identified as Ryan Loffler, 32, an editor at Jameson & Lord Publishing. He'd been stabbed to death in the stairwell of his downtown condo building. No suspects, no motive. An anonymous Toronto cop was quoted as saying he was surprised at the location as "there's virtually no crime in the area."

That grabbed my attention for three reasons. Ryan Loffler's employer was Clayton Thompson's publisher. His job was not one that immediately sprung to mind as a dangerous one, right up there with, oh I don't know, being an elderly English Lit professor at a small liberal arts university. And his violent murder had taken place in a neighbourhood where such events were rare to non-existent, like, say, the bucolic campus of a small liberal arts university. These three facts didn't add up to much, just wisps, really.

Armed with these faint—to the point of being illegible—connections, I decided to invest about fifteen minutes of my ever-dwindling life to filling out the context of Ryan Loffler's death.

The Distillery District was just coming on as a cool place to live when I quit the entire city of Toronto—except its airport—more than ten years earlier. Except for occasional stays in the Royal York, I had abandoned downtown Toronto a decade before that. What had been a desolate and ugly industrial area on the lip of Lake Ontario was now trendy as fuck with a shitload of renovated Victorian-era factories and warehouses housing a shitload of art galleries, boutiques, coffee houses, natural food stores, and fashionable restaurants, all complimented by a shitload of modern condo buildings, and all linked by cobblestone streets in the pedestrian-only district.

Was there any connection between Loffler and Thompson? If I wore shoes, I would've claimed to have applied some good old-fashioned shoe leather to my strenuous act of pushing away from my shitty laptop in the porch and walking all the way to my bookshelf in the living room to find my copy of *The Returning*. There were a page and a half of Acknowledgements stretching back to his Grade Three teacher in which Thompson profusely thanked a bunch of people including Patricia Morland, his agent, Publisher Truscott, his editor Henry Blake, and a few others by name, as well as "the rest of the gang from Jameson & Lord."

But no specific mention of Ryan Loffler. So, on the face of it, no apparent connection.

I walked all the way back to my "office" in the screened-in porch (I was whipped) and on to the Jameson & Lord website where I found the very recently deceased Mr. Loffler listed as a

Junior Editor with a very short list of unrecognizable writers with whom he was involved in some capacity or other.

But it was his brief bio that grabbed my attention.

BA (Honours) from Trent University.

Well, well, well. Another one of them thar wisps.

I checked the writer of the *Sun* piece. Sure enough, my buddy, Steve Golding, had e-penned the piece.

Note to self: Even if Loffler's murder had no relation to Clayton Thompson and therefore maybe Ted Bromley, have a chat with Steve to see if there was anything odd about it. And see what he thinks about the case after I gather up my wisps to show him.

Oh happy, happy day when Alex returned during the first week of July. She hadn't told me when she was coming back so I had been on high alert for a request to drive to Toronto to collect her. Instead, she just turned up one afternoon in a white Hyundai Tucson hybrid.

Joyous reunion completed, she expressed her dismay at all the crates forming a half wall around my seldom-used dining room. She was even more dismayed at what they represented: I was yet again knee-deep in the hoopla of another murder investigation.

"I'm reading, babe, just reading and thinking," I said, trying to reassure her.

What I was reading were Bromley's journals and what I was thinking was that, as a book editor, Ryan Loffler's Trent degree was likely in English which meant he likely took at least one course from Ted Bromley. I guessed at the years Loffler would have been in university given his age at death and fished out Bromley's corresponding journals.

It took a while to find them but find them I did: Bromley's candid assessments of his seminar groups. I was to learn he wrote something about every class he had. I assumed he recorded his often-bitchy evaluations to compensate for not being able to say them out loud.

One of my favourites was: *BW is extremely fortunate that his wealthy father was born before he was.*

But 'RL' was one of the few students spared his character assassinations. "*Excellent work from RL. Total grasp of the milieu and its implications.*" A year later he wrote: "*RL made the seamless transition from fin de siècle Paris to Erewhon, turning in quality papers and confidently leading discussion groups with insightful, fulsome commentary. He is worthy of my annual gift.*"

So, young Ryan had been teacher's pet in Bromley's pet literary period and in his survey course on Utopian novels starting with Samuel Butler's *Erewhon*. He'd also become the second winner of Ted's clandestine award for excellence that I'd found out about, joining Terrence Childers who won it a decade later.

July with Alexandra was as wonderful as May had been. Only warmer and less rainy. She had me back doing things with her that to the casual observer looked like physical activity. I enjoyed some, endured the others. Both of us had a gas amongst the flowers and shrubbery, whipping the garden into eye-pleasing shape. Earth-covered and too tired to shower, we savoured sunset evenings on the deck.

But our best time in my book was when we weren't even vertical. And that included lying in bed with our morning coffee doing crossword puzzles together.

"Dad?"

"Daughter! How the hell are you?"

I'd been back in Canada for more than two months and I hadn't spoken to Halley. We'd exchanged a few short e-mails of the "Welcome back" "Christ, the weather sucks" variety but that was it for contact. I understood why. She was an up-and-coming Detective on the Homicide Squad in Toronto, so she was always busy and I'm a shitty father.

"I'm fine, pops. But I missed going south this year."

"So you start with the passive aggressive shit right away?"

I actually did feel bad. Halley had visited me in the DR every March for five years until last year when my move to Florida and the resulting murderous chaos put the kibosh on our father-daughter tradition.

"Mind if I come up this weekend? I miss the old place. And its old owner."

"That'd be wonderful! Alex's here. She'd love to see you. And so would I."

"Great! Is it OK if I bring someone?"

"What, like another cop? You got a rookie detective working for you who now does all the work while you handle the press conferences?"

"Not exactly. But he is a cop."

"Fuck, I love it when you're coy….Wait! You're seeing someone?"

"Yeah."

"Who is this young punk?"

"You remember Detective Farisi."

"You asked me that last year."

"Well…."

"You're dating him? How is that young punk? What are his intentions?"

"Dad, I'm twenty-eight."

"What?! Twenty-eight! When did this happen? Why wasn't I told?"

If eye rolling had a sound, I'd be able to hear Halley making it. I live for moments like that.

"I'm happy for you, Hal. Drag him along and I promise not to make him sweat too badly."

"See you Friday after work. And please try to be nice."

She had reason to warn me; I hadn't always behaved around her dates. As a teenager, she didn't go out with boys that much. I do remember one instance in particular. I guess she'd have been sixteen, maybe seventeen. I sort of knew the young lad in question. Neighbourhood kid whom I'd met before, hanging around our rec room in the Toronto 'burbs. This was about the time when young people started banding together in packs instead of breaking off into pairs.

He came to pick her up for a movie and burger. Halley wasn't quite primped enough, so I figured I'd chat with young Bobby or Billy or whoever the fuck instead of leaving him in the driveway, slouching against his mom's Buick while she finished her rare make-up and hair chores. I sauntered out and stood right beside him, leaning on the car.

We exchanged pleasantries; the lad was nervous. I felt the need to comfort him as he looked up at me.

Falling squarely in the category of Why The Fuck Do I Do or Say Some Things?, I casually threw an arm over his scrawny shoulders, closing my hand on his insubstantial bicep.

"Now Bobby (or Billy) I like you. I really do. But you must remember: I know where you live. Are we clear?" I said, tightening my grip on his arm.

For some reason, he didn't calm down.

Halley was pissed at me for some hours for killing her sure-to-be life-long romance by scaring the shit out of her jittery suitor such that he don't come around here no more.

As an adult (her, not me), Halley didn't date much either, not that I knew anyway, but then again, as I may have mentioned, I'm a shitty father.

I didn't have a real beef with Farisi. He had been one-half of a team of Toronto Police fraud investigators who had grilled me until I was well-done over a murderous land development scheme I had uncovered. I didn't blame him for being sort of a dick during the inquisition as they had to establish that I wasn't just making shit up.

They arrived before dark. I was instantly overjoyed to be hugging my daughter again and equally happy when she and Alex embraced. Detective Farisi (actually his first name wasn't Detective but Ron) stood around looking awkward as new dates almost always are on the outside of a family circle.

For some primal reason, I almost turned our handshake into a standing arm-wrestling match—a match that both of us knew he'd lose.

We settled into a swell evening. Snacks and drinks on the deck then in the porch. A fast-moving conversation during which Ron acquitted himself well with his staunch and knowledgeable defense of recent Raider roster moves—although I wasn't convinced Halley hadn't prepped him.

At one point well into the evening and out of the blue, Halley said: "Dad, that must've been terrible news for you about the murder of that prof at Trent."

"Yup, shitty thing to happen. I took a course from him back in the Jurassic period."

"So, are you nosing around it?" she asked

I could see Alexandra giving me the side eye—with a mixture of the stink variety. I also got the distinct impression that Halley was playing her old man with her innocent-sounding comment. Why the hell was she keeping tabs on a murder months earlier and in another jurisdiction? How'd she even know about it? And why hadn't she mentioned it in any of our earlier e-mail exchanges?

"If by nosing around," I said, "you mean conducting a rigorous if somewhat unofficial investigation with all the hallmarks of Sherlock Holmes' best work, then yes."

"No, I'm pretty sure I meant nosing around."

"The answer's still yes, witch. But, for some reason, I'm thinkin' you already knew that."

"OK, OK. I talked to Les Macgregor. He said you were helping them. Didn't sound too happy about it."

"Les is a bitter, bitter man. You caught the case of the editor in the stairwell, I gather?"

"How'd you know?"

"Wild guess."

"So, unofficially, do you mind if we compare notes?"

"I originally thought they might be connected too. But it's a real stretch. As far as I can see, Stairwell Guy had nothing to do with Thompson; he wasn't his editor or anything. You know something different?"

"No, not really. Just checking all the angles."

""Not really"? C'mon, Hal. You think you're playing with kids? You saw the Bromley case file."

"Yes."

"And in it, you saw something more than the coincidence that the editor worked at the publisher whose star author had just been appointed writer-in-residence at Trent where Bromley was murdered."

"Yes, again."

"Could it have been the fact that Ryan Loffler took not one but two courses from Bromley when he was at Trent?"

"Really?"

"Really. Or was it the fact that Bromley died on the same night Thompson was speaking at the main campus?"

Here, Halley paused, obviously surprised.

"I did not know that. Are you sure?"

"Yup. About two hours after Thompson got off stage. So what similarity did you see? Was it the weapon?"

"Ordinary kitchen knife. Used from behind. It went in sideways through the rib cage. Four wounds like Bromley."

"But Bromley had a fifth. Through the heart."

"So did Loffler."

"You think it was a shitty copycat?"

"Maybe."

"Let's see."

"Oh, let's not," Alexandra said, speaking for the first time in a while and looking right at me.

"Any chance we're both full of shit even imagining the murders are somehow linked? Could the attack on Loffler be completely random?" I asked.

"Sure, it's possible," Halley said. "But highly unlikely. Loffler lived on the 28th floor. He used a bike to get to work every day, always left at exactly 8:30. He kept it in a ground floor locker just inside that stairwell. We figure the killer was waiting for him when he took the bike through the stairwell to the outside door."

"So who knew his schedule?"

"Co-workers, probably. Or anyone who just watched the building for a few days."

"Did you talk to anyone at Jameson & Lord?"

"Of course. We started with the publisher—Truscott—who seemed really broken up by it. Promised full co-operation but he didn't seem to have too much insight into Loffler. So we talked to a few of his co-workers there. A picture emerged of Loffler being quiet, intense, and conscientious. Nobody seemed to have a problem with him. Another junior editor said Loffler was getting frustrated with the job."

"Why?"

"I guess he wasn't happy that he hadn't managed to get many of the manuscripts sent to him published. Said it was killing his career. And costing him money."

"I can see that. The juniors get the slush pile. Every goddamned manuscript from every goddamned aspiring writer or agent. Odds are pretty low—like lottery-win low—that a book comes out of it. But how was it costing him money? A salary's a salary."

"Apparently, there's a commission for sales from authors you worked with."

"Oh. Never heard of that. How'd the guy get into Loffler's building? There's probably some kind of security."

"That we don't know."

"Cameras?"

"None in the stairwell."

Farisi had not been contributing to this conversation. I gathered that in the pecking order of cop etiquette, fraud investigators learn to shut the fuck up around murder detectives and their cases. But he seemed like a pretty good guy rather than the on-the-job dick he had been when he questioned me last summer. Although I grew quite alarmed when, after a few beer, he professed to not really following the NFL, preferring—of all things—English Premier League soccer, for fuck's sakes. Halley *had* planted his NFL knowledge. The witch.

We said all there was to say at the moment about people killing people. We chit-chatted a bit more and then packed it in. Alex took Halley to the guest bedroom. Farisi and I cleaned up the bottles, glasses, and dishes.

"I'll make up the couch for you." I said.

"I beg your pardon," he said, looking shocked as hell.

"My house, my rules."

He stood there kinda stupefied. As an act of mercy, I cut the schtick short.

"Just fuckin' with you," I told him.

Our bedroom was cool, mostly because Alexandra was cool.

In bed, I said to her back: "What's going on, babe?"

"I want you to be safe. *I* want to be safe."

"It's just a hobby now. Like collecting stamps or ceramic bunnies. Nuthin' to worry about, OK?"

I wake up earlier than most people. Something Halley said the night before got my interest. So, coffee and smokes in hand, I adjourned to my office, skipped my usual news scan, and went back to the original *Sun* article on Ryan Loffler's murder.

Going by the address given in Steve's news story and then its Google image, Ryan Loffler's apartment was in a towering condo building recently put up to house the horde of hipsters descending on the latest "it" neighbourhood. I could see that True Spirit (the actual name of the complex, for fuck's sake) soared over the recreated quaintness below it by about thirty stories.

Usually, anybody who lives on the 28th floor of anything in a major city pays heavily for that view. But how heavily? A few more clicks and the answer came. Everything above the 20th floor were two-bedroom apartments. If he was renting, he'd been paying about $4500 a month or 54K a year. If he owned, the joint it would've set him back about million bucks, and then tack maybe $1000 a month in condo fees to a mortgage of say 800,000 that would demand monthlies of about $5500 to stave off foreclosure.

That's a lotta dough. Not a chance a junior editor's salary covered that nut of about 55K a year after taxes just to keep enjoying the view and elevator rides. Not much left over for luxury items like food.

Our house guests didn't even have a chance to enjoy their first coffee when I was on Halley.

"How the Christ did Loffler afford his condo?" I asked.

"Good morning, father."

"Yeah, yeah. Now I repeat..."

"We're working on that."

"Big savings account? Lottery win? Luck at a casino? Stock market? Inheritance? Loan shark?"

"Dad, why don't you watch me take my *second* sip of coffee while you ponder the answer I just gave you: we're working on it!"

I was jonesing for an answer but let it drop.

"Like collecting ceramic bunnies, huh?" Alexandra said as we were cleaning up the kitchen.

To my credit, I didn't bring up the Loffler case once during the ensuing day we spent with them. There was a stretch there when Alexandra and I sat on the deck and watched Halley and Farisi—sorry, I may have to get used to calling him Ron—energetically splashing about in the lake. I patted Alex's hand.

"Ah, they grow up so quickly, don't they?"

She looked at me and smiled and I knew she was thinking exactly the same thing I was. At that moment, we both felt like we were an old married couple overjoyed to see an adult child happy.

It was a wonderful feeling.

CHAPTER SEVENTEEN

I am not a big fan of autobiographies. There aren't many where authors hold up the mirror and show themselves to be assholes, despite the fact that, statistically, there has to be a relatively high number of said assholes in that bunch. I should know.

Alexandra was otherwise occupied on her phone and computer doing something productive for her ethical investment brokerage. As a study in contrast, I was pissing away my time reading more Bromley journals

But poring over his self-documentation fascinated me. Sure, there was a ton of minutiae and a further tonnage of his frequent lack of self-awareness—particularly about his three kids whose non-attendance at his funeral indicated that they took his alienation a little more seriously than his dismissal of them as "annoying," "…a disappointment, every one of them," and "…shocking in their complete lack of perception." But, over time, you could trace the tortuous path of what he described as "the most important work of my life." [Sidebar: A lot of artists—just like a lot of people with all-consuming corporate jobs—don't even try for the ol' work/life balance. Kids are bound to get the short end when mum or dad shutters themselves away in front of an easel or keyboard or leaves them for twelve hours in an office cubicle or out on the road touring with a band 250 nights a year.]

Bromley's novel, as far as I could tell, had been variously entitled over the years *City of Light, The Rise and Fall of Simon Tate, The Phoenix on the Seine,* and *Turning Back.* It appeared as though he began the novel seventeen years earlier.

It reminded me of the old civil servant in *The Plague* who never got beyond the first sentence of the great novel he was writing once the epidemic had swept Algeria and made civil servanting pointless. Camus has the guy revising and revising that one sentence—each version perfectly fine—until—you guessed it—he dies from the plague.

I could picture Bromley hunkered down, at first on the ancient Underwood manual, the keys loudly clacking away, because that'd be the machine he'd used for years. Then making the transition to a computer and Word, maybe skipping the IBM Selectric stage.

At one point, about five years earlier, Ted was finally pleased enough with the first chapter to send it out with a query letter to the list of usual publishing suspects.

In total, he probably had a book length's worth of commentary on the book he was writing, instead of just writing the fucking thing.

Rod Serling voice-over: "Picture if you will, a man spending year after year as a virtual slave to tinkering."

But finish it he did. In August of 2019 by his account.

"*There*! [he wrote] *It is done! And I am done with changing it.*

Swelled by its completion, Ted was pretty goddamned proud of what he had accomplished. And so he should have been, just as I bet Hercules gave himself a little self-praise after the day he spent cleaning out the Augean Stables with their thousands of cows.

And then came Bromley's inevitable self-doubt as he tried to get published. Was *City of Light* (his final title choice) any good? Were people going to think it was any good?—two completely different questions, by the by.

James Lee Burke famously took it on the chops one hundred and eleven times over *The Lost Get-Back Boogie*, his fourth novel (after bombing on his third book thirteen years earlier). He had nine years' worth of rejections from agents and publishers before lucky #112 paid off, leading to a Pulitzer nomination and a well-deserved career elegantly making shit up.

Unpublished writers—I know—sustain themselves with this story. Not a lot of time goes into thinking about the anonymous scribe who, after one hundred and ten fuck-off letters, asks: "What the hell am I doing?" And then goes back to their day job. No difference between that and the undrafted college football player who hopes to walk on at a college training camp, then improbably make the team, before turning pro, then ending up with a Hall of Fame career.

Bromley had eleven rejections (each one commented on in his journals with increasingly despairing and bitter words) until a nibble! From Jameson & Lord.

Huzzah! He wrote on October 11, 2019, *Jameson & Lord is interested. I am to e-mail the entire manuscript to them "immediately." They've had a draft since 2017 so it appears my extra work and prompting of RL has paid off!*

C'mon, folks; you can't be surprised. Former Trent grad, former student of Ted Bromley, and now formerly living Ryan Loffler had done his former teacher a solid. But what exactly had he said?

I switched to Ted's computer and the Inbox of his e-mail account, searched 'Ryan,' and up came a string of correspondence, maybe ten, with the first one coming three years ago. I started there and worked my way up to the most recent. The second to last one sounded final:

For what it's worth, Professor Bromley, I didn't want to write that rejection letter. I was told to; it was my job. I recommended your novel. I believed in it and fought for it at the Publishing Board meeting because some members had changed from when you first mailed your query and draft a few years ago. Marketing and Sales overruled me again. They said it was too tough a sell. Just as they had indicated years ago.

I'm sorry but there's nothing else I can do. Best of luck somewhere else.

But there was one more message Loffler wrote. Its subject line was in bold showing it was unread. It was timed and dated as 11:06 March 23, about the same time Ted Bromley was being stabbed to death in the university parking lot.

I opened it.

Please stop writing and calling me. I will no longer be polite.

I switched to Bromley's Sent folder, searched 'Ryan' again. There were a lot more e-mails Ted sent to his ex-student than what he had received from him. Over thirty of them, some to his work address and some to his private account. In the beginning, they were lengthy, polite, and beggarly. But they became shorter and more demanding. The last one, dated this past March 20th was telling.

By your refusal to talk to me or address the issue, I can only conclude that you are involved in this conspiracy against me. Be assured I shall implicate you along with the others when I unmask that charlatan. As I intend to do soon.

Ho-ly shit!

Buckets of bad blood. But over what? What was the 'conspiracy' Bromley raged against?

I reckoned that his submitted book was the source of his acrimony towards his former star student, which meant I should have at least some familiarity with it.

I searched his files and found that he kept every draft, all twenty-two of them, in a file marked BOOK, followed by a date like in his Journals. In his filing cabinets we had lugged up here, were pages, hundreds of them, in bulging manila folders representing the hand-written and typewriter origins of his magnus opus, dating back to the mid-90s.

Might as well see what all the fuss was about by actually reading the book. I chose the file marked 'Book Final.' Being an old fart resistant to any change, I don't much care for reading novels on a computer screen, but that's the only place it existed.

It was good. A pleasure to read, mainly because the sentences were crafted so carefully. Setting aside the oh-so predictable story line, it was a decent reworking of familiar themes. Ever read any Henry James? Be honest. Well, *City of Light* was like that: meticulously constructed but bloodless, devoid of any honest human emotion that would make you give a good goddamn about any character or what happened to them.

But something did stand out: six, maybe seven other bolded sections, one lasting more than a page. I recognized them all, as obviously Bromley would have too.

They were contained in Clayton Thompson's book.

Zero wonder that Bromley had a hard-on for Thompson.

CHAPTER EIGHTEEN

This whole plagiarism thing boggles my wee brain. Ol' Tommy Stearns Eliot once said: "Good writers borrow. Great writers steal." While I didn't think that this defense of plagiarism would stand up in a court of law, it raised a big-ass question. What's a rip-off and what's an homage? What's original and what's a thinly disguised copy? What deserves to be decided by a court and what deserves a loud "fuck off!" for even trying to sue?

That famous musical jurist, Keith Richards, points us to an answer. He and the Stones have always respectfully acknowledged that without the American blues legends of the 40s, 50s, and 60s—Howlin' Wolf, Buddy Guy, John Lee Hooker, Robert Johnson, Jimmy Reed, Elmore James— their band wouldn't exist. They recorded and played with them (just the living ones), and they indirectly got them finally paid by promoting the hell out of them. But there's no way in hell any one of the American legends would be mistaken for Mr. Jagger and his blues band

Or let Kurt Vonnegut explain his defense against the accusation that his first novel, *Player Piano*, was far from original. I'm grossly paraphrasing a comment he made in his *Playboy* interview from the early 70s (when the articles *were* really good, I swear!) that I'm too lazy to look up. Kurt proclaims that he "cheerfully ripped off the plot for *Brave New World* that Huxley had cheerfully ripped off from Eugene Zamatyan's *We*."

You cut Vonnegut some slack because all he's doing is pointing out that the plot line for just about every male-centred dystopian novel is the same. Rebels against authoritarianism, rages against the machine, meets and falls in love with a sympathetic woman. They either escape to uncertain freedom or one or both of them are crushed. The end.

Likewise with music. Señor Google says there are just over 4,000 chords in music. Apparently, most pop music—where the big money is—uses about four of them—although the Ramones built a career knowing *maybe* half that number. On the other hand, the English language contains 170,000 words with most people regularly using about 20-30,000. Let's assume writers know the upward limit. (Asterisk for Hemingway who evidently employed less than 10% of them).

Like I said, it's how you piece together those words, those chords (or those brushstrokes or camera angles) that make a made thing yours and yours alone.

I don't have a lot of principles. I mean, if pressed, I couldn't sit down and write out a long list of them. But I react strongly to situations as they come up. And sometimes, those situations themselves dictate my reactions. For instance: stealing instantly pisses me off a lot. From garden-variety break and enters to knifepoint muggings, all the way up to the swindling and defrauding that routinely goes on in the more refined corporate world where nobody gets blood on their white collars.

Most people aren't anywhere near this kind of skullduggery. But a lot of people steal. Cheating on your taxes, lying in an insurance claim, pirating movies or music—it's all stealing from somebody. And it all rankles me because it violates one of my simple rules: don't take other people's shit.

But the theft of someone's idea, something they wrote down or recorded, a real thing they made out of nothing, that makes me nuts. I've got some notion of what it takes to sweat out a book. How much it matters to you, how much time you devote to it, how much it consumes you, how goddamned great you feel when a sentence, a paragraph, a few pages, a chapter truly come into being so that when you re-read it in the next dawn's early light and then read again and fix the little fuck-ups, you know—you really *know*—you done good.

But then to have somebody—a complete fucking stranger— see the same thing and think: "Say, I really like that. Yoink! It's mine." That's just monstrous.

So I could pretty easily see how apeshit Bromley would've have become knowing that he'd been ripped off.

So what exactly was Bromley going to do about it? And what did he expect to have happen when he was done whistleblowing?

I remembered Rob Byford had told me just before he died that Bromley had contacted Thompson. Back to his computer for a search for any e-mails. There was a brief exchange that laid out the whole accusation.

On March 14 of this year, Bromley wrote:

I finally read your alleged book today. You have stolen from me. Multiple times.

Here is one example. It's the turning point for your clichéd, card-board hero in your facile book:

> *"He stepped off the train in a small village not twenty minutes away from the New York outskirts. And was transported. Such a great distance from the side streets and alleyways of the city that never sleeps. He saw that now behind the station as he lay in the pasture in the tall golden wheat, the fragrance on the*

slight breeze, the meadow larks singing, the sky an enveloping azure sea. A universe away from the fetid smells, the garbage, diseased prostitutes, the danger.

Now here is what I wrote over ten years ago:

"He stepped off the train in a small village not twenty minutes from the Paris outskirts. And was transported. Such a great distance from the backstreets and alleyways of the city with no light. He saw that now behind the station as he lay in the pasture in the tall golden wheat, the fragrance on the slight breeze, the meadow larks singing, the sky an enveloping azure sea. A universe away from the fetid smells, the garbage, the poisoned prostitutes, the danger.

Any chance you see the similarity?"

Thompson had replied two days later with: *I have no idea what you are talking about.*

Bromley had responded that same day with a similarly terse reply: *Then you shall find out when the world knows, you thieving bastard.*

I assumed that Bromley felt the least, the very least Thompson could do is acknowledge his theft. Announce it, apologize, and let the proverbial chips fall where they may. A bunch of journalists had done that; copped to everything from inventing sources to just cutting and pasting from someone else's speeches or articles. And I could almost see the pressure on journalists to do so. They're on a schedule, having to regularly file columns or think pieces even when they'd maybe hit an irregular unscheduled wall of writer's block. The fall-out for them hadn't been pretty, at least publicly, because the stink of plagiarism follows you.

There was a cartoon by the great Stan Mack in *National Lampoon* many, many years ago that's on point. Guy named Murray Oxe who, while addressing the crowd at his wedding reception, lets loose with a truly bombastic and malodourous world-class fart. In utter shame, he leaves his town, crosses the country, changes his name, and lives a quiet life. After ten years, he deems it safe to return home. He was happy to be back and walking around his hometown when he passes an open window and overhears a young girl speaking. "Momma," she said, "I can never remember the date of my birthday." "That's easy," her mother replied. "It's two days after the anniversary of Murray's Fart."

Well, that's the effect of being caught copycatting.

I imagined the consequences for Thompson would be just as severe as Murray's Fart. I could only guess at the motivation. Most obviously, he must've done it to help create a multi-million-dollar enterprise. His continuing silence was in the service of protecting that giant cash cow. But that was true well after the fact. He might've hoped to become mega-rich when the word theft took place, but it wasn't a sure thing. So why'd he do it when he was first writing the book?

I had become incensed on Bromley's behalf. Particularly after our shooting-the-shit session on my dock where Thompson fed me that line of bullshit about training himself to be a good writer.

I sent him a short e-mail.

I understand from Ted Bromley's correspondence that you and he shared something in common: his writing. I think we should talk. Let me know what's a good time for you.

I can't say I felt triumphant about sending my "*J'accuse!*" note. For one thing, what came out of my note was the only thing that mattered. And for another, the last guy who called bullshit on Clayton Thompson's originality found himself bleeding out in a deserted parking lot.

But the fact remained: In black and white pixels we had a darn good motive for Thompson or somebody close to him to slip out of his post-lecture meet n' greet and follow or walk with Ted out to his car.

Except.

Except how the fuck would that someone get his—or her—
hands on the Viking meat skewer from Ted Bromley's house? I'd
put serious money on the fact that the only Viking skewers in
Peterborough at that time belonged to Ted Bromley.

I tried to put that detail aside, feeling comfortable in believing
that what had started out as a hunch that Bromley's death was
somehow linked to Thompson's first Trent lecture that same night,
only a few hundred yards from the murder scene, was now heading in the direction of becoming a solid-gone fact.

CHAPTER NINETEEN

But I couldn't put that one detail aside; it was bugging the shit out of me. If Thompson was the killer, he somehow had to have come into possession of the skewer that we knew was the murder weapon. And either he'd visited Bromley's house, or it had been given to him, or he had taken it from Bromley on the night of and used it on him. I quickly discarded that last possibility as I didn't think Ted routinely tooled around campus with a foot and a half of Norse steel tucked into his dad jeans.

There had to be some previous connection between the professor and the alumnus. But when? The only immediate source of a possible answer lay in Ted Bromley's detailed journals. Realistically—and sadly for me—the time frame for that connection was some day between the murder and Clayton Thompson's university days. I found his graduating class in his bio then forlornly stared at the half-wall of milk crates encircling my dining room. More than twenty years since Thompson's probable time as a student translated to about two hundred journals to go through. Pitter-patter, Jake.

I worked backwards for a while, scanning rather than reading for any notation of 'CT.' I stopped after five years, reasoning that Thompson's *Returning* wasn't likely even an idea in his brain before that. And it had only cost me a whole goddamned day and some eyestrain. No mention of CT. Fuck!

Although I was pretty sure Alex didn't want to hear a goddamned word about my snooping, I did want to tell her about what I'd found out at that point.

So far, I hadn't been very specific about what I'd learned from all my reading of the Bromley papers.

To my utter surprise, she offered to help when I told her about the potential mass-scale plagiarism. A former English grad herself, she had the same sense of outrage that I did.

We divvied up the load, me starting in journals from 1999, her picking up where I'd left off with the most recent volumes. We worked towards the middle. I got the impression that Alexandra was actually enjoying the literary tomb raiding. I was more or less just scanning for the initials, but Alexandra would chirp out various entries she found amusing.

But at the end of all that, we had fuck-all. No CT. Well, one. But it didn't take very long to disqualify that CT as being Clayton Thompson. Here's what Bromley wrote: *CT is obviously smart, but she is far too sensitive to criticism. Twice in seminars so far, she has broken down crying at mild arguments by her classmates of her position on Hugo's obsession with the architecture in* Hunchback. *Unless she toughens, I find it difficult to see her in front of a class of high school or even university students, the likely destination of most English graduates.*

The only other possible explanation I could think of was in the ten days between Ted's accusatory note and his demise Thompson had confronted him in person at his home and lifted the skewer then. No way in the fucking world Bromley wouldn't have commented on that visit in his most recent journal.

The problem was, I didn't have the goddamned thing.

I was certain there had to be one. No chance Bromley would have abandoned writing about himself after about half a century of self-recording. Most likely, I had missed it in my search of Bromley's place.

Bromley's house had been listed and already sold. I figured the real estate agent might know what happened to the rest of its contents that weren't already cluttering up my hovel.

I still had his business card in my wallet. Along with several lottery tickets from two years earlier. I hadn't checked the numbers and wouldn't now. Because lottery winnings are a key—perhaps the most critical cornerstone of my business and retirement planning—I couldn't deal with knowing that I'd blown collecting millions just because I'm too fucking lazy to look up the winning numbers.

After I informed him I wasn't in the market for a new house, ol' Doug told me that none of the kids showed up, so the executor had to deal with "all that old shit," as he put it.

"And the name of that executor?"

"Gordon Wellsley, that old lawyer in town."

I got off the phone thinking that maybe my luck had changed. That old lawyer was my old lawyer. All I'd have to do is put up with his string of corny puns and jokes and I might get somewhere.

Turned out, I was wrong.

Gord wasn't in a jokey mood. Lawyers get that way when you ask about another client's business.

"C'mon, Gord; it can't be a state secret."

Begrudgingly, he told me that the contents in the house had been "disposed of." The everyday shit had been donated to Habitat for Humanity. The antiques had been auctioned off at an estate sale. Except, he said, the Viking battle gear.

He explained that the professional assessor had determined that all the Viking stuff was, indeed, authentic.

"By law he had to let the Norwegian government know that these historical items were without provenance in our province."

"Good one, Gord."

"So we shipped everything back."

"You have an inventory list?"

"You mean a table of contents?"

"Another good one, Gord. Yes."

"Yes, I do."

"I just need to know how many meat skewers were on that list."

"Let me take a stab at it."

I could hear him rummaging around paper and the slam of a cabinet drawer.

"No meat skewers," he said. "But I see daggers accounted for. Five of them."

A thought occurred to me.

"What about what was his in his car?"

"Junk as I recall, except for some books, oh, and a leather-bound journal."

"I need that! Do you know where it is?"

"Right here in my office. But I don't think I can give it you."

"Of course, you can," I assured him. My explanation—that I was working with the police—he could call them—and the fact that I already had more than fifty other journals, had him wavering. I wore him down with a volley of cajoling, wheedling, begging, and pleading. That tipped the scales.

"Come and get it," he finally said.

I was there in half an hour, and reading it minutes later at a table in The Red Dog. Beginning with his March 13 entry, right up until his demise ten days later, Bromley railed and raged about the word theft he had discovered. Page after page of articulate anger, all devoted to one simple idea: "I'm mad as hell and I'm not going to take it!"

But no mention of Thompson showing up at his place.

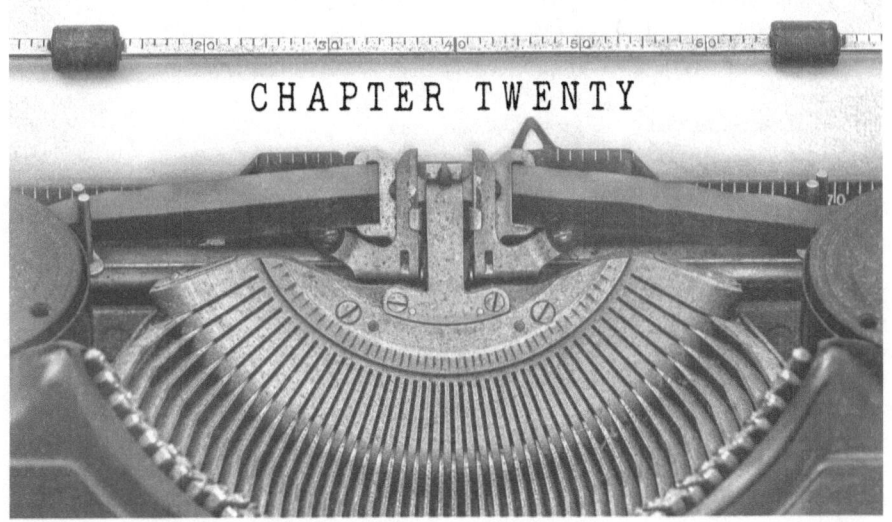

CHAPTER TWENTY

At the best of times, I despise answering the phone because the caller always wants something. Except middle of the night calls. That's when the caller usually only wants one thing: to tell you shitty news. That's what I was thinking as I stumbled out of bed in the dark to answer the incessant ringing. The stove clock said it was 11:03 (I'm old, OK? Most of us seniors consider 11:03 the middle of the goddamned night). I was relieved it wasn't Halley or about Halley, but concerned that the nasally voice talking at me was Les Macgregor's.

"Jake, we just got a 9-1-1 from a hysterical woman, said her boyfriend was threatening to kill her and then himself."

"That's terrible. But why tell me in the middle of the god-damned night?"

"I guess you know the boyfriend."

"Who?"

"Clayton Thompson."

"Holy shit!"

"He asked for you."

"Me? Why the fuck would he ask for me?"

"No idea. Maybe he wants to be weirded to death."

"I can get there in twenty minutes."

"I'll send a car."

"No time. I'm on my way."

"Don't you want the address?"

"Place out off 28, just past the bait shop?"

"How'd you know?"

"Because I'm fucking smart, Les!" and I quickly hung up.

I laid it out for a disturbed Alexandra after I got off the phone.

"You're going, aren't you?" she said.

"Not too much of a choice, babe. Before you get all pissed at me, you have to tell me what you'd do in the same situation?"

She considered it, but I knew what her honest response had to be. If the roles had been reversed, she'd already have been out the door. Like I said, she's waaaay nicer than I am. She didn't answer; she didn't have to.

"Maybe he just wants you," she said as she watched me take four beer out of the fridge and put them in a plastic bag.

"Doubt it. Can't see how he'd know I know. Plus, if he wanted to mess with me, all he'd have to do is drive up here and wait."

"Please, *please* be careful."

I hadn't been looking to add Hostage Negotiator to my CV but what the hell else could I do, I thought as I drove away. It was mighty tempting to just turn around and head home. We'd hear about the hostage drama tomorrow—no matter which way it turned out. And we'd either think: "What a tragedy" or "Glad it worked out." And we'd move on.

On the other hand, I felt guilty at the possibility that my e-mail to him may have caused Thompson to snap. Maybe I had convinced Alex that he wasn't after me, but I wasn't completely sure myself. She didn't know about the e-mail I sent him two days earlier.

The scene wasn't at all like I expected. I passed two cops cars sitting at Stone's Live Bait Shop on the main road but saw nothing and nobody else until I turned down Rob's side road carved into the thick forest of pine, spruce, or whatever the fuck. Yellow police tape finally stopped me just before the clearing where Rob's cabin was. Behind it weren't the ten cruisers you usually see in movies with the black SWAT truck and the place ringed by combat geared-up snipers. Instead, just one cop car.

Two officers were watching the house, more or less loitering, their guns holstered. No unintelligible megaphone, no search lights bathing the cabin in blinding light, no thrill-seeking crowd unless you count the possibility of some casually interested raccoons lurking in the forest.

One approached me. An officer, not a raccoon.

"Constable Dysart," I said. "How are you on this fine summer night?"

"Jake. Macgregor down in Peterborough said you were coming."

It was good to see Dysart. After a rocky start a few years back, he'd proved to be a stand-up guy during some near-fatal unpleasantness the previous summer. With him on the scene, there'd be some calm and some common sense.

"You're the cavalry?" he said.

"I know; goddamn scary, right? Anything going on?" I asked, motioning towards the cabin.

"Not a thing."

"Anybody talk to him?"

"No. A couple of hours ago, he came out onto the porch with the woman sort of in a headlock and the gun at her temple. Just yelled that he was serious and to stay back. So we're staying back. Letting things calm down."

"Any idea what he wants?"

"None. We tried talking to him, called on her cell. Used the megaphone. Nothing. We've got eyes on them through that front window. Hard to see because he's just got an oil lamp on."

"There's no electricity in the house."

"So we discovered. Looks like they're just talking. She's probably trying to get him to settle down too."

"No shots?"

"We would've been in there."

"You guys ready if this shit gets real?"

"Sure. Got these flak jackets, got a battering ram. Two more cars just down the road."

"Where are the snipers? There's supposed to be like thirty snipers."

"None of that made sense to the brass. We're keeping a lid on it. No need to panic the neighbours. Or him."

"I'm going in."

"Sure you're OK with this?"

"Gotta do it. Beer's getting warm."

"Clayton! It's Jake!" I shouted as I walked towards the cabin. "Want to talk?"

I was almost at the front steps when I heard the lock turn on the door.

"You alone?" he asked from the other side of the wood slab.

"I'm pretty well always alone," I answered.

"Wait there ten seconds."

Impatient little fucker that I am, I counted off seven and turned the door handle. He was standing behind an easy chair that Jan Morris was sitting in. He had an arm around her neck, his gun pressed into her temple. None too surprisingly, she looked terrified.

"Lock the door and sit down over there," he said, indicating another easy chair flanking the couch on the side.

I did as told and sat down. He parked himself on the couch between us. There was an awkward silence where we just stared at each other. There was no real tension in the air, more like expectation that somebody better say something to get things rolling.

"So," I said. "I suppose you're wondering why I called you here tonight…"

I've been told that I have this fucking annoying habit of joking around in serious situations.

Tough crowd. Nary a chuckle.

"Alright then," I said. "Maybe we can start with an easy topic."

"Sure."

"Where'd you get the gun and why?"

"I used to get many very graphic threats—particularly when I was in the States," he answered, almost wistfully. "My agent thought it would be a good idea, just in case…"

"So not for special occasions like this?"

"No."

"Ever use it?"

"Good lord, no. Why are you asking?"

"Just curious. Now, maybe you can tell me what you want."

"I want…I want to work some things out."

"Fine, let's do that. But first, let her go. You got no beef with her."

He waved her away with his gun. Without hesitating, she got up and walked to the front door, glancing back once.

Little alarm bells started ringing in my wee brain. Something wasn't right. She didn't scramble to get the fuck out of there. He didn't take more than a few nanoseconds to consider my toothless order. And she should've been a lot more relieved. Or concerned about what was going to happen to her boyfriend once she was gone. It also struck me as stupid to have a hostage on either side of him, making it tough to cover both.

Then I asked myself what she was doing during at least ten seconds as he walked to the door to unlock it for me, spoke to me, and walked back again. Because she was living there, she had to know—just as I knew when we were building the cabin decades ago—that there was a set of French doors off the bedroom at the rear of the small house. The instinct to fight or flee is just a fact. She could've been out those doors in about five seconds and into the dark bush. None of it was adding up.

"Was it your idea or the PR lady's?" I asked.

"What?"

"Who came up with this fake hostage shit? I'd really like to know."

"What are you talking about?"

"Oh, I see; you're going to make me guess. OK, what about this: You knew the jig was up about your plagiarizing after you got my e-mail on top of Bromley's. Career finished forever in disgrace if I went public. You're a smart guy so you ruled out murdering me because you could get caught—most people do. If you did get arrested—boom!—a twenty-five-year sentence. And a really, really ruined career. This way, you prove severe mental distress; we struggle because the hero moron—that would be me—attempts to disarm you. Gun goes off. Bye-bye, Jake; hello, maybe five years for manslaughter. Gets me dead and you off the hook for the next book. You now have five years to write it. And talk about a simple life; prison's may be the simplest of all lives. You come out in triumph, rehabilitated, ready for your redemption tour. That close enough?"

The rueful little smile that popped up on his face confirmed my theory.

"Fuckin' philosophy majors," I continued.

"What?"

"Big picture, it's a plan, maybe even a good plan. But in the *real* world, shit like this doesn't work. Heard of GSR? We'd both be covered in gunpowder residue if we were grappling. I've got forty pounds and maybe a four-inch reach on you. Do you actually think you can get close enough for that gun to be touching anything but my hand?

"I can if you're dead."

"And you explain the long-distance shot how?"

As our eyes locked. Clayton paused. He was a smart man. He had to be imagining possible outcomes. In seconds, he would've run through his options. In seconds, he would've understood he didn't have any. His shoulders slumped. In seconds, he saw an inescapable truth: there was no way he could rescue his original scheme. And there was no Plan B.

"So what now?" he asked quietly.

"You put the fucking gun down."

"And then?"

I posed the universal question that signifies a desire to talk: "Want a beer?"

Thompson gently placed the pistol on the dining room table and stepped away. He sat down in the opposite easy chair, took the beer I'd placed on the coffee table between us.

"Were you really going to kill me?" I asked. "I mean, did you actually think you could bring yourself to do it?"

"Not my first choice. I wanted to talk you out of going public. Pay you, if I had to."

"But then you realized neither probably would work on me."

"So after I got your e-mail, I saw I had no choice but to disprove F. Scott Fitzgerald's claim that there was no second act in America."

"For fuck's sake, his actual quote was: "I *once* thought that there were no second acts in American lives." There isn't much Americans—and Canadians—hell, anybody—admire more than a second act. Rise, fall, redemption, triumph. Why, the book practically writes itself, don't you think?"

"Funny."

"Did you know about all the plagiarized parts?"

"No. Not before publication."

"I call bullshit!"

"I didn't," he insisted." Henry Blake, my editor, would send me these lengthy suggestions for rewrites. Most of them very much better than what I had done. I had never published a book. I thought he was doing what an editor is supposed to do."

"But you found out different?"

"*After* the book took off. When Bromley sent me a note last March, well after it came out. But it was too late by then. What choice did I have?"

"Yeah, I can see how it'd be quite the ethical and philosophical dilemma. Having to pick between all that money and fame or the goddamned truth. Gee, I wonder what Socrates would've done? Wait! I know. He'd man the fuck up! Take the hit."

"I'm not Socrates."

"No shit. Who else knew?"

"Henry. I confronted him and he admitted it. He had to. I had Bromley's pages."

"Anybody else?"

"My agent. I told her about it. I also told her that every word of the new book would be mine."

"Sorry, but you don't get a fucking hero biscuit because you decide *not* to commit a crime in the future."

"I know."

"Was that publisher dude, Truscott, in on the scam?"

"Not that I'm aware. I don't think so, but maybe. He and Patricia are close."

"Did you kill Bromley?"

"No!" he said, with a heap o' emphasis.

"Did you kill Ryan Loffler?"

"No! Who? I didn't kill anybody!"

Even though he appeared ready to whack me, I believed him. One of the very few things I'm good at—besides smoking and gardening—is being able to instantly tell if someone's lying. There's always a moment, just a split second, when you catch their eye, and you *know*.

"So you weren't in on it, but you did find out."

"Yes. By then, what was I supposed to do?"

"For Christ's sake, two innocent people would still be alive!"

It was as if he considered that fact for the first time.

"I'm…sorry."

"Isn't that just fucking wonderful of you? Now, let's get this over, OK?"

We drained our beer.

"You go out first," he said, "Calm them down."

That made sense, I thought, as we walked to the door together. It'd be a pretty shitty way to end the evening, getting accidentally gunned down by an over-excited cop.

"Careful where you step, Jake. There's poison ivy out there," he said, just as the door closed behind me. "And hemlock."

I was at the top of the steps when I heard those words. I froze. Aw fuck! I thought, just as I heard the deadbolt slide into place behind me. I wheeled and ran to the door, pounded pointlessly on the solid wood. Yelled for the cops to come, just as the single shot rang out. Dysart swung the heavy battering ram and the door frame splintered.

I knew what we'd find once inside. Thompson was sitting in the chair. His head hung on his chest as if he were sleeping. Except there was no top to his skull, just a bloody mess where most of his hair should've been.

I could hear the screams from Jan Morris. Dysart's partner turned to intercept her on the porch, held her as she sobbed.

"What the hell just happened?" Dysart said.

"Socrates happened."

I wasn't in the mood for a history tutorial and didn't supply any more information. It was pretty obvious what had just happened. Instead, I changed the subject.

"Nuthin' for us to do here, right?" I said. "Go look after her."

"We will."

The initial shock had worn off. That's when I considered the fall-out from this sad, sad night.

"You have to hold her at the station," I said.

"For what reason?"

"I don't know. Anything. For her own protection, suicide watch. She just lost her man. But don't believe a word she says and don't let her talk to the media, to anybody."

"We'll see what the higher-ups say. But we need a statement from you, Jake."

"Understood, but I gotta get home. Can it wait until tomorrow?"

"Welll…"

"And besides. You guys are gonna be up all night figuring how you're gonna play this."

"Any suggestions?"

"Try this: 'We can't say much. It's under investigation. Looks like Mr. Thompson snapped under some kind of pressure. We'll update you as soon as we can.' And tell your bosses not to take any questions. Same goes for Peterborough. Can you call Les Macgregor?"

"I'll pass that along."

"Can you keep me out of this for the meantime? Like I wasn't here."

"Hey, Corson!" he called out to the other cop. "You seen Jake Lydon around? You haven't? Me neither."

I drove and thought, my hands gripping the wheel to keep them from shaking over one inescapable fact. It was all my fault. If I had only pocketed the gun.

And that mistake led to such a waste, such a shame. The weight of expectation, the enormity of the business, the sin of fakery had crushed Clayton Thompson. Clichéd as hell but not hard to understand.

At least, that's what I hoped as I sat in my driveway until I was sure I had calmed down enough to talk to Alex. It was 3 a.m. and I could see her in the window, waiting.

Yet again, I was about to lie to her because I didn't want to alarm her. She meant more to me than anything or anybody. She had almost kissed me good-bye a few months ago because she just couldn't take the high-stakes dramas I was regularly involved in. I didn't blame her. I was truly scared shitless that the night's she-nanigans would end us if she knew.

We didn't start off talking. We hugged and not one of those casual, brief affairs either, more like a death grip where you couldn't tell which person wanted to end it.

"Are you OK, babe?" she asked as she pulled away to study my eyes.

"I'm fine, darlin', just fine."

"What happened?"

"I need a drink. And beer ain't going to cut it."

My lovely lady instantly grabbed the Cazadores tequila bottle and poured me two fingers—if those fingers had belonged to Andre the Giant.

"Clayton Thompson's dead," I announced after the first gulp pleasantly burned its way down my throat.

"A shoot-out?" she asked with alarm.

"Didn't get that far. Self-inflicted."

"And you watched this?"

"Pretty awful...I should've done more."

"You can't blame yourself. You could've been killed."

"Naw. Never felt threatened. Not once. His beef was with himself."

We went to bed and lay in each other's arms. And I was comforted.

It, of course, wasn't close to the whole story. And there was another issue on my mind. I believed Thompson when he told me he hadn't killed either a senior professor or a junior editor.

But sure as fuck, somebody had.

CHAPTER TWENTY-ONE

The next morning—a sunny and calm morning—I was struck, for the first time in recorded history, with the wish, no, the burning desire to go canoeing.

Alex was suspicious and why wouldn't she be? Having picked the two-toed sloth as my spirit animal years ago, my sudden interest in voluntary physical activity had to be alarming.

It was one of those lake-surface-as-glass mornings when you almost felt guilty for shattering it with paddles. The silence was complete, broken only by our rhythmic splash and the occasional cry of an early-rising loon.

We toured a large part of the eastern shore of Mississauga Lake. Devoid of human presence, the pristine, changeless wilderness cast me back centuries. And a million miles from troubles and entanglements and needlessly dead writers, I focused solely on the water and sky and tree line and the supple strokes of my lady in front of me.

We did not utter a single word.

We docked and then reality happened. Waiting for us on the

deck were Constable Dysart and a woman in plain clothes whom I didn't recognize. Alexandra went inside.

We settled into the deck chairs as Dysart introduced me to Inspector Lena Wilson of the Peterborough Police, a stout, kindly-looking woman. I was instantly on my guard because you don't get to be a police inspector through kindness.

"I don't know how much more I can add to what happened last night, Inspector Wilson," I said. "Constable Dysart must've filled you in."

"First off, how are doing?" she asked, all concerned and motherly.

"Not great, I guess. But I'll be fine."

"Good," she answered as the maternal look disappeared. "Now. We think you can tell us more."

"OK…"

"Let's start at the beginning of the evening," Inspector Wilson said. "Hostage takers have some kind of demands. We aren't aware of him saying anything. Her 9-1-1 call also didn't say anything, beyond telling us he wanted you there. You were in there for close to an hour. Do you know what he wanted?"

It was at that second that I decided to spill the whole goddamned can of beans. Who the hell was I kidding that professional investigators wouldn't be professionally investigating, picking at any thread in what was to be my bullshit story? The inspector had just yanked on one of the biggest threads.

"He wanted me," I said.

"What?"

"Jan Morris and Thompson cooked up the whole thing. Except the end part."

At first and understandably, they were gobsmacked. I laid out exactly what had happened.

"What you haven't told us is why he had it in for you," Wilson said.

"Here's the tricky part. I suspected he had plagiarized huge chunks of his best-seller. Actually, I had proof. So did Ted Bromley. And I told Thompson that in an e-mail. Three days ago."

"I'll need to see that e-mail. Any reply?"

"No. I mean, of course I'll forward the note and, no, he didn't answer."

"We can't sit on that. Even if Thompson is dead, that's fraud on a massive scale. And then there's the matter of Professor Bromley's death."

"Let me tell you why you have to keep it quiet," I said. "I don't think Thompson was in on the rip-off from the beginning and I don't think he killed Ted Bromley. He said he wasn't, and I can't think of a reason he'd have to lie. If he was going to waste me, what did it matter if I knew or not? If he switched horses and was going to kill himself then why get all deceptive about his involvement?"

"So, Jan Morris?"

"No. If Clayton was telling the truth, the book was already a best-seller when he found out. Jan Morris would've likely only been assigned his personal PR duties *after* it became a hit, so obviously, long after the plagiarizing."

"Leaving…?"

"Someone at Jameson & Lord, likely a senior editor named Henry Blake and probably Thompson's agent, Patricia Morland. And let's bet, whoever that person is had a hand in killing Ted Bromley up here and probably Ryan Loffler in Toronto."

"Who?"

"A junior editor at the same publisher. Stabbed about a week ago. He may have been involved somehow. By the by, my daughter Halley is running the investigation for TO Homicide. Morris might be a key."

"We'll talk to her. The OPP in Apsley transferred her to us early this morning. Said we could handle it better."

"Sometime today, Inspector—if it hasn't already—a shitstorm's going to erupt. World-famous guy whacks himself. That's capital 'N' news."

"We know," Wilson said. "We'll be ready."

"No offense, Inspector, but I seriously doubt that."

"Why?"

"Two reasons. First, this is a media situation like you just have never seen. Do you remember substitute teachers back in high school?

"Of course," she answered, puzzled at my colossal non-sequitur.

"During my university days, I used to be one. There's nothing quite like thirty minds united in their attempts to mess with you on every front about anything. Tack on maybe thirty more trained adult minds trying to find a story beyond your prepared statements."

"And the second thing?"

"It'll sound like I'm asking for a favour but, really, it's a deal breaker."

"And that is…?"

"You have to leave me out of it. Dysart, are you OK with that?"

"Yes."

"And your partner?"

"He's my junior partner. I'll talk to him again. Shouldn't be a problem."

"Stop right there!" Wilson said. "I don't think we can do that either."

"For fuck's sake, Inspector. I'm serious. I did this media stuff for thirty years. You do *not* want me talking to the press otherwise."

"We can handle it."

"Oh, really? Here: try handling this," I said, acting out a possible interview:

'I didn't really want to go but the police insisted. Honest.'

'They sent a civilian in there?'

'I know, right? I didn't think I had a choice.'

'They let you go in with alcohol?'

'I was surprised too.'

'Couldn't you all have died?'

'That's what I thought the whole time.'

'Wouldn't you say that was a pretty weak police response?'

'Frankly, I was surprised as you. They just seemed to not care very much.'

"See my point yet, Inspector? And that's just off the top of my head."

"You'd do that?"

"I swear ta Christ, I will."

"Inspector," Dysart said, "with all due respect, I know him; he's not kidding."

I took their silence as agreement.

"That leaves Jan Morris," I said. "You said you have her?"

"Yes. But we can't hold her forever. She's pretty messed up, but she wants out."

"It's a gamble but you have to talk to her first. Don't arrest her. Not yet. Spell out her situation for her. What's the maximum penalty for faking a kidnapping?"

"False report, obstruction, maybe fabricating evidence…could be as much as ten to fourteen years."

"Once she knows that, I'm pretty sure she'll shut the fuck up about what really happened. She'll play the same role that got everybody out to that cabin to begin with."

Inspector Wilson looked dubious and pissed off.

"You want us to blackmail her into lying."

"Such a harsh word," I said. "More like extortion. Blow open the plagiarism stuff and you've got one or maybe two killers on high alert. I assume you're investigating Bromley's murder."

"Yes. Sergeant Macgregor and I."

"Getting anywhere?"

"Not really. But we just started looking into the Thompson connection."

"Like I said, I don't think he was involved. The real killer's still out there."

She was considering that probability when I gave her a nudge.

"Look, I know this sucks, but what's the downside of playing it this way? Constable Dysart and his partner had a shitty night. The folks at his detachment and you people down in Peterborough had a shitty night. To go along with all your other shitty nights."

"I have to tell the Chief the real story."

"Sure, but I think he has a lot of reason to keep it to himself too. Same with your detachment commander, OK?" I said to Dysart who nodded.

Nobody walked away from my interview feeling good about it. Nobody really won anything. I had lied to Alexandra about the threat I was under and then I'd pressured the police to protect that lie. The cops had to live with a cover-up of sorts, and they didn't get to do the cop things they get paid to do, like punishing criminals. Jan Morris wasn't going to get to follow her PR instincts by talking—probably for money—about what happened in that cabin in the woods. In exchange, she wasn't going to be forced into a single wardrobe choice for the next decade or so. Ironic as hell but Clayton Thompson would come out the best—except for the dying part. There would be public sympathy for his apparent situation. Who doesn't understand pressure at work? And there would be the sad ironic point of this morality play where the guy advocating a simpler lifestyle got killed by the expectations of a complicated world.

Real life is messy. Seldom are there quick and neat endings, no matter how badly we want them and how badly the media wants us to have them. This happened and then this happened and—bang—The End. Next story.

But this was the closest thing. And with zero guarantee it

would remain that way.

By noon, the expected nuclear media explosion detonated. I didn't watch any of it, at least not right away. Far from ground zero, Alexandra and I were out on a long walk (Please note the severity of my distress: Canoeing *and* walking on the same day, for fuck's sake!). We must've spent four hours tramping the bush, lugging a packed lunch after I had performed a detailed cost/benefit analysis: The number of beer bottles I brought along in my personal-sized cooler was directly related to the amount of extra weight I was willing to carry. FYI: That number was four. With a little weight training or a switch to loathsome cans I was positive I could get that number up to five easy, maybe six.

At any rate, during our safari through the pine, spruce or whatever the fuck forest, we saw all sorts of distracting wildlife. Screeching blue jays letting us know how pissed off they were for us invading their green sanctuary, a not quite Harvey-sized rabbit frozen on the narrow path in front of us until it put its fuzzy pedal to the metal and booted out of danger, a furry tank of a raccoon waddling in front of her string of insufferably cute young'uns.

We found a bit of a clearing overlooking the lake and set up our mobile canteen. The bugs weren't bad, and the conversation was swell, chattering away about everything except the events of the previous evening. I studied Alexandra, blown away by her kindness, her patience, oh, and her hotness—plus she made a mean chicken salad sandwich. The more I looked at her, the more convinced I became that, for mostly selfish reasons, I'd made exactly the right choice in downplaying the danger I had been in.

We didn't get back to the Hovel until early evening.

Alex returned some calls while I did a media scan. Nothing like the death of a celebrity to grab headlines and coverage. Clayton's death played big. Everywhere.

So far at least, the bullshit storyline the cops had agreed to seemed to be holding and my name hadn't appeared anywhere.

But it wasn't over by any stretch. Those outlets with the budget and the inclination would be on their way to Peterborough, if they weren't already there.

I checked my blinking phone. Just one message that wasn't a fucking telemarketer. It was from Steve Golding at 11:49 that morning. "Call me. I'm fucking serious."

Back to my relic of a laptop. I had one unread e-mail. It too was from Steve.

Whaddya know? And don't bullshit me! he wrote.

The simplest way to not bullshit him was to not talk to him. So I didn't. Steve Golding was the digginest news dog I'd ever met. As a crime reporter for the *Toronto Sun*, Clayton's hostage drama and death were completely in his wheelhouse. He'd relentlessly pursue this story. The time stamp on his note was 12:03. It was now 8:28. Those eight and a half hours are an eternity to a reporter on deadline. Especially these days, when the deadline is always two minutes from now.

Did I mention that I have a real difficult time lying to my dear friend? Oh, and that he knows it.

Carl swam over. We watched him from the deck as he broke the full glitter of the lake's surface. Ingenious man that he is, he towed behind him a small cooler he'd rigged up with floats—Carl liked to keep it fair by not drinking all my beer.

"Steve's looking for you," he said after he toweled off, pulled on the 2XL T-shirt he keeps here, and took his position in *his* old wooden Adirondack chair. "He called me. Sounded pretty antsy."

"What time'd he call?"

"Around noon, I suppose."

"He can wait. I got a sunset to watch."

And watch the blazing glory we did. As per usual, I was blown away by how that daily event could rivet attention and end conversation, forcing you inside yourself to contemplate something as simple as the motion of the sun's descent or as complex as everything that baffles you.

As the sun sank entirely behind the pine, spruce or whatever the fuck, snapping the spell, I couldn't resist:

"So, what'd you say to him?" I asked Carl.

"Not much. Shot the shit for a bit."

"He ask about Clayton Thompson?"

"Yup."

"Annnnd....?"

"Might've mentioned that fella was up here a while back."

"Shit!"

"Sorry if I fucked up, son."

And he was. That much was obvious.

"You didn't. Forget it, bud," I said.

"What's the big deal, Jake?" Alex asked.

"If you knew Stevie like I know Stevie, you wouldn't ask. He smells a connection between Thompson and me, he'll keep rooting."

"So?"

"Nobody—except a few cops, you, and now, Carl here—knows I was even there last night."

"You were?" Carl asked.

"Hello!" a familiar voice called out in the dark.

"Steve!" I said in response. "What a pleasant surprise! Good to see ya, bud."

"Yeah, yeah, yeah," he said as he stepped onto the deck.

"Quoting the deepest Beatle lyric already?" I said.

"Fuck off. Got a beer?"

"No, you fuck off and get it yourself. Oh, and while you're up... the lads could use one and Alex here's out of wine."

His serving duties over, Steve plopped himself down in my chair that I'd vacated for one of those collapsible camping/director's chairs that threaten to trap you and swallow you whole.

"So, how was your day, old buddy, old pal?" Steve asked.

"Just great! Went canoeing *and* then walking with my lady. Now I'm trying to enjoy a magnificent summer evening with my closest friends. And yours?"

"Well, for starters, I had just a grand time driving out of Toronto at rush hour to be here because a close friend of mine wouldn't answer his fucking messages."

"That blows."

"You want to do this here or should we go somewhere?" he asked, his tone becoming dead serious.

"Here's fine."

"Good. I'll start. While you were busy avoiding me, I got busy too," he began. "Talking to cops mostly. All the big cheese gave me the same bullshit, but I got an interesting detail from an OPP officer named…here it is…Constable Wayne Barrett," Steve said, flipping through his note pad.

"Never heard of him."

"He was working last night. Pulled back-up duty for some kind of hostage situation. He was on Hwy 28, sitting in the parking lot of…of the Stone Bait Shop. Like a good soldier, he said he didn't know anything and that I should talk to the PR people. But he did want to be helpful, so he told me he noticed a particular car. Once before and once after the drama was over. Wait… yup. An older model silver Pontiac Vibe. Much like the one I just passed in your driveway."

"There must be thousands of them on the road."

"I'm betting there are about six in all of North America," he said. "But, turns out, there's only one with the Ontario license plate that Constable Barrett jotted down. And wouldn't you know it—that license plate would appear to match the one I just passed in your driveway."

See? What'd I tell you about our digging reporter?

It didn't even cross my mind to ask him to kill his angle on the story and to forget I existed. Number One: I knew he wouldn't.

Number Two: Facts are facts. And he had them.

Sidebar: my complete and utter hypocrisy was not lost on me. The set of "facts" Steve had, everybody was going to have, was horseshit. Only Jan Morris, a few cops, and I knew what led up to the faked drama in the cabin. I didn't think, no I was sure, Morris wouldn't voluntarily implicate herself. And the police had no incentive for public dirty laundry-washing.

"I gotta make some calls," I said.

"Why?"

"Because I said so; that's why!" I snapped. "These are good cops, good people. I owe them a heads-up. They did me a favour by keeping me out of it."

"And you did them a favour by disappearing."

"See! That's how it'll look! 'Incompetent local cops send in civilian. Culture Hero Dies.' Fucking writes itself, doesn't it?"

"I'm not going to write it that way."

"That's the way it'll get read. And you know it."

"Not necessarily."

"Bullshit! Everybody talks about how militarized the cops have become, all geared up in army hardware like they were sweeping the streets of Kandahar with tanks, mortars, attack helicopters, all that army crap. Yet everybody still expects to see it. Movies, TV, real life. That's what they get."

"Ya gotta admit, it was a pretty low-key tactic last night."

"Cops out here understand that maybe a whole lot more people get to live if they dialed it down."

"I'm just guessing here—correct me if I'm wrong—but there was a pretty high fatality rate last night."

"And it wouldn't have made the slightest bit of fucking difference if there had been an assault force outside."

"Are you worried about how you'll come off?"

"Yeah, right. Any negative press might really hurt my brand-new hostage negotiation business," I said. "I couldn't give a shit what people think of me. And you know that too. What's really pissing you off is that, after I make those calls, you're scoop ain't one anymore."

Steve didn't say anything; he glared.

I went inside, called OPP, left a voice message for Dysart, then the Peterborough police and was put through to the chief. Even though it was almost 10 o'clock, all hands were on deck dealing with the hubbub. I told them I'd been busted—for driving an American classic car no less—and that it was coming out some-time tonight.

I suggested they hold a joint media briefing revealing that fact to all and I gave the Chief some holding lines. 'Against our better judgment we agreed to contact Mr. Jake Lydon as Mr. Thompson requested. Mr. Lydon volunteered. The police had eyes on them the entire time, first with Ms. Morris, the hostage, and then Mr. Lydon. The hostage was released safely. Mr. Lydon and the po-lice were out of danger. The situation was de-escalating exactly as planned and hoped for. Tragically, it all went bad at the end, such was the extent of Mr. Thompson's personal distress. We offer our condolences to his family and friends.'

It would enrage the gathered throng, but I told the Chief to again not take questions while promising more info would be coming soon.

When I went outside, Carl had already gone back home, and Alex and Steve weren't speaking to each other. Steve had his laptop open and was furiously typing away. Alex looked like she didn't know where to be. She knew how well Steve and I got along and was pained by the friction.

"So everybody's going to get the story?" Steve asked.

"Yes."

"You just brought a shitstorm down on yourself, my friend."

"It was going to happen anyway when your piece came out, my friend."

"Now I need to ask you some questions."

"Understood."

That was Alex's cue to get up. She bent to kiss me, told me to come to bed soon. I couldn't think of anything else I'd rather be doing.

"Before we start," I said to Steve, "two things."

"Which are?"

"You should pretend this is a courtroom and treat me as a hostile witness."

"And the second thing?"

"Can I get you a beer?"

Yes, I was pissed, but I did remember my manners. Plus, it would give me some time to get my shit together.

"I agree to both."

As I went to the beer fridge, my mind was racing, trying to imagine the situation if it had occurred the way I was about to describe it, guessing at the questions that had to come.

"Now," Steve began, "Why were you there?"

"He asked for me."

"Why?"

"I have no idea."

"Best guess."

"He didn't really know anybody around here. He needed to talk; I suppose I was the only name he grabbed onto."

"How did you know him?"

"Met him after his lecture a couple of weeks ago."

"That's all?"

"I invited him up to the Hovel to see what slow living looked like in action. Well…inaction," I replied, knowing he already had that fact and was trying to trap me in a lie. I wasn't surprised by the questions so far. What took me aback—and shouldn't have—was the complete change in our normal two good friends shooting the shit way of dealing with each other into rapid-fire investigative reporter badgering a wary and defensive witness.

"So he was here?"

"A couple of weeks ago. Spent a few hours bullshitting on the dock. The quiet and the loons impressed the fuck out of him."

"Did he strike you as a desperate man."

"No. But he was a man under heavy pressure. There was a lot of weight on him for his follow-up book. He seemed almost lost."

"OK, now. Was there pressure on you to go?"

"No. I volunteered. Thought I could help. Cops didn't like the idea, but they also didn't like the idea if it came out that they hadn't called me."

"Were you nervous?"

"Of course. But once inside, it didn't seem all that, I don't know, threatening."

"You convinced him to let Jan Morris go?"

"Didn't take much. I believed he didn't want to hurt her."

"How was she through all this?"

"Pretty composed under the circumstances. She was frightened. Who wouldn't be? But she kept a lid on it."

"Cops have her in custody. Know anything about that?"

"I heard it was protective custody. She was pretty messed up. Evidently, their relationship was a lot deeper than just professional."

"So, he lets her go; then what?"

"I asked him to put the gun down. He did."

"Where was the gun?"

"On the dining room table."

"You didn't think to grab it?"

"No."

"Why not?"

"What was I going to do with it? Shoot him to stop him from killing himself? I thought it was over."

"But it wasn't, was it?"

"Gee, do you think?"

"You're a helluva lot bigger than him. How did he get the gun?"

"We agreed that I'd go outside first, tell the cops everything was alright, and that Clayton was coming out to surrender."

"So you didn't see him…fire the gun?"

"No."

"Then what happened?"

"I tried the door. It was locked. By then, the cops were running up the steps. They used their battering ram."

"Did you see him? Clayton, I mean."

"Yes."

"And?"

"And we're done here if that's the kind of shit you're interested in."

"OK, OK, let's back up. What did you talk about?"

"Almost entirely about the heat that was on him. From all sorts of places. He wanted to figure shit out."

"If he just wanted to sort things out, why create this hostage crisis?"

"Fuck knows. Cry for help, maybe."

"That makes no sense."

"Of course it fucking doesn't make sense! That's why this shit happens. I can only guess—you can only guess—what he was thinking, what he was feeling."

Steve was flipping through his notepad.

"Are we done here?" I asked.

"Yeah…I suppose. For now."

I had learned over the last several years, that anytime a reporter—or a cop—uses the phrase 'for now' it usually means they are pretty sure they're being fed a steaming pile of horseshit. But, in the absence of any other evidence, they're handcuffed and have to go with what you've said.

"Any overall thoughts?" he asked, putting aside his pen and

pad (another old reporter trick to lull the interviewee into thinking the interview was over).

"Just one: it's all just a goddamned shame. Including what
we're doing right now."

"Why?"

"Your story'll come out. Lots of others will and everybody will
pick them over for the details. Analyze the fuck out of them. And
then move on. Meanwhile, there's just one fact that remains. A
guy is dead who didn't have to be."

"And that's somehow my fault how? He made a choice."

"Oh for Christ's sake! Wild guess here: In retrospect, it looks
like he didn't think he had a choice."

"I'm not going to apologize for doing my job."

"And I'm not going to apologize for thinking that, right now,
it's a pretty shitty job."

"Can I crash here?"

"I'm really tempted to say no."

"No?" Steve said. His expression was stunned disappointment,
then maybe sadness as he began to see the chasm that had opened
up between us.

Looking back, it was obviously an arsehole thing for me to say.
I knew it was a moment when I didn't want anything or anybody
around that was involved in the shit that had just happened. I was
glad I relented.

"You know where your room is," I told him.

With that, I left Steve reading his notes and clicking away at
his keyboard. I went to bed, utterly bagged and craving dreamless
sleep.

I got that kind of sleep—for about four whole hours until 7
am. That's when the phone calls started. Steve slept through it all,
rousing himself just before 10. By that time, I had disconnected
the phone and was busily deleting the messages in my junk mail
folder from every media outlet large and small. *Times of India*?

What the fuck?

I did not look at any news stories.

Steve and I said little. He asked me if I had read his story. I told him I hadn't. He choked down a coffee, packed up quickly, and left.

He was back at the front door in minutes.

"Do you mind asking your friend to move his car?"

Puzzled, I followed him down my long driveway. There, by the road, was an OPP cruiser parked sideways across my driveway.

There was quite the protesting hubbub from some of the reporters who obviously recognized Steve. Even though they all crave it, they despise favouritism or early access exclusively given to one of their colleagues.

I thanked Dysart.

"No problem," he said. "I figured there would be a crowd after the Peterborough chief's press conference last night. We owe you for going into that cabin."

I asked if his perceived debt might last another hour or so and could he let Steve out.

Before he got into his car, he addressed the group.

"Folks, I will again warn you. If you come onto this private property, I will arrest you for trespassing and being a public nuisance. And you, the vans over there, you're blocking a fire route. You should've guessed that because the road is called Fire Route 162."

Walking back up my driveway, the sound of their shouted questions receding, I thought that time would either patch things up or it wouldn't with Steve and me. But at that moment, I had other things to worry about.

The news beast had not finished feeding off this story. Jan Morris turned out to be the next available media meal when they tracked her down in Toronto. Even though, as far as they knew, she'd just gone through a pretty traumatic and horrifying event, she handled it like a true PR pro, appearing to co-operate while pleading for understanding and privacy. She gave the kind of sincere answers that make it difficult (but not impossible, as some questions proved) to be dickish towards her. And as I hoped, she didn't give any hint about what really had happened.

I picked up some pointers from her and used them with the few reporters who persisted in my driveway after Dysart left. You could see that my non-answers pissed off the straggler journalists.

One even told me: "I waited hours for this?"

"You're right; you deserve more," I said, conspiratorially leaning into him and pausing for a bit. "I know where Hoffa's buried."

He walked away, so I yelled after him.

"Saskatoon! And you're welcome!"

To his credit, he waved a single-finger good-bye over his shoulder.

CHAPTER TWENTY-TWO

I decided to do my worrying by myself. Alexandra had been a champ so far but, Jesus, enough is enough, I thought. She didn't need to hear me babble on about Steve and the rest of the crapfest.

What she did need—or for sure deserve—was a little peace and quiet.

She pressed me of course—because that's the kind of selfless person she is—about how I was doing. I said I was fine and asked if she wanted to play a little tennis.

"First, canoeing, then walking and now tennis? All suggested by you? *Obviously,* you're not fine. What the hell is going on?"

"Nuthin', I swear. C'mon. I'll kick your ass."

"I doubt that, old man."

"You change. I'll see if the coast is clear."

It was, nary a newshound sighting. We drove to the community courts on the other side of the lake. They were empty too and in the same state of disrepair as they'd been in the summer before. Installed years earlier by a well-meaning service club or the early lake owners' association, they'd been left to settle. The resulting bumps and depressions made for very scientific play; you aimed for the undulations hoping for crazy bounces. Leastways, that's what I did to achieve a level playing field on the unlevel playing surface against Alexandra who was a way better player. I had accused her of having taken the Kicking Old Men's Asses at Tennis course at Bryn Mawr. She had obviously excelled because, as per usual, she ran my paunchy sweaty self all over the goddamned place.

But I got to tell ya, she was a helluva sight, crouched, twirling her racket while she got ready to pounce on my anemic serves. She recalled Sharapova, only without the god-awful sounds, as she tried to ram the ball down my throat.

Despite the 6-2, 6-3, 6-3 beat-down, the games were delightful there on the secluded shitty courts surrounded by trees whose shadows dappled the heaving asphalt. I wanted to keep playing—forever, if possible—despite being on the verge of coughing up bits of lung. Down 5-2 in the fourth set, I was barely mobile, having tried to run down shots I had zero chance of returning—a shockingly wasteful expense of energy from someone who always looks like he's ready for hibernation. Alex called it off and looked alarmed at my frantic breathing as I lit a cigarette.

"You need to calm down, Jake," she advised. "Promise me you'll relax today—read a book or something. I have a bunch of work to do anyway."

The reading I chose to do was not found in the pages of a book but rather, in the pixels of my shitty laptop. I caught up with some of the stories filed by those media on the road in front of my place that day. They were pretty well evenly split thematically between "Just who the fuck did I think I was by ignoring them?" and "What are the police hiding?"

I spent a good portion of that evening calling back forty some odd media outlets and either left messages or spoke to the reporters, giving them all the same brief message. "Jake Lydon will not be commenting on Clayton Thompson's death, not today or in the future." Click.

Other than quickly dealing with a few reporters who took my initial message as an invitation to keep calling me, I had a welcome respite from the tiring media storm. At least for the meantime, things got quiet.

A couple of days later, Patricia Morland called and left a short message: *I'll be in Peterborough tomorrow. There's some business I have to clear up. Wondering if we might meet. Rob Byford passed along that chapter and outline of yours. Loved it! I would like to talk about how we might work together.*

She left her phone number and e-mail.

I was pleasantly surprised. I wanted to talk to her, and Rob had inadvertently given me the opportunity. I had to remind myself that, at the moment, I wasn't looking for any agent beyond this one but only because she may have been involved in one or two murders. Hard not to ask the obvious question: Was I the business in Peterborough she was coming to clean up? I was also pretty sure that she wasn't really interested in having me as a client—I mean, who in their right-mind would be? Smart money said she was keen to find out what I knew or suspected—if anything—about the plagiarizing caper I'd stumbled upon.

I went the e-mail route, asking her to meet me next day at noon at the Red Dog (she might as well see me in my preferred public environment).

Dive bars at that time on a non-payday are usually pretty subdued. The majority of the clientele was made up of the pro drinkers—all of them skinny and trembling. They go to places like that to drink, not carouse. And they sure as hell weren't going to hang around until the music started in the evening.

Patricia Morland caused quite the stir when she walked in, looking more as though she should be entering an upscale fashion boutique. At least the sparse crowd had the collective politeness to not break into a chorus of "Hubba! Hubba!"

"Going full Bukowski, are we?" she said, her eyes again sweeping the large dingy room as she sat down. As she gazed around, the noon-time drinkers all averted their eyes at once, which was kinda sweet.

"Here's to all my friends!" I said as I hoisted my draft glass to cheer. I hoped she'd see the humour in quoting Mickey Rourke's line from *Barfly*. She looked like she hadn't.

"Just be clear, Ms. Morland," I said, "I'm not a big fan of writers celebrating the filth and despair of urban life. I live in the bush on a lake. I go south every winter. I'm closer to the black-socks-and-sandals set than I am to the residents of big city shitholes."

The waiter slid up to us. For the forty-five or so years I've been seeking out joints like this, the waiters are of a type. Generally as thin as their customers, they speak little. None of this "My name is Bradley and I'll be your server tonight and if possible, your friend for life" shit. No "Can I take your order?" either. He's a goddamned waiter; everybody knows why he's standing by your table. And for sure, he wasn't going to either say "Awesome" or "No problem" after he took our order, him being a goddamned waiter as I mentioned and therefore unlikely to be impressed by our request or compelled to assure us that our order could be filled without a hitch.

The only concession to modern times that our nameless and apparently mute waiter had made: he no longer had a shiny metal coin dispenser strapped to his belt, puking out nickels, dimes and quarters to make change for the 20-cent glasses of draft, (yes, I'm that old).

"I've let my sommelier papers lapse, but I wouldn't trust their wine list," I said.

"I'll have a beer."

Kudos to you, Patricia, I thought, either for liking beer or for at least making the effort to pander to me.

"Shall we turn to business, Jake?" she asked.

"Of course."

"I must tell you, there are exciting possibilities with you. I've done some homework. We could go to a national publisher with a two-book deal."

"Jesus, let me finish this one first."

"I'm talking about *On the Rails*. I took the liberty of contacting your local publisher, Frank McCann. He quite likes the book. But—to be honest—you, not so much. Said you were—what was his quote?—unnecessarily difficult."

"I get that a lot. That doesn't concern you?"

"Not particularly. I've been involved with many difficult authors. Comes with the territory."

"I have to warn you that I work overtime against my own self-interest."

"That's where I'd come in," she said, not missing a natural-born segue. "I will protect your interests as if they were my own and fight to ensure that you, like all my clients, get the maximum possible returns for your work. Your publisher said there'd be no problem assigning the publishing rights to *On the Rails* to us…for a nominal fee."

"But it's an old book," I said, again arguing against my own self-interest in going country-wide with a book that I more than liked.

"It's also a long book. 638 pages, I understand. We remove at least one hundred and fifty pages, and it'll be a brand-new book."

"Not sure I know how I feel about that," I said, knowing exactly how I felt about that. I fucking hate being edited. Right or wrong, I had been able to convince myself that I wrote *exactly* what I needed to be written.

"We'll talk."

"No, let's talk now. Do you exercise this kinda control over how and what your writers write?"

"Not usually. But new clients need to know what will work in this market."

"New clients like Clayton Thompson?"

"No, no. Clayton hit the sweet spot right from the beginning."

"So he didn't get help or direction from you."

"He got that from Henry Blake. That's an editor's job. But nothing like that from me."

"Hmmm," was my clever comment.

She paused at that. I thought I'd hate like hell to play poker with this woman. Her expression was difficult to read. Sadness, for sure. A wistfulness, maybe. Regret, who could tell? She seemed to will herself to snap out of it as she re-focused to me, her eyes full of business.

"Why are you asking about Clayton? Did he say something different?" she wanted to know.

"Not at all."

"Well, what did he tell you?"

"When he visited me at my place or…at the end?"

"Both."

"He talked about how the book came to be, his writing 'process' for *The Returning*."

"And?"

"I didn't much care for it. Sounded a bit too, I don't know, scientific."

"But the results. You must be able to see the results."

"Yeah, the narrative chapters had flashes of brilliance…Frankly, I was surprised at how good they were. So I guess his so-called process worked for him. That last night, he said he was going nuts with all the pressure on him from everybody."

"And you've concluded that 'everybody' means me?"

"I didn't say that. I took it to mean the general everybody, mostly his fan base who really wanted a follow-up."

I don't know if my answer satisfied her or not, but she dropped the subject of my discussions with Clayton.

Instead, she said. "Now if this works out and I get you a deal, I trust you'll put this whole Clayton thing behind us. It's so…ugly."

She was staring right at me.

"Can you put this affair behind you?" she wanted to know.

"Yes. Yes, I can."

"Good. It's very important that you do."

She finally dropped her steely-eyed gaze down to her watch. I was relieved. I was starting to feel like a weak-willed mongoose hypnotized by a Queen Cobra.

"I really must be going," she said.

"Before you do that, I'd like you to tell me why I should hire you."

She seemed insulted by my request. I could see why. As probably the top agent in the country, she wasn't used to being interviewed for a job. Especially not when the interviewer hadn't done shit in the publishing world and looked derelict enough to blend right in with the lunchtime patrons of a seedy bar.

"What do you know about me?" she asked.

"What I read in your website bio."

"So you know I originally—more than twenty years ago—was an editorial assistant at a major house."

"Yes."

"What's not in the bio is any idea of how soul-destroying that work was. I was a glorified gopher. I made lousy money and I was treated terribly by the mostly male staff and mostly male authors. All for the opportunity to be involved in what I believed was the glamourous world of book publishing. So I vowed to change all that, to get the respect and the money I wanted. I couldn't write but I could negotiate, so I hung out my shingle and I nearly starved for years. I kept at it. I finally got a good deal for a nobody and then another and another. Word quickly spread and soon I couldn't handle the volume of writers like you, desperate for a publishing future."

"Good for you; I mean that," I said.

"Damn right good for me," she said, her eyes lit up with pride. "I built a staff of topnotch agents, and I became the top agency in the country for one simple reason: If I decide to take you on, I can guarantee you access to every major publisher on the continent and a more than fair hearing with Jameson & Lord because of my connections there. That's why you need me."

"I've got to think about this."

"While you're doing that, think also about this: how many copies of *On the Rails* did you sell?"

"I dunno. Two or three hundred."

"273 to be exact. With my help, you'll see a minimum of at least twenty times that many, probably a lot more. You think about that."

With that, she got up, turned smartly, and left the bar followed by a wave of forlorn gazes.

While there had been no music at the Red Dog that afternoon, it was pretty clear—I think to both of us—that we had been dancing. She'd offered me a kinda mushy quid pro quo. I shut the fuck up about Clayton—"put this whole Clayton thing behind us"— and she'd make me a star.

She was smart and tough. You had to be in that business. I was dumb and soft. You had to be, in the business of being me.

CHAPTER TWENTY-THREE

That afternoon, I got an e-mail from Patricia. *Daniel Truscott wants to meet you. He has time tomorrow morning 10:15, Suite 4000, Commerce Court West. Please confirm. I can be there if you'd like. Otherwise, good luck (and don't be late).*

Well, that was some pretty fast work. I wrote back, telling her that I'd show up, but preferred my chit-chat be one on one with Truscott.

Then I got jumpy. First, over the fact that I knew squat about the publisher who was likely going to pretend to be interested in my book while I pretended to be interested in having him publish it. Nor did I know much about the Patricia Morland Agency beyond what they said about itself. Time to head down a literary rabbit hole!

Jameson & Lord was one of the oldest but not the biggest publishing houses in the country. But the book biz was changing—just like every other industry was changing. Everybody was swallowing up everybody else in the name of "sector consolidation." Translation: "Bigger is better and biggest is the fucking best." All in the name of growing quickly. All that merging and acquiring actually looked like is a frantic game of musical chairs, only instead of one pissed-off kid at a birthday party you get big winners and losers. But why, oh why? Time to trot out more bullshit PR phrases. To "optimize operational efficiency" and "achieve economies of scale that eliminate resource redundancies." Translation: "Sorry, buddy. You—and millions of others over the years—are out of a fuckin' job." And what is really driving all this merging and acquiring? Why, you have the "fiduciary responsibility to maximize shareholder value." Translation: It always helps that all the executives with shares maximize their own value.

Sidebar: And just how do I know these comfortably bland but authoritative-sounding expressions? Because I used to write the fucking things when I was gainfully employed. I have no idea how many lifetimes I'd need to atone for that maltreatment of the English language. I've also been able to convince myself that, back then, I was young and keen to succeed—two features I gave up a very long time ago.

It surprised me to learn that Jameson & Lord was not playing that buy-out game, staunchly refusing to eat or be eaten. They stuck to their one-hundred-year-old business model of producing quality books that sold moderately well and won far more than their share of prestigious literary prizes. And over the years, they would occasionally land a blockbuster book from an unknown new writer who had been spotted by an eagle-eyed editor. Not quite Thomas Wolfe showing up at Max Perkins' office at Scribner's with three boxes crammed with 330,000 scrawled long-hand words that eventually were hacked down to become *Look Homeward, Angel*. But close.

Their only apparent concession to the pursuit of filthy lucre was the appointment of Daniel Truscott as Chairman less than three years earlier. Truscott was an anomaly in that he did not grow up in the publishing industry. He came from the world of fashion retailing where he had been a senior financial officer for a major clothes manufacturer.

I went back to the announcement of his appointment. Quite the fucking kerfuffle in some quarters about an outsider, "an émigré from the rag trade" as one snotty letter in an industry newsletter put it, taking over the venerable reins of Jameson & Lord.

Such grumbling died down when reports surfaced that ol' J&L, which had been skating on thin financial ice, but had righted itself under his command. The pissing and moaning disappeared altogether after Truscott made a big splash by announcing his signing of Clayton Thompson. Soon after that, Truscott took J&L public. Largely on the strength of Thompson's book, the share price had gone up 190% since then before settling back a bit. One analyst said that the shares have stayed up because the anticipation of Thompson's second book had been "priced in."

On to who and what wanted to represent me. There was little I could find out about Patricia Morland that raised questions about the portrait she painted of herself and her company. Her success rate and the size of the contracts she negotiated set her apart. She was a fixture on the literary scene, giving talks, showing up at book launches and swell social outings. Nobody said anything negative about her, although maybe that was because they were afraid of the power and influence she wielded. Her position allowed her to be as picky as vegans about what they eat when it came to deciding who she took on as a client.

The biggest literary agencies like hers got that way by representing a roster of best-selling authors. And, boy, was that profitable. Get a million-dollar advance, that's a 150K commission. Sell it to a movie production house for the same number, g'day, another 150K. You also get your cut from every speaking engagement. And unlike, say, an agent for a football player with a five-year career, writers can keep cranking 'em out for fifty years. Easy. Oh, another major difference between the two sets of agents. The jock ones took home about 3% while the literary representatives fetched themselves 15.

Now there aren't of lot of writers in this category, any more than there's a ton of superstars in the NFL. But you don't need many. Just a couple and you've got your reputation cemented and your retirement well-financed.

You're working on spec, like a real estate agent, so how much time are you gonna spend trying to find the next Grisham or Stephen King? Where's the better pay-off: a completely renovated 15-million-dollar New York brownstone or a $200,000 fixer-upper in the wilds of New Jersey?

Does that make agents lazy? Doubt it. Why wouldn't they work like mad bastards to ensure their prize ponies are happy and continuing to get paid so they do too?

OK, that was a general sense of who and what I would be dealing with the following day. Next question: whatever was I to wear?

Wardrobe selection was key. I figured Truscott should see exactly what he was getting so I went with Hawaiian formal, (an understated black and yellow number), paired with my best (i.e. non-frayed) cargo shorts and matching black flip-flops. I always pride myself on being peccably dressed.

I may have mentioned that I don't like big cities. The longer I'm away from them, the more virulent the case of the heebie-jeebies I get when I have to be in one. Traffic, lots of people, one-way streets and underground parking garages, they all fuck me up. Even the simple act of getting on an elevator—as I was doing in the lobby at Commerce Court West—now freaks me out.

I was late (which I also fucking hate) because I had already been to Commerce Court *East* which, I discovered, was about thirty stories short of my destination. That would be the 44th story of Commerce Court *West*. And I, of course, lost more time while I waited by the bank of elevators that only went to the 25th goddamned floor.

So I was properly flustered and sweaty by the time I made it through the huge oak doors of Jameson & Lord, keenly aware of the loud smacking sounds my flip-flops were making on the dark polished parquet flooring. Immediately, I was ushered into Truscott's massive, paneled office overlooking Lake Ontario. From that vantage point, I swore I could see most of upper New York State.

Even though my apologies were as profuse as my sweat, Truscott had to register his displeasure at my lateness.

He opened with: "I am *only* seeing you, Mr. Lydon, because Patricia—by the way, why isn't she here?"

"I haven't decided to hire her yet."

"I suggest you do. As I was saying, Patricia said I should meet the author she insists I should be publishing. I must say, this isn't a great first impression."

"Stick with me, bud. My second and third impressions are even worse."

Nary a chuckle. I was dying out there. [Note to self: Jake, ya gotta get better at reading a room]. I had already lost points for punctuality, and I *always* start out in a deficit based on my appearance. Now, my comedic genius wasn't paying dividends either. Might as well raise the stakes.

"I was hoping you'd be primarily interested in publishing great goddamned books. And *The Sixth String* is a great goddamned book," I said.

"I am told your first chapter is good and that the outline shows promise."

"You didn't read it?"

"Not yet. Henry Blake did, and I trust my editors, just like I trust my mechanic. If he tells me the car is fine, I believe him."

"You should know that the chapter is more than simply fine."

"And what about the rest of it?"

"That will be too. When I finish it."

"Rather confident, aren't you?"

"I prefer true arrogance to false modesty."

After years of practice, I can act like a pompous asshole with little effort, although many—including me—would argue that it's not really an act.

My cocky answer elicited a slight smile from him. I took that as permission to plough onwards.

"Obviously," I said, "I hope that we can reach a deal to publish the book. But I wouldn't mind getting a better idea about with whom I might be doing business."

"Fair enough. Ask away."

"I've heard a bunch of things about how J&L is doing under your management. A lot of them not good."

"Such as...?"

"Well, for starters, it's been said you don't really understand the book biz, coming from another industry."

"That's a load of snobby rubbish. Jameson is a business like any other business. We make one product. A book. It may have a million variations but it's still just a book. With a cover design and squiggles inside on paper or pixels. Ultimately, it becomes an inventory number, an SKU that the computer can't distinguish from a line of dresses. Both of them have predictable costs and a solid distribution system. And believe me, there is no difference between how you treat a superstar fashion designer or a famous writer."

"Like Clayton Thompson?"

Here, Truscott swiveled in his chair to stare out the window.

"An unspeakable tragedy," he finally said, turning back to me. "The saddest day I have ever experienced in business."

"You were close?" I asked.

"Not especially, but I admired him tremendously."

"So you didn't hang out? You know, visit him at his cabin."

"Good lord, no. I had never even been to Peterborough until

the night of his second lecture there."

If he was telling the truth—and I had no reason to believe that he was—that would immediately rule him out as a suspect in Ted Bromley's demise

"I gather you were with him…on that last night," he said.

"I was."

"What did he tell you?"

"He was under a lot of pressure for the follow-up. I wanted to ask if that's something you feel at all responsible for. I mean, I'd like to know if this is standard procedure here."

"No, it is not. Of course we were eager to see a new book from him. But I can assure you that we did not exert any pressure on him. He was a perfectionist. It would appear he put that load on himself."

"Had you seen any parts of the second book?"

"No. But Henry, his editor, had. He told me it was every bit as good as the first draft he saw of *The Returning*."

Technically, I thought, Blake wouldn't have been lying to his boss if Round 2 from Clayton was just as crappy as his first effort.

"So tell me about the changes around here," I said. "I understand you're cutting staff, changing the way books are readied for publication and what you expect from writers."

"Yes, it's true that we have fewer editors than we used to—just like every other publishing house. Yes, we lay off more costs, such as proof reading, on authors—just like every other publishing house. Yes, we rarely pay advances of any size—just like every other publishing house. You'll find it's the same everywhere as there's more line-by-line budget scrutiny; it's the only way we'll survive. But we have more editors than most. We expect less contribution from our writers, and, in total, we advance more than most. Did I mention, we're actually making money? Just like an actual business and not a benevolent charity."

"I hear you brought in a system of incentive bonuses for your editors."

"Yes, and I'm quite proud of it. A portion of an editor's compensation comes from sales figures on books he or she had edited. Just as it is for the marketing and salespeople. Why shouldn't they get rewarded for their role in making a successful book?"

"But…but isn't that just another way to choke off new writers getting a shot? Editors won't bust their onions promoting them because there's a whole lot more reward and whole lot less risk in working with the established crop."

"Do you think that only the very best books are published every year? Or that every book on the slush pile deserves to be there? It's not perfect, but it is a business. And a good business invest its time and money with the greatest return. We and every other publisher and agent each get probably 5000 submissions a year, that's twenty *a day*. We and every other publisher actually print maybe twenty *a year*. We have to choose wisely. Why wouldn't you go with proven winners? And you know what? That's what most readers want. Books that win prizes, books that are on best seller lists, books by people they've heard of because they're the real gamblers with their twenty or thirty dollars. Did they just waste it? Or do they pick tried and true?"

"But what about really good new writers?"

"Enough get through to keep the pond stocked."

"Like turtle hatchlings scurrying across the sand to get to the ocean."

"Precisely."

"You gotta be getting pushback."

"Not from the editors who are producing winners."

"And the rest?"

"They tend to be gone."

"Where?"

I sensed it was time for more glossed-over corporate bullshit. I was right.

COPYCAT   201

"Did you know," Truscott said, "there are about two million writers who self-published books last year on Amazon? Two *million*. The smart ones, the good ones, hire freelance editors to polish their manuscripts. Jameson & Lord—and all the other traditional publishers—are contributing to the talent pool of available experienced editors by letting them go. At the same time, we're giving those editors new careers as entrepreneurs setting up their own new businesses."

"In other words, you were going to fire Ryan Loffler."

That took him aback. He was pissed. After a pause during which our eyes locked, he trotted out the ever reliable "We do not discuss individual personnel matters."

"Even if this particular individual personnel is way past caring?"

"That's not the point. Can I ask you what your interest in Ryan is all about?"

"We both went to Trent."

"No offense, but you're easily old enough to have been his father."

"Once an alumnus, always….et cetera…So how did he take the news?"

"I think this chat is over, Mr. Lydon."

"Maybe I should have a talk with Henry Blake while I'm here. If I'm going to be working with him and all."

"No," Truscott firmly said, rising from his chair. "That would be quite premature. We haven't even decided to publish you. *If* we do, it's unlikely you'd have him as an editor."

By this point, he'd come around his desk and was making for the door. Instead of telling me to get the fuck out of his office, he dismissed me with a quick handshake and the ol' "we'll be in touch."

With Truscott shadowing me, I was subtly bounced through the front doors. I waited for a while by the elevators, then re-entered the J&L offices. At the reception desk, I asked if I could see Jan Morris.

"I'm sorry; Jan doesn't work here anymore."

"Oh, I said. "Any chance you know where she went?"

"Sorry. I really don't."

Waiting for an elevator, I wasn't surprised that Jan had moved on. The traumatic events of Clayton Thompson's last night alive would be all the reason I'd need to escape the memories of working with him at Jameson & Lord. I did want to talk to her to find out how she was doing and to ensure that her story was still holding.

Riding down the elevator (still weird) I was perplexed—as I often am. On the personal front, even though this whole trying to get published bit was bullshit, it was oh-so fucking tempting to play it straight. The prospect was seductive as hell. I defy any obscure writer to feel otherwise. Even if Jameson & Lord might put a half-hearted effort into promoting it and were publishing it only to appease me and cinch my silence once I was in their stable. Self-deluding little fucker that I am, I saw the book going gangbusters on the strength of its merits and excited word of mouth.

And all I'd have to do in return was forget everything I knew about the copycatting and everything Thompson had told me, oh and the fact that there was still at least one murderer out there, maybe sitting in the office I'd just left.

I had to remind myself that when this whole thing blew up—as it had to—Daniel Truscott, as well as Patricia Morland and likely more, wouldn't have anything left in a way of a career in the biz. And, in the short term at least, there wouldn't be much left of Jameson & Lord either.

As with every other industry, the book business was changing. Even established writers were expected to deliver near perfect products, edited and proofread on their dime. Then, when it came out, they were pretty well required to do everything in their power to market and sell it.

There were three perfectly persuasive reasons why I am oh so ill-suited to this new way of doing things: I fucking hate change, I'm bone lazy, and I couldn't sell shit to a fly. I liked it when the job of the writer was simply to write. Their hard work ended with a finished manuscript. The publisher then, gee, as their name implies, published it after their, gosh, aptly named Editorial department edited the hell out of it at which point their Marketing and Sales departments, lemme guess, marketed and sold the goddamned thing.

It was partially like our new responsibilities at a grocery store where it is no longer enough to simply select and pay for your food; you must also scan and pack it. To beat the living shit out of this analogy, you do not yet have to make yourself known and sought after as a premier grocery packer. Nor do you have to grow and ship your own fucking food. But, in effect, that's what was now expected of writers.

So what? I thought. Businesses change and life goes on. Western civilization somehow managed to recover from the collapse of the whalebone corset industry and fall of the buggy whip manufacturing empires.

As far as my half-assed nosing around went, I had a bit more to chew on. Both Truscott and Patricia Morland wanted to know about my conversation with Clayton Thompson just before he blew his brains out. Neither had asked: "What did you talk about?" But both had posed the identical question: "What did he tell you?" That struck me as odd phrasing.

Truscott's non-answer on Ryan Loffler's future actually was an answer. But if he was going to can Loffler, why be involved in killing him? Unless his soon to be ex-junior editor was part of the plagiarizing enterprise gone sour and he had threatened to reveal the whole thing or attempted to extort more money out of him.

But Truscott had betrayed nothing about his possible involvement. Like my old boss, he was adept at not showing his cards, playing the long game by leaping ahead to silently plot strategy and outcomes while hiding his intentions behind a steely gaze. Or he was dreaming about an upcoming Cabo vacation while he wasted his time with a low-rent writer as a favour to his agent friend.

I was nervous about who knew what when. I was pretty well relying on the close-to-deathbed confession of Thompson, a guy who'd already admitted to doing his fair share of lying. He had flat-out implicated Henry Blake. The pirated prose came through him. Could Blake possibly not have known the word chunks were stolen? Seemed to me that was somewhere between improbable to impossible on the likelihood scale.

That meant that my next stop had to be an encounter with Clayton's editor/prose supplier. Or I could let the police do their job and conduct a thorough investigation using proven methods and techniques while I fucked off back to the lake and minded my own goddamned business.

Nah! Where's the fun in that? Besides, it *was* my goddamned business. Sort of.

Right there, I committed to filling Halley in on what I'd learned and suggesting questions to ask Patricia Morland, Daniel Truscott, and Henry Blake while generally being a helpful son of a bitch. But only after I talked to the last of my suspect triad: Mr. Blake.

There was no good way that I could think of to "officially" meet him at work. That left the only other option: an apparently chance meeting after I indulged in two of my favourite activities: lurking and stalking. A slight drawback was the fact that I had no idea what the object of my lurking and stalking looked like.

I remedied that tiny issue by strolling up to the Toronto Library at city hall and messing around on one of their PCs. In a few keystrokes, I found out that he closely resembled "Animal," the photographer in the great *Lou Grant* TV series. Mid-40s, big glasses, longish wavy dark hair that was neatened up for his portrait on the Jameson & Lord website but that was longer and wilder in other photos on Facebook and Google Images. Those shots also gave me his build. Tall, lanky, he was easily the tallest figure in any group. Surprisingly broad-shouldered and obviously athletic. Think swimming greats like Michael Phelps or Mark Spitz. There were pics of him in T-shirt and shorts playing yuppie-type sports like Frisbee football in a city park. Probably a hell of a rower, I guessed. He cleaned up real good for book awards shows and literary galas, but mostly, he was shabby-chic.

For sure, he didn't look like someone who lived in the 'burbs. So if I did manage to spot him and then managed to track him, it would likely be on foot or his bike or mass transit of some description. I feared the two-wheel option because he'd lose me after the first twenty or so feet. There was no time to retrieve my car and besides—and I don't know if you've ever noticed this—decade and a half-old Pontiac Vibes are rarely used as movie chase cars.

So I worked at lurking for a bit at the base of the Commerce Court elevators. 4:45, Thursday afternoon and the eight elevator cars were disgorging throngs of people. Typically a pay day, the office workers were streaming out like a giant school of smelts freed from a fishing net.

Mercifully, Blake stood out, at least half a head taller than most. I fell in behind him, picking up my pace as I feared being on the losing end of a trampling, like the running of the bulls in Pamplona, to switch to land-based similes.

I followed him for just under two blocks south on Bay Street and he turned into a bar, the Harp and Clover. Huzzah! Drinks after work with colleagues was still apparently a tradition. I stood outside and watched him through the big front window as he made a beeline to a table with a woman sitting there. She had her back to me but turned sideways and lifted her face as Blake gently put his hand on her shoulder. He bent his lanky self over and planted a lingering kiss on the lips of Patricia Morland.

Well, well, well, I thought. Ain't that interesting?

I had two options. Head back to the car, drive home, and ponder what I'd just witnessed or go inside and stir the pot a bit more. Guess which one I chose?

I faked acting surprised at seeing her and quickly moved to their table.

"Patricia!" I said, chock full of warmth and excitement. "What an amazing coincidence? I was going to call you. Thought I'd have a beer first to celebrate my meeting with Daniel Truscott. It went really well. Mind if I join you? Sorry to interrupt," I said to Blake, extending my hand. "I'm Jake Lydon. You are…?"

"Henry Blake," he stammered.

"Say, I've heard of you. Terrific to meet you. Let me get the next round. I insist. What are you having? Waiter!"

The thing about these occasional bursts of rapid-fire speech is that they leave little room for resistance. Just shock and awe. Well, shock anyway.

I pulled out a chair and sat down.

Sure, it was awkward but, contradictorily [and if that's not a word, it should be], I'm comfortable with awkward.

"Yup, I think I really nailed the interview," I said.

"I talked to Daniel," Patricia said. "I must tell you, he sounded less convinced."

"A few rough spots, I'll admit, but that's why—drum roll, please—I've decided to hire you!"

Her face didn't exactly light up with unbridled joy.

"That's…that's wonderful," she managed.

"Maybe you could work Truscott a bit, so I get Henry here as my editor. Word is he's quite the magician."

"I can't promise anything."

"Patricia," Blake said, "we better get going. We'll be late for that book launch."

"Oh, right. *That*," she said.

"Mind if I tag along?" I asked.

"It's…it's invitation only. Sorry."

"You two kids run along then," I said. "I got the check."

"Thank you. We'll be in touch," Morland said. Now where had I recently heard that line?

They got up without finishing their drinks and skedaddled out of there. I watched them leave. Patricia was a good 5'9"and she was dwarfed by Blake, although barely outweighed. I watched them through the plate glass front window. Boy, oh boy, they were having a humdinger of an argument as they walked away.

Mission accomplished, I thought. The old grey fox went crazy in the hen house, or something like that.

I was left with a bunch of questions and the absurdly strato-spheric bill. Among those questions was: Eighteen goddamned dollars for an "artisan-crafted" Bloody Mary and twenty god-damned dollars for two beer? What the fuck? With tip and tax-es, that was almost enough for *two* cases of Yuengling in Indian Rocks Beach where the three of us could've choked down sixteen beer—*each*—amid palm trees and not in a hoity-toity ersatz Irish pub that a native Irishman wouldn't even recognize, let alone pa-tronize.

Now, normally, I couldn't give a good goddamn about who's zooming who—both on video conference calls or of the more in-timate variety. People will find love or an approximation of it or just plain ol' lust where they can. But the Morland-Blake union had a few, oh, let's call them issues.

Depending on how long they'd been an item and how pub-lic it was, the biggest question was, again, who knew what when? Clayton Thompson told me on the night he died that he had let his agent in on the plagiarism caper *after* he had been confronted by Professor Bromley. But I couldn't see Henry Blake, the apparent original copycat, keeping that secret from his love for months and months while the book was being readied. And that meant that she was in on it right from the start and just pretended to be surprised when Thompson told her. Further, she could've actually been the driving force behind getting Henry to juice her client's manuscript when she saw it was nothing special.

I gave my head a literal and figurative shake as I sat and finished my beer—and then Henry's, and then Patricia's drink. All this speculation was down in the weeds, separate from the much bigger central question of the day: Did I just have partial drinks with one, two or zero murderers?

CHAPTER TWENTY-FOUR

B ack at the lake, I started a search for Jan Morris. I wanted to see if she was wavering at all from our deal to stay quiet. I also reckoned she might be able to tell me more about what was going on within the paneled walls of Jameson & Lord. It was far from a needle in a haystack scenario. I know these folks. PR people gotta do PR. Especially if it's for themselves.

I once worked for a big agency—occasionally still did—after my regular job ended. I was classified as an Associate which meant they could hire me for overflow writing assignments and crisis events but didn't have to pay me a salary or benefits or give me office space or tolerate me being around. For years, I had a slew of blue-ribbon clients with whom I worked, usually in a crisis capacity. Pet poisonings from tainted food, pilots' strike at a major airline, murders at a famous hotel, big company acquisitions with a ton of lay-offs, protester accidentally dying at an oil refinery, that kind of shit hitting the fan.

I wouldn't work for a pharmaceutical company, and I got fired by a fast-food giant after I pointed out the absurdity of them spending way more on publicizing a donation they had made to a national charity than the actual donation.

But in all my years on the agency side, I had never, not once, met a dumb person.

I found her through LinkedIn after tortuously reviving my long-dormant account by proving my identity to some algorithm. She was the new Communications Manager for a medical devices company in Oshawa, a city south of Peterborough and touching Toronto's eastern boundary.

I called her, asked if we could meet. She hesitated, no doubt debating which was more desirable: seeing me again or having a root canal without an anesthetic. But she agreed to a get-together at her place after work.

For some reason, Alexandra failed to see the importance of me leaving her to see a young pretty woman at her place in the evening. So I reminded her of her angry reaction to my jealous hissy fit in her driveway in the spring and then invited her to come along. She passed.

My personal exposure to Ms. Morris had been limited to watching her shepherding Clayton Thompson, her client, around after his lecture and then being traumatized on the night Clayton Thompson, now her lover, died.

She met me at the door to her apartment with the same kind of warmth reserved for those roving driveway asphalt guys who "happen to be in the neighbourhood" and could make you a sweet deal. It was instantly obvious that she was crisp, totally composed and impressive as hell. Any company would be lucky to have her.

"How are you?" I asked when she answered the door.

"Fine."

"I just thought I should check."

"Great. You've checked," she said, looking pretty eager to slam the door in my goddamned face.

But she relented and decided to show me at least the appearance of hospitality by inviting me in.

Her place was small and newly furnished in late-year IKEA. I perched at the edge of her couch, likely named after a lesser Swedish mountain range.

"Are you happy where you are now?" I asked

"I am. Not too much glamour but way more money."

"And you left Toronto and moved here."

"Not much there for me anymore. Especially after all that media heat."

"I saw your interviews. Thank you for keeping me out of it."

"Sure."

"But I also know about the threat to prosecute if you didn't."

"You do?"

"It was pretty much my idea."

"Shit."

"Look, you don't get to be too upset, OK? You played a pretty active role in getting me in Thompson's sights."

"I swear I didn't know anything about the possibility of you getting hurt! Clay said he wanted your full attention and for you to see how serious he was. He was obsessed with keeping all this quiet. He figured that with Bromley dead your silence would do that, and he wasn't worried about the others."

"The others?"

"Patricia and Henry. You didn't know?"

"I assumed Henry and guessed Patricia. Did you know they were an item?"

"Not for a fact but it was an open secret around the office for years. No one cared; why would they? Both were single. It was their business."

"Alright. Getting back to the plagiarism: Was Ryan Loffler involved?"

"Ryan?"

"Yeah, Bromley first sent his manuscript to him."

She thought for a bit.

"Maybe he did know what was going on, but he forwarded the first chapter of the Bromley book to the whole Publishing Board for discussion. Any one of them could have asked for the complete MS, then cut and pasted."

"Why did you leave J&L?"

"Memories everywhere I looked. I mean Clay—he was in our offices a lot—and then Ryan."

Her voice was trembling. Her eyes had misted up.

"That's hard, Jan. Can you tell me about Ryan?"

"He was just a sweet, little guy. Quiet, very smart. A bit quirky; that's what was endearing about him."

"Quirky how?"

"He used to do these cheesy magic tricks—you know, pick a card, any card. Anytime, anywhere, he'd trot them out. He was actually pretty good."

She was lost in remembrance.

"Oh, and he used to play with this dagger thing he kept in his office."

"Dagger?"

"Yeah. He said a professor of his had given it him. Some kind of Viking thing. He used it for a letter-opener. But every once in a while, he'd toss it up into the acoustic tiles above his desk to see if he could get it to stick."

"Tom Hanks, *Nothing in Common*."

"I beg your pardon."

"Hanks worked at an ad agency. He'd flip pencils into the ceiling tiles when he was thinking. Never mind. Jan, do you know where it is?"

"No idea. I saw it in his office after…after…"

"Any idea what happened to all his stuff?"

"His father came around and collected it. I think his name was George. Why?"

"That dagger thing may have been quite valuable, that's all. Was that the only reason you left?"

"Mr. Truscott made me nervous."

"What, like in a lechery kind of way?"

"No, no, nothing like that. More like suspicious of me when he was around me."

"Do you think he knew? About the plagiarism."

"Clay said not, but he had no evidence one way or the other, and I was out of that loop."

"Was Clayton involved in the murder of Ted Bromley?"

"Absolutely not!" she exclaimed, getting instantly amped up. "I was with him most of the night after the lecture. There's no way he could've slipped out. And besides, he wasn't the kind of person who would do that. He just wasn't!"

I let her declaration hang there. At that moment, there was zero percentage in pursuing it. That didn't stop me from reminding myself that "most of the evening" didn't exonerate him, or that Jan had been part of the scheme to get me to the cabin, or that, under pressure, Clayton Thompson had proved that he was *exactly* "that kind of person" who could commit murder. He'd almost done it to yours truly.

"What happens to me now?" she asked.

"It kinda depends on you. I looked it up. There is no statute of limitations for kidnapping and forcible confinement."

"I know. I looked it up too."

"Think you can keep that secret about what really happened that night?"

"I don't have much of a choice, do I?"

There was no point in leaning on her again. She was smart enough to know that the sands of time would likely do its work, drifting over and obscuring the actual events until they became irrelevant or completely forgotten by everyone. Except us. And a court of law.

"I have to tell you," she said, "I'm surprised the plagiarism thing is still a secret."

"It won't be forever. The cops are sitting on it until they get a fix on who killed Bromley...and Ryan. But you're safe," I said as I got up. "Unless of course if you were involved right from the start," I added.

"I wasn't!"

"Take care of yourself, OK?" I said.

"I'd just as soon not hear from you again."

"Understood."

I drove away with a general sense that Jan would—for self-preservation reasons—keep up her end of the bargain. And the very specific bit of information that Bromley awarded things like Viking meat skewers to star students. I could think of another scholar who might have also been a recipient. Terrence Childers.

First though, I had to account for the whereabouts of Ryan Loffler's skewer. Was it still resting in a box at his dad's place, or had it been removed from Ryan's office earlier and perhaps used as a murder weapon on Ted Bromley?

In running down that little detail, I reminded myself how little I envied actual police detectives. Laborious and time-consuming, the task still had to be done. There were eight George Lofflers listed in metropolitan Toronto. I got lucky on the fifth one who turned out to be dickish right from the start. I could see why. He'd recently buried his son and now a complete stranger was quizzing him out of the blue about his boy's possessions. Yes, he assured me, he had the skewer and why did I want to know. When I told him it might be worth a lot of money, he wanted to know how much, as if I was the fucking *Antiques Roadshow*.

I let him know he could expect a call from the Norwegian embassy and hung up.

CHAPTER TWENTY-FIVE

It turned out that Alexandra's attempt to spend two months—May and then July—at the lake had been a tad ambitious. While she had mostly cleared the decks for our delightful May together, July wound up to being far more demanding of her time. For one thing, she had twenty-two employees, many of them recent hires as the trend to ethical investing had gathered steam (but not steam generated by a fossil fuel!). And that meant twenty-two human beings with issues, jealousies, petty complaints, and real or imagined indignities piled on them that needed attention. All these personnel problems had, of course, nothing to do with actually running a business that had paying clients, things to produce to keep them paying, and a bottom line to worry about.

I couldn't do what she did. No sane boss would ever give me staff to manage, such is the extent of my empathy and patience. For some reason, my management philosophy was always: "You're getting paid to show up and do your fucking job. So do it. Figure out on your own time how to deal with Angela for swiping your yogurt from the lunchroom fridge and don't ask for a day off because your goddamned cat died and stop fucking badgering me for a promotion that I know—and you should too—you don't deserve." These days, perhaps justifiably, I would, at the very least, be fired and publicly pilloried for an attitude that resembled General Patton's on a bad day.

Alex said she was sorry for the amount of time she was spending on the phone and computer. I was OK with it as it gave me a bunch of time to delve deeper into Bromley's journals. I read them more carefully than before and found all sorts of interesting stuff. Take this from over twenty years earlier:

I am beside myself with rage. Today, Vivian tearfully confessed to a dalliance with PH, that middle-aged libertine. I so wanted to be angry with my dear Viv but could not summon the ire. She was distraught and devastated. Surely, she was seduced by that amoral roué. I shall not be the laughingstock cuckhold. His day of reckoning shall come.

I had no choice but to elevate another name to my roster of potential killers: Philip Harder. It was a stretch, but maybe he had acted in self-defence before Bromley had a chance to fuck him up.

Finally, Alex had to give up. Her long-distance managing of the company wasn't working. It just wasn't letting her keep on top of things and deal with all those messy humans. Early into the third week of July, she folded, making neither of us happy.

"You have to drive me to the airport," she told me as she finished packing.

"Sure, babe…But why take two cars? And if we don't, then what do I do after I return the rental?"

"It's not a rental."

"What?"

"It's yours…ours," she said, plopping the keys into my hand while I was otherwise busy being stunned.

I collected maybe half of my wits to tell her: "No way!"

"Way," she insisted. "I had a very good year."

"That's not the point."

"Listen, you can look at this one of two ways. Call it a gift to my barely adequate Canadian gigolo for services rendered."

"Barely adequate?"

"OK, how about: it's a gift to my *superbly* adequate Canadian gigolo?"

"Much better. What's my second choice?"

"It's an investment in your lover's personal safety and comfort. You know, the lover who refuses to drive another fucking mile— let alone all the way to Florida—in that…that silver deathtrap!" she said, disdainfully pointing at the Vibe, which, I swear, shrank in humiliation.

"I…I don't know what to say."

"Well then, it's worth it just for that. Now, c'mon; let's go; we'll be late. Insurance and registration in the glove compartment," she said, opening the passenger door.

I was nervous, as I always am when I get behind the wheel of a strange vehicle. Sidebar: Have you noticed I get messed up by the tiniest things? No, it's true.

Given that the last time I'd owned a new car was when I popped the wad for my brand-new Pontiac Vibe almost fifteen years ago, back in the automotive Stone Age before they developed the slew of gadgets to amuse and confuse a world of ADHD drivers. Sitting behind the wheel of my new ride, I was bewildered by all the new thing-a-ma-bobbies in front of me, starting with the large multi-coloured display screen where—sigh—the ashtray and lighter used to be.

"Can you turn that fucking thing off?" I asked.

"It's useful."

"For Christ's sake, how'd we ever manage over the last hundred years or so of driving? What's it good for?"

"For one thing, it has a map."

"I know where the goddamned airport is."

"It's got lane assist if you start to drift."

"I know how to stay in my own goddamned lane."

"It can tell you if there's a traffic jam ahead."

"I can probably figure that out as soon as we come to a stop on the highway and are surrounded by a bunch of other parked cars."

"Let's you know outside *and* inside temperatures."

"Let's bet I can feel the temperature walking to the car and then get a pretty accurate idea once I was inside."

Suddenly, there was a loud ringing, like a phone, only underwater. She answered the steering wheel and spoke for a garbled few seconds with someone from her office.

"Can you also turn that fucking thing off?" I asked when she was done with her call. "You may have noticed that I don't have a goddamned cellphone."

"I do."

"I've been meaning to talk to you about that. Ever wonder why state and provincial governments are spending millions and millions to get people to shut their fucking phones down? And don't give me that 'hands-free' bullshit; a distraction is a distraction. You might as well drive drunk."

"Why are you being such an old-fashioned asshole about this?"

"Let's set aside the fact that I actually *am* an old-fashioned asshole. Think of it as—what were the words—oh, yeah, as an investment in your lover's personal safety and comfort to not have me distracted by any of that crap while I'm driving."

I have to admit that as loyal as the Vibe had been and how much retro-fun I had in the ancient beast of a Cadillac awaiting me in Florida, tooling down to Toronto with new wheels was kinda luxurious after Alex silenced some of the distracting bells and whistles.

All that comfort didn't make our good-byes any easier. Although she said she'd try, I probably wouldn't be seeing her again until I drove to Framingham to pick her up for our drive to Indian

Rocks at the end of October.

The second I got back to the hovel, I called Les Macgregor. Wait, I just lied. I got myself a beer first.

"Les, how's it goin,' eh?"

"To what do I owe this folksiness?" he asked warily.

"It's kinda a palsy-walsy way of giving you your next assignment."

"Fuck off."

"Oh, Les, Les, Les. That's not even remotely plasy-walsy."

"What do you want?"

"Glad you asked. To start with, I need the names and numbers of that seminar group you interviewed. I need to talk to them."

"That's easy. I'll e-mail you the list."

"Thanks. Oh, and there's something else."

"What?" he asked suspiciously.

"Are you guys starting to see a connection between Bromley's death and Clayton Thompson's appearance at the campus that night?"

"It's a theory."

"Well, so's the rumour that Elvis is alive."

"OK, OK. We just talked about it again this morning."

"Great. Then you know we need to recreate the evening of March 23 as close as you can get, minute by minute."

"Oh, that'll be a snap. Do you want all of Ontario or just Peterborough?"

"I can narrow it down for you. Backstage in the Great Hall at Trent."

"Well, why didn't you say so? Piece of cake."

"But wait; there's more! We need to know the movements of just a few people, for a couple of hours after Clayton Thompson finished speaking. Minute by minute. Above all we want the exact time when Bromley left."

"I already have that—9:45. More or less."

"How much 'more or less'?"

"Based on the autopsy, given the body temp, time it'd have taken to walk from the hall to his car, fifteen minutes on either side. Who else?"

"Patricia Morland, Jan Morris, Henry Blake, and Thompson himself. You can't miss Blake, he's at least 6'6". Also, could you check if a Daniel Truscott was there? And while you're at it, our friend, Terrence Childers. Oh, and a Ryan Loffler."

"Jake, give me a fuckin' hint where you'd start if you were actually doing the work instead of sitting by a lake with your thumb up your ass?"

"If I were you—and believe me when I tell you, I thank the living lord, sweet bleeding Jesus that I'm not—I'd interview the English professors; they were all there. Start with the oldest ones. They'd likely remember Loffler because he was a student and Childers still is. They'd probably know *of* Morland, Blake, and Truscott. Jan Morris was the very pretty young brunette attached to Thompson that night."

"Why don't I just ask them what they were doing?"

"Why? Because one of them probably killed Bromley. That's why."

I had a thought.

"Les, one more name for you."

"Shoot," he said wearily.

"Philip Harder, old philosophy dude."

"That's it?"

"Like I said, minute by minute from, say eight until nine. And also, if anybody was beefing with anybody else on that list."

"Are you sure that's all?"

"Now that you mention it, maybe *exactly* what they were all wearing—including their footwear. And I need all this info by tomorrow afternoon."

To his credit, Les told me to fuck off and hung up

I then was onto clearing up a small detail that maybe might matter: how many Viking skewers had been arrayed behind that shield over Bromley's mantle? I knew Ryan Loffler and now his estate had one. Lawyer and punster Gordon said five were accounted for. None of those six had been the murder weapon. So at least one was missing. But were there more? The only way I could think of to find an answer was by spending a large amount of time working my way through the list of seminar attendees that Les e-mailed me. Most of an entire fucking day was eaten up by tracking them down, waiting for call-backs, just to find out that all I really learned was that eyewitnesses were unreliable.

Maybe six. Or seven. Definitely five. Six, for sure. I even got a three. No one picked eight as the lucky number.

Les called two days later.

"How'd you make out?" I asked.

"Pretty good, I think. I talked to five profs. Like you said, they all knew or knew of everybody on the list except Jan Morris. But she made quite a first-time impression on the old hounds. She was probably the most watched of the bunch. Amazing memories, those profs have. But holy shit, they can yak."

"Whattya got?"

"There wasn't much they didn't agree on. To start with: no one remembers Childers or Loffler being there. But they were sure Morland was."

"What about Truscott?"

"All five knew who he was and all five said he wasn't there."

"You sure?"

"I'm sure. Anyway, Morland disappeared twice during your timeframe—both times alone—ten to fifteen minutes each time. They didn't recall this big galoot Henry Blake, so I guess he wasn't there. Thompson talked to a lot of people but longest with Morland."

"Everything all friendly?"

"Not quite. Seems as though Bromley got himself agitated with Thompson. Two of the witnesses said their conversation wasn't longer than a minute but it looked pretty hot."

"Know what was said?"

"Nobody was close enough."

"Thompson get into it with anybody else?"

"As a matter of fact, Thompson had a longer chat with another professor type that didn't seem all that friendly."

"Who?"

"That Philip Harder."

"Well, that's interesting."

"I'll take your word for it. Maybe this tidbit will fascinate you too. Bromley and Harder mixed it up a bit. Again, nobody heard what they were scrapping about. One of the profs I spoke to, well, a former prof—Sanford—said there had been bad blood between those two for years."

"Know why?"

"Sanford said—I got his quote here—"I shouldn't want to speculate." Whatever that means."

"Was Thompson there the whole time?"

"Nope, he left the room with Morland for about twenty minutes. They were both on their phones walking out."

"When?"

"About ten, maybe fifteen minutes after Bromley left."

"Hmmm."

"That's it? Hmmm."

"For now. I gotta think. Excellent work, Dr. Watson!"

"Oh and I suppose you're fucking Sherlock."

"What the Christ are you talking about? Doc Watson was my GP when I lived in the Bahamas. Smart guy. He had a knack for—"

Hearing Les hang up was almost as much fun as me doing it

first.

The suspect pool was getting to be Olympic-sized. At least five possible evildoers involved in two murders a hundred miles apart. In the deep end, maybe Patricia Morland and/or Henry Blake. I had a no-call on Daniel Truscott. He couldn't have wiped out Bromley if he wasn't there, but he may have had a bloody hand in Loffler's demise. Paddling around in the shallow end we maybe had Terrence Childers. And now, after Les Macgregor's survey, maybe Philosopher Philip Harder. Or maybe someone else for completely different reasons that I hadn't yet stumbled over. They all couldn't have killed Ted Bromley and/or Ryan Loffler unless this somehow morphed into an Agatha Christie novel—only with a lot more fucking potty words—where the characters joined in a group effort.

I was starting to feel like one of those South American performers that used to be on *The Ed Sullivan Show.* You know the guys, the lads in the puffy shirts and tight pants who kept plates spinning on top of these long poles. They would add a plate until they had seven or eight whirling away and he'd race from one pole to the next keeping the plates from crashing down. Just like the crowd at a NASCAR race does, the audience was crammed with expectation, maybe even hope, that at least one of those plates shattered on the stage.

Something was bugging me. Why wasn't Henry Blake in Peterborough that night with his lover for a dirty out of town get-together? Or maybe he was. Maybe he was spending time stabbing people while Patricia was at the lecture and following reception.

I figured I should clear that detail up.

After a little research, I found the most expensive hotel in town, figuring that Patricia would only stay there. I also guessed that hotels don't automatically give out info on their guests just because someone asked. I called Les Macgregor.

"Les, old buddy. We need to get together."

"For what?"

"Can you meet me at the Hilton this afternoon, say around three?"

"Why?"

"I just think we should, you know, get a little closer, what with working together and all."

"What the fuck are you talking about?" he asked.

"Actually, it's for *our* case. What I really need is your badge for a little law enforcement authority."

"I'll be there." Click.

I printed out Morland's photo from the agency website as well as Henry's from J&L. His was on the Officers of the Company page, one of six.

The Hilton was nice but certainly not deluxe as Peterborough isn't a deluxe town, no 500 buck-a-night broom closets next to the elevator shaft. Les was waiting for me in the lobby.

I suggested that Les introduce us, flash the badge, and then shut the fuck up.

Courtney at the long front desk greeted us with a dazzling 1000-watt smile that winked out the moment she saw Les' shield.

"I'll…get my manager."

"No need for that, Courtney," I said. "We just want to know if a person we're investigating stayed here one night."

"I'm really not supposed to give out that—"

"I know, I know, but this is a serious crime, Courtney. Now, we could go the subpoena route, come back and cause a scene or you could just give us a simple yes or no."

She went to her terminal.

"Name?"

"Patricia Morland. March 23rd this year."

Her flying fingers clicked away.

"Yes. Here she is."

"This woman?" I asked and showed her picture.

"Oh, I remember *her*. I checked her in. Stylish lady but, boy, was she a bossy rig."

"Do you remember if she checked in alone?"

"No. There was a man with her."

"Him?" I said pointing to Blake's picture.

"No."

She paused.

"Wait. *That* was the guy," she said.

She had run her finger up the page to a head shot of one Daniel Truscott.

"Are you sure?"

"Sure I'm sure. Classy older gentleman, hotel restaurant said he was a big tipper."

Can I get a "well, well, well"?

"Ya know, maybe I should think about becoming a cop," I said to Les out in the parking lot

"How old are you?"

"Sixty-three. And don't give me that ageist shit."

"You wouldn't reach retirement age."

"Cop school last that long?"

"No, it's just that you'd be beaten death in the squad room within a week."

CHAPTER TWENTY-SIX

Driving home, I drew three conclusions from our little foray. Morland's rendezvous with Truscott might help explain her publishing success rate at Jameson & Lord. It also re-elevated Truscott back to the suspect list. While I couldn't care less who pairs off with whom, his wife and mother of his three children might. Maybe that's why he had lied to me about never having been to Peterborough. Or maybe he was out at remote parking lot getting a different kind of thrusting exercise. And finally, I could strike Henry Blake's name off the list of possible Bromley killers. No way he was in town if Patricia and Dan the publishing man were being horizontally adjacent.

I went back to that list to see if I could eliminate somebody else.

Professor Sanford, I decided, might be able to shed some light on the Bromley-Harder feud that Ted had mentioned as early as twenty years ago, and Les had confirmed was very much alive until Bromley wasn't. Sanford was still in Peterborough, over eighty years old, I reckoned, and obviously hale enough to have been at the first Thompson lecture.

I had truly liked him when he tried to drill the relevance of Jonathan Swift and Alexander Pope into my wee young student brain when I was a pupil of his. Soft-spoken, polite, always smiling, he tolerated me as a student even though back then I wasn't nearly as fuckin' sophisticated and goddamned classy as I am now.

Professor Emeritus Sanford was easy to find. I just showed up at his door one afternoon. And a darn nice door it was, attached to one of those big old brick houses like the one I had lived in with Beth.

He answered that door, instantly recognized me, and, what's more, actually seemed happy to see me, a reaction I didn't seem to inspire a lot these days.

He hadn't changed much that I could tell. Slightly more rotund, his movements slower, his hair wispier but the same dancing blue eyes and perpetual smile. Even though he was retired, and it was the middle of a Tuesday afternoon, he remained immaculately dressed. From his polished brogues, black dress socks, to his dark grey dress slacks, crisp white shirt and understated striped tie. I guess for him he was going casual by exchanging his usual charcoal suit jacket for a knit argyle vest.

He ushered me into a formal living room where I perched on an antique overstuffed chair that was probably worth more than my goddamned house. The home was decorated as elegantly as I remembered with expensive but comfortable antiques, the obligatory bookshelves, marble fireplace, period artwork, thick brocade rugs bordered by shining maple hardwood floors. The whole place looked like it had just been the scene for an army of cleaners toiling away.

We were joined by his gracious wife, Sandra, whom I had met only once, at a dinner the professor had invited Beth and me to. She seemed even more delighted to see me and I started to suspect that they were both in mid-stage dementia and had forgotten what an irreverent and boorish arsehole I had been.

At that dinner, I distinctly remembered thinking that the grace-filled life he and Sandra had fashioned was exactly the sort of way I wanted to play out the string with Beth after a lifetime of teaching and reading and writing. My, my, the years had different plans.

"Beer, if I remember," Sandra said. "John?"

"Oh, why not?" her husband answered. "This is an occasion."

"Here, let me help," I offered and followed her into the kitchen.

I poured my Tuborg into a chilled mug while Sandra half-filled a short highball glass with scotch from a cut crystal decanter.

"I am so happy you dropped by," she said in a whisper. "I worry about John sometimes. Since he retired, he mopes. He does so much miss teaching and being with young students."

Her comment made me happy and sad at the same time. Sanford had spent his lifetime teaching, just *teaching*. I knew he had turned down the chairmanship of English departments at several universities and he had steadfastly opposed a graduate program at Trent that would've diverted professors to the pursuit of being published in order to ensure that the school stayed focused on teaching undergrads. He had never lost his enthusiasm for being a true educator and now he had no place to put that enthusiasm.

Sandra didn't sit with us ("You boys have some catching up to do."). And catch up we did, although most the conversation consisted of me answering his questions about what I'd been up to for the last four decades. It seemed to really matter how it all turned out for his students.

He pointed at his bookcase. I spotted the spine of my *On the Rails* that I hadn't noticed earlier.

"I do know something of what you've been up to, Jake. And I must say, I was impressed."

I know I blushed, something I almost never do.

"Now tell me, my boy, why did you decide to pay a visit to an old goat of a superannuated teacher?"

"Well, professor," I started, but he insisted I call him John.

"I just can't do it," I said. (And I couldn't). "You will always be 'professor.'"

Meant only to be factual, my answer seemed to truly please him.

"One of the reasons I'm here is that I understand you were recently involved in the police investigation into the death of Ted Bromley."

That took him aback and I quickly explained my low-paying part-time job helping the cops out in tracking down people who do nasty things to other people.

"Shocking, that," he said. "We weren't close friends, but Ted was a trusted colleague. We'd been through all the department wars together for decades. Unimaginable what happened."

"I was interested in your observation about the set-to he had that night with Philip Harder."

"I simply confirmed what others had noted: they had a spat."

"I understand that what you said was you "shouldn't want to speculate" about the cause. I'm thinking, given your precision with language, that you *do* have some thoughts about what led up to it, but you felt it was inappropriate to share them. Am I close?"

"Dead on, I'd say," he admitted.

"Care to share them now? It could be important."

"I wasn't trying to be evasive. I simply don't enjoy salacious gossiping about ancient history. Never have."

"Understood. But like I said: it could be important."

"Very well," he sighed, looking as though the whole exercise was thoroughly distasteful to him. "In the early days—perhaps even when you attended classes—Ted and Philip were good friends. So were their wives. They'd socialize, even vacation together. Then the Harders divorced; it was all rather surprising. She left town and he underwent something of a transformation."

"An early onset mid-life crisis?"

"Precisely. All the signs were there. He lost weight, changed his wardrobe, bought a sports car and fancied himself quite the dashing figure on campus. The truth is, I never much cared for him. He was always even more pompous than me, if you can imagine. But this reconstituted cliché of man was unbearable. It seemed to me that Philip had wholeheartedly become a member of the most pernicious race of little odious vermin that nature ever suffered to crawl upon the surface of the earth."

"Ah, Mr. Swift had his way with words, didn't he?"

"Well done. I'm glad some things I taught sank in. At any rate, while he may not look capable of it now, Philip cut quite the swath through our corps of female teachers and faculty wives about a quarter of a century ago. And he made no secret of it. He would claim that his middle name was Harderand, if you can imagine."

"And Mrs. Bromley was one of his conquests?"

"Yes. That was the truly unconscionable part of all this. He and Ted had been friends. And Vivian was really quite a lovely person, but rather delicate and shy. Harder actually said—to anyone who would listen—that she was a shrinking violet that he had made blossom. What he did was callously use and discard her, leaving poor Ted to pick up the pieces. Bromley actually threatened to kill him at an inter-department symposium some years later. But it would have had to be done at a great distance. Poor Ted was no physical match for Harder."

"Looks like Ted hadn't reached the 'let bygones be bygones' stage yet."

"So you think Harder may be a murderer?"

"Oh, I shouldn't want to speculate."

"Clever."

"OK, if you insist. It's *possible*. Maybe Ted kept up his campaign of threatening harassment over the years and maybe Harder just got so fed up or maybe even afraid that he decided to put an end to it by putting an end to Bromley."

"It doesn't seem reasonable."

"Oh, you Age of Reason guys are all the same," I joked. "I've learned, first-hand unfortunately, that reason frequently doesn't have much to do with murder."

I left with a warm handshake and a promise to drop by again at any "reasonable" time.

There wasn't much danger of Professor Sanford spreading around any of my speculations. Guy like that was way too discreet and classy.

I also came away with a bit more detail, some context for Bromley's rage against Philip Harder. But I also had the fact that they had once been friends, so Harder could've swiped a Viking skewer or maybe Bromley had given it to him years earlier. If he kept it in his office, he could've left the reception, nipped down and retrieved it, then followed Ted out to the parking lot.

In this sweepstakes to determine a winner in the Most Likely to Take the Life of an Old English Professor category, Philip Harder was bringing up the rear, a true dark horse.

But he was definitely in the running.

CHAPTER TWENTY-SEVEN

"Does Childers have a car, Les?" I asked.

"I don't know. Why?"

"Well. If he didn't and if he also went to Thompson's lecture, then maybe he bummed a ride back into town with his prof. You know, the guy who didn't get a chance to start his car 'cuz he was busy dying."

"Lemme check."

The checking shouldn't have taken as long as it did. Les was fucking with me, but it didn't upset me. I've developed a foolproof strategy for passing time while I'm on hold 'til I die with banks, cable suppliers, credit card companies, airlines, government departments and any other outfit which are *always* "experiencing higher than usual call volumes" but want to assure me that my "call is important to them." I play solitaire. Not your usual solitaire but a match between me and invisible opponent known as The Fucker that involves games to ten using a complicated scoring system. I amuse the fuck out of myself, and the time just passes. I was up 7 to 5 on The Fucker when the lower-case fucker got back on the line.

"Sorry for keeping you waiting, Jake."

"No problem. Why, I didn't even notice you were gone."

"Childers owns a car," he grumbled. "Suzuki Samurai 4X4. Old one. 1986."

"What was that?"

"He owns a car," he said louder.

"…Sorry. I've…bad connec…"

"I said he owns a car!" he almost shouted.

"Geez, Les, no need to yell. I'm not deaf."

There was a pause before the inevitable "Fuck off" and the click.

I needed to skinny down the suspect list. With Blake in the clear, the possible Morland-Truscott assassination duo from Toronto would, like my strings of Christmas lights, take some time to unravel. Jake, how about you look at the individual local possibles and either eliminate them or not?

I sent Childers an e-mail, telling him I'd read his stuff, liked it a bunch and wanted to talk to him about next steps. I suggested the Red Dog at noon. No way was I meeting that big, temperamental bastard anywhere but in a public place.

He wrote back saying it'd have to be a Saturday or Sunday because he couldn't get off work at his summer job installing swimming pools.

Our mid-day rendezvous at the dive bar started out contentious and went downhill from there. I tried to praise his writing, citing enough passages to convince him I'd read the stories. That part wasn't bullshit.

But I did actually want to talk about the bleakness of his work.

"I'm curious why there is no evidence of empathy or understanding or even judgement about what happens to the people in your stories," I said.

"They don't require empathy or judgement; no one does," he stated. "There are only actions, reactions, and consequences."

"So you're fine with a completely immoral world?"

"*Amoral* world. And yes. Morality is a comfortable human invention we use to tell us we should be good and that we must punish the so-called bad people. We're kidding ourselves."

"Yeah, but—"

"Look, this is tiresome," he said, cutting me off. "There are some French thinkers—Georges Bataille, Jean Baudrillard or Charles Baudelaire in *Flowers of Evil*. Or Thomas de Quincy for that matter; he wrote *On Murder Considered as One of the Fine Arts*, and Marquis de Sade. You should read them closely and then we can discuss. In the meantime, what can you tell me about publishing my stories?"

He grew even more impatient when I didn't seem to add anything to my hollow claim that maybe my connections to the publishing world could be helpful to him. That was the bullshit part, and he knew it.

"You didn't come here to debate philosophy or pretend you're some publishing guru. You want to tell me the real reason you're fucking with me?

"Straight up?"

"I'd like that."

"I think you may have had something to do with Ted Bromley's death."

There was only the slightest of pauses.

"How the fuck do you figure that?"

"How? You drove out there and waited."

"Bullshit. That didn't happen. Piece of crap was in the shop. Radiator was shot."

"Where?"

"Usually at the very front of the engine compartment," he said with a slight smirk.

"I meant what shop?"

"Oh. Al's on Lansdowne."

"We can check."

"Check away. I got a lift out to campus and *back* with Richard somebody or other in my class. You can check that too while you're at it."

Well, that put a screeching halt to my brutal interrogation. Oh, and there was still the immediate matter of getting out of there alive. But he surprised me.

"Are we done here?" he asked. Instead of beating the shit out of me for accusing him of murder, he stared at me.

Jake be nimble, Jake be quick, I thought. Whoa the fuck down; Jake be none of those things.

"Yeah…sorry," was all I could manage.

He didn't say anything but wore something that looked like a slight self-satisfied grin.

"So….what about them Expos?" I said into the more than awkward chasm of silence.

"For shits and giggles, do you want to tell me why you decided I was a murderer?" he asked, as if he was marginally amused at my rash accusation.

Where to begin? I thought.

"I'm curious. Did you come up with this crackpot dog-eat-dog, fuck everybody else French philosopher theory before or after you were in JTF2?"

That startled him.

"How the hell would you know that?"

I explained stumbling onto the story and accompanying photo that got those journalists kicked out of Afghanistan and how his ear injury gave him away.

"Clever."

"The ear. Gift from Afghanistan?"

"Yes. Sniper bullet."

"You were also in Iraq with the Americans," I said.

"How'd you know that?"

"I didn't, until just now."

It was my turn to grin at my own goddamn cleverness.

"So how long were you there?" I asked.

"Briefly. "

"Forty or fifty of you."

"A few more than that."

"Doing?"

"Doing none of your business."

"And now here you are—an English major and a writer."

"I wanted to get as far away from it as I could."

"Mission accomplished."

As soon as I said that, I realized it was an incredibly stupid comment. Childers stared past me, through me actually, and thought.

"That would be about the only mission I did truly accomplish."

"What do you mean?"

"Over there, right from the start, every mission was bullshit. They didn't have uniforms, neither did you. I wasn't behind enemy lines; there were no lines. You'd sit in a briefing, get all sorts of maps and pretty pictures and "intelligence." Then you'd get out there and it was all FUBAR. You've heard of that?"

"Fucked up beyond all recognition?"

"The only way to describe it. There was no normal way to do things. A completely different reality. The only thing that kept you going, kept you safe were the other guys in your platoon. You made up the rules as you went along when you were in-country. And every minute, you're worried about stepping on a mine, or getting shot at by a guy you thought was just a translator. Try living that way 24/7."

"How'd you handle it?"

"Not well, obviously. But thank God for the relief some of us got."

"What kind of relief?"

I truly wanted to know. My conversation with his ex-wife had only hinted at the extent of damage done to this man by war. Maybe he answered my question because he sensed my genuine interest.

"The dope," he said.

"What?"

"The heroin and the coke, both easy to get. A line of smack to let you nod off when it was your turn to grab some sleep, coke to keep you up and alert."

"You could function?"

"You still had job, a mission, to carry out so you tried to do that but, really, all you were doing was just trying to stay alive. And you were trying to take as many of them off the board as you could. After a while, you were just settling accounts."

"Revenge?"

"No…well, maybe. The locals would point out a fighter who maybe got one your guys. And you'd settle his account."

"That bothered you?"

"Fuck, no. Like I said, I had a job. I was good at it. We were trained to not think of them as humans. They were just targets."

"Even the innocent ones?"

"It was a whole lot easier to see everybody, including us, as guilty. Except…"

"Except what?"

"Our dogs."

"Dogs?"

"We had a canine unit. German shepherds and Belgian Malinois. Magnificent animals. They had no choice. They did what we trained them to do. Bomb-sniffing, patrolling, defending us. They just wanted to please. And then you watched as they got blown to bits by IEDs, shot, or poisoned. They were blameless."

I was sure I could see the eyes of this hardened man mist up.

"I saw shit; I did shit. I quit. Let's leave it at that," he said.

"You should know that I spoke to your wife."

"You had no fuckin' right to do that!" he said suddenly, loud enough and angry enough to attract a bunch of stares from the drinkers around us.

"It wasn't a great thing to do; I'll give you that," I said. "But that Charter of Rights you were over there defending says I can freely associate. I was freely associating."

"So you know our story. I met Eleni in Cyprus. She was a nurse there."

"You were sent there after your tour was up but before you came home."

"It was my first R&R in three years."

"Were you in a hospital?"

"They said it was a facility but, yeah. They called it decompression. Know what they gave us for decompression in that facility? Video games."

"Not those first-person shooter games?"

"Yup. Can you imagine that?"

"Like a bricklayer comin' home after work and playing with Lego all night."

That earned a rueful smile that disappeared with my next question.

"Were you still using?"

"Yeah."

"You could find it?"

"We got day passes. In a port city of about half a million you could get just about anything. But Eleni got me clean. We fell in love, and she wanted to come to Canada. That took a bit of doing and she couldn't practice nursing here."

"So she went into dental hygiene."

"How is she?" he asked.

"She seems fine."

Childers had a far-away look in his eyes. He was back there, maybe in Afghanistan or Cyprus. Maybe on his wedding day in Montreal, maybe on the day they split up. I was just the embarrassed bystander, watching him react to memories I had dredged up.

Seemed to me like a good time to get the hell out of there.

Well, damn, I thought as I left the bar. Swing and a miss, Jake. Childers was pretty restrained in his defense, but I doubted he was lying. Lad that smart wouldn't be making alibi claims that weren't easily corroborated.

I came away more or less stunned by the personal revelations I had heard. For once, I was sorry I had the ability to get people to talk. It wasn't much of a chore to imagine the strange and terrible world Terrence Childers had survived, a world which absolutely no one who hasn't inhabited it can possibly understand.

Now knowing as fact that Childers was a highly trained warrior who had "seen shit and done shit" made me awful glad we hadn't scrapped on the first day I met him.

This revelation also told me that he'd learned to do a lot of unsavoury things. Like, oh, I don't know, how to efficiently stab people to death.

CHAPTER TWENTY-EIGHT

Everybody uses the term PTSD and there's a sense that just by using this shorthand we know what actually happens to its sufferers. We don't. It didn't take me long on the web to learn a little more. Like most mental or physical conditions, there is no one-size-fits-all. Different causes, different symptoms, different treatments. More often than not, it's triggered by a traumatic event; Childers had years' worth of traumatic events that he not only witnessed but caused. How did anyone think he could return from a war zone and casually resume everyday life? He probably had nightmares and flashbacks; I couldn't say. But he seemed almost detached from reality, quick-tempered, alienated from humanity and to some degree, paranoid. I knew my amateurish analysis was just that, but the sum total picture of the man suggested I ought to look closer.

I decided I should check out his alibi anyway, just to be sure. I had Richard Harper's contact info and spoke to him again. I called him at home in Hamilton where he lived with his parents in the summer.

I identified myself and told him I was working with the police, looking at all angles in the Bromley murder investigation. I asked about Terrence Childers that night.

"Do you suspect him?" he asked.

"No, no, no. Nothing like that. I've got the joe job of running down all the loose ends. I understand all of you weren't too happy about being out at the main campus."

"No, we weren't; we all liked the professor's place better."

"Bromley was pissed too?"

"Probably more than us. He told us two weeks earlier and we all groaned. He groaned the loudest. And when we got out there, he moaned about having to park in the boonies."

"So tell me about Childers."

"To start with, he bummed a ride with me. Out there and back, right after class."

"Wonder why he didn't take the shuttle."

"Shuttle?"

"Yeah, doesn't the university provide a free shuttle from down-town?"

"No," he said, making me feel like I was an out-of-touch time traveler from the past—which I was. "They give us a bus pass as part of our tuition. City bus goes out there."

"OK, so why didn't he just take the bus?"

"Don't know. Maybe he didn't have a pass because he already had a car and didn't want to spring for the fare that night. He made a big deal about how pissed he was that his had broken down."

"While I got you here, can you tell me—generally—about Ter-rence in the class. How was he?"

"Pretty assertive, if you want the truth. He's smart, no doubt about that, but he's sort of a douche. Not too hard to see why he didn't have any friends, at least not that I could see. Please don't tell him I said that."

"How was Bromley towards him?"

"Almost deferential. He was the teacher's pet, but I think Professor Bromley was a little scared of him. Heck, we all were. He was a lot older than us…and a lot bigger. He'd have this weird way of looking at you if you disagreed with him. You *do* think he did it, don't you?"

"No, Richard. Like I said, just checking out some details. So you are absolutely sure he drove with you back into town?"

"Positive."

Damn. Childers' alibi checked out. Sure, there were other ways he could've made it back out to campus—cab, bus, hitchhike, even run out there—but all of them presented a whole lot more opportunity to be seen and remembered, something he just wouldn't have risked. I ruled out him renting a car because the paper trail and ID requirements I knew were somewhat akin to gaining access to a top-secret nuclear facility.

I had been convinced that, given his volatile character, he was a highly likely suspect. But at least I could strike one more name off the list of possible dastardly deed doers.

On to Philip Harder.

I called Harder, got him on the first try, and identified myself as the alumnus whom he had spoken to earlier about Clayton Thompson. I might as well have told him I was going to drop around with a free dose of ebola for him.

But he agreed, however reluctantly, when I said I needed some basic philosophy tutoring for the bullshit story I was allegedly writing. Sitting in his office again, I tried my damnedest to picture the pudgy, garishly dressed—predominantly white plaid golf slacks of the sort the PGA makes its golfers wear to humble them and a banana-yellow shirt tucked in to make him look like a giant, well-fed canary—old guy as the big dashing hound on campus. Couldn't do it.

I copped to being a fake as the phrase "working with the police" tended to get co-operation from most people.

"Terrible thing about Professor Bromley," he offered.

"I understand you two weren't exactly bosom buddies."

"Who said that?" he demanded, which pissed me off.

"That really doesn't matter, does it? A fact is just that."

"Alright. No, we were not close."

"Why not? I understand you once were."

"A bit of messiness a long time ago. Ancient history."

"Really? You and he got into it the night he was killed."

"Ted never got over it."

"We know about his death threats; we know about your fight at Thompson's reception. I'd like to understand if there were more problems you had."

"He was annoying. He'd pull these childish...pranks. That's what they were. Pranks that irritated me but that's it."

"Such as....?"

"His most egregious was during my attempt to achieve full professorship. That was five years ago."

"Tell me about it."

"My first application was denied—on spurious grounds. I appealed. He actually came to the faculty hearing, almost yelling that I was "morally unfit" for tenure. Probably helped me more than it hurt."

"How so?"

"Everyone knew—or thought they knew—what had happened between Ted and me. I believe they discounted his objection as being the result of jealousy and emotional distress."

"And since then?"

"As I said: pranks. His latest was slipping into my office and gluing together sheets of a paper I was working on. As if he'd never heard of computer files."

"Were you afraid of what he might do?"

"Don't be silly. Me worry about Ted?"

"Know anything about Viking skewers?"

"As a matter of fact, I do. Ted was awfully proud of his Norse shrine."

"Did he ever give you one?"

"Now why in the world would I want a Viking skewer?"

"I wasn't looking for another question, Professor."

"No, he didn't!" he said, summoning up that temper I'd seen at our first meeting. "Wait—you cannot possibly think I had anything to do with Ted's death!"

"Did you?"

"I will not dignify that question with an answer. Is there something else?"

"You got into it with Thompson too. What was that about?"

"I gave him bloody hell for perverting the discipline of philosophy."

"Where did you go after the reception that night?"

"Home. To my wife. We watched *Nova* on PBS."

"What was it about?"

"The plastic waste in the Pacific," he answered with no hesitation.

0-2 at the Peterborough plate of suspects. Philip Harder may have a bit of a temper but he wasn't a killer. The answer to who rubbed out Bromley had to lie in the Toronto publishing world.

CHAPTER TWENTY-NINE

On my news scan the next morning, I was surprised to read about Peterborough's second murder of the year. As the brief news item pointed out, the year was barely half over and already the city's average murder rate of two had been reached. Usually, cops will start by describing a "suspicious death," but in this case, they jumped right to homicide. Good guess, I thought. At 4 AM, the body of Darren Nelson was discovered by a delivery van driver in the alley running behind the businesses on George Street. Not too many people have business in an alleyway before 4 AM, and even fewer die there of natural causes.

I was also more than a little surprised to get a phone call from Patricia Morland a couple of days after that.

"What are you doing tomorrow late morning?" she asked.

"I don't have my daily planner with me, but best guess? Nothing."

"Why don't you meet me in Daniel Truscott's office at eleven and we can sign your contract for a two book-deal with Jameson

& Lord?"

"What?!"

"Daniel was convinced by me and by Henry that *On the Rails*—once it's re-edited—is a very good book and that *The Sixth String* will be even better!"

"Well, Daniel is right. That's great news! Thank you. What kind of advance are we talking about?

"Well…the standard advance is five thousand, but that's what J & L paid your publisher for the rights to *Rails*. They never give a big advance to a first-time author."

"How about some hollow, meaningless gesture?"

"I'll see what I can do."

"Great. Can you also send me the contract? I'd like to look it over before I show up. Oh…and your contract with me?"

"Of course. I'm happy to," she said, sounding very unhappy.

"Swell."

"Congratulations, Jake…oh, and remember, Truscott was quite upset last time, so you're not to bring up Clayton Thompson with him."

"Who?"

"Excellent! See you tomorrow. Eleven A.M. *Sharp*," she said, with altogether too much emphasis.

I wanted to be elated. Every writer dreams about this happening. But I couldn't be. Morland's ham-fisted warning about Clayton Thompson was all I needed to remind myself that it was total bullshit. My silence was the price I'd pay for hitting the publishing jackpot. They still didn't know what I knew, but if they could get me to shut the fuck up by offering this prize then they didn't really care.

At the very least, I now had a solid-gold reason to be in Toronto and among some potential killers. Oh, joy.

Unfortunately, I had to sound jacked when I told Alexandra. There was no choice, it seemed. The tangled web of a deception had to be continued. Not because I was worried she'd blab anything but because I was scared shitless she'd give me the boot if she found out I was up to my bloodshot eyeballs in something that had been—and still could be—injurious to my health. I felt like a grade-A shitheel when I called her that night to let her know the "good" news. She was unabashedly thrilled for me.

"Jake, you don't sound all that excited," she said after she calmed down.

"Oh, you know me. I worry about stuff until it's done. And I gotta lotta work ahead of me."

"You'll knock 'em dead."

Interesting choice of words, I thought.

The drive downtown went easily, and I was early. By about an hour. I pissed away time nursing an overpriced coffee in a bistro-y sidewalk café, getting up from time to time to step off their patio corralled by a three-foot black wrought iron fence to stand on sidewalk on the other side of that fence, lean over, grab my smokes off the table and light up a good nine inches from the forbidden zone. I watched the torrent of people rushing by me. Everybody looked as though they were practicing for that goofy-looking Olympic speed-walking race, but in their civilian clothes.

Could I get used to living in a city, I asked myself. *Don't be an arsehole, Jake*, I answered as I was jostled and harumphed by young go-getter on the phone who wanted to share the content of his fucking phone call with anybody within a ten-foot listening radius but, by his expression, not my cigarette smoke, all the while he was sucking in tons of hydrocarbons from the trucks, cars, and buses whizzing by him.

Just because I'm a dick, I decided to be fifteen minutes late, complaining about the traffic as I bustled into a boardroom. Seated around the marble table were Patricia and Truscott and, a discreet distance away, Henry Blake.

"*Finally*!" said an apparently jovial Daniel Truscott as he got up and came to greet me. "Jameson & Lord's newest author!"

A hearty handshake from him followed, a whole lot livelier than the limp rag affair I'd been treated to last time.

A lot of smiles and congratulations all the way 'round. I'll admit to being more stunned than usual. Even if one, two or all three of them were faking it, it'd been a while since I heard more than one person at a time say anything nice about me.

"Let's get the business out of the way, shall we?" Truscott said and he handed me a sheaf of papers…First, your contract with Patricia…"

I had read it the night before. I fought back the urge to beef about the 15% off the top. I signed.

"And now your deal with devil," Truscott said. I looked for any trace of irony in his description; there was none.

I had read that bundle last night too. Well, most of it. I'd kinda nodded off poring over all the ways in which J & L covered their asses, clause after clause protecting them against the miscreant they were signing up.

"Yeah, about that. I've got an issue," I said. "I'm sure you could fix it right here."

"And what's that?" Truscott asked, the veneer of that joviality being eroded.

"The split of any movie or TV rights," I answered, aware of Morland's look of concern.

"What's wrong with 50/50?" Truscott wanted to know. "That's industry-standard."

"That may be. But that doesn't mean I have to like it," I said. "I'd really like 60/40 a whole lot more."

"If I may," Henry piped up, "Both properties would likely be prohibitively expensive to film. The location shooting alone is a huge barrier."

"If they're unlikely to attract buyers, then what's the harm in changing the contract? It shouldn't be a big deal."

Everybody got real quiet and serious all of a sudden. Truscott silently surveyed the other two.

"Done!" he announced, his smile returning.

He took out a pen, changed and initialed the terms in about thirty-three places and slid the pile over to me. Again, I signed.

"And now the finale!" Truscott, the ringmaster, said, as he presented me with an envelope.

"What's this?" I asked.

"Your advance. Ten thousand. Patricia was most persuasive."

I opened the envelop and saw the cheque for eighty-five hundred dollars.

"Less her commission, of course," Truscott said. "She earned it."

"So what you're saying is if I had signed with you first, you'd be giving me the whole ten large right now?" I said.

Truscott and, for sure, Morland looked alarmed.

"Just fucking with you," I said. "Thank you."

"Good one," Truscott said. "Patricia and I have to discuss another project, so we'll leave you with Henry here to talk about next steps."

He actually clapped me on the shoulder and wrung my hand again. "Welcome aboard, Mr. Lydon. We expect great things from you."

Henry was instantly business-like as I supposed he always was with a new pony in the stable. He was regarded far and wide as one of the best editors in the biz and I'm sure he wasn't used to taking shit from a no-name like me. If I were him, I'd want to get his ground rules clear from the jump. If I were me—which, as it turns out, I am—I'd want to get my ground rules straight right off. This might be fun, I thought.

"You've got two big projects ahead of you," he said. "Writing a book and editing another one with me. That's the only thing I've got on the go. So let's start there. How soon can you send me the word doc of *On the Rails*?"

"I'd rather not do that."

"What?"

"I'd prefer to send you the printed copy."

"Why?"

"You can't be too careful these days."

"But it's already a copyrighted book."

"That's the old one. The new one won't be yet."

"We don't do the old red ink bit anymore."

"Just call me an endearing piece of nostalgia. Humour me, will you?"

"Alright. When can I expect it?"

"Next few days."

"Pony express can make it down here by then?" he asked with a touch of an edge showing.

"Guaranteed. What else?"

"How far are you along with *Sixth String*?"

"Quite a bit more than what you've seen," I lied. "But I write in chunks then assemble them. They won't mean much, so I'd rather send you the whole goddamned thing when it's done."

"When will that be?"

"Not sure."

"Look, there are some publishing realities you have to understand. It's August now. We have the first one scheduled for the spring which means you have to get me your draft by the end of October at the latest. With *The Sixth String* following a year later. We have to stick to that. Otherwise, you'll get bumped 'til God knows when."

"I'll try."

"You have to try very hard. If you don't deliver according to our schedule, you have to give your advance back. All ten thousand of it. It's in the contract."

"I knew that," I said, pissed at myself for skipping over that part above where I had signed on the dotted line.

"Well, I suppose that's all for now," he said. "You've got work to do."

Once again, I had a strange elevator ride back to earth. On the one hand, I was struck by how authentic the ceremony had seemed. Was there any chance at all that everything I thought, everything Thompson had told me the night he died, was complete and utter bullshit? That I had built this rock-solid case on loose sand and convinced myself that all my elaborate scheming and acting in service to this fucking case had actually been a shadow play? Could everything and everybody else have been genuine? Had Patricia and Henry and Truscott really just given me the break that every writer dreams of?

No way in hell, I decided. All three of them had motive in spades—a motive that I couldn't truly nail down for Childers or Harder. I just had to figure out the how. Piece of cake.

On one hand, I was on shaky ground and somewhat blinded by this whirlwind courtship and marriage as if it was real. On the other, it was difficult not to see that I was like an actor parachuted into a strange play during one of its performances. All the other actors knew their lines cold, hit their marks in a tightly choreographed show while I just sort of mumbled gibberish and wandered around crashing into the scenery.

No time for rehearsals, Jake. Catch the fuck up! And start writing your own lines.

The first order of business was printing out the 638-page book. Getting it down to Henry right away was important to keep the charade going with little ol' me being all eager and co-operative. And it would keep him busy. But I knew my cheapie $70 Canon inkjet printer wasn't up to the job. It'd probably be quicker for me to chisel out a stone copy—although the shipping costs would be killer. Long before that however, I bet that my printer would overheat and explode in a great ball of fire round about the third chapter.

"Les, dear heart, how are you?"

"What do you want?"

"Well, seeing how you asked, do you folks have a high-speed printer? And would you mind printing off a little something for me…I mean *us*. Oh, and ASAP?"

"Send it to me." Click.

I dug the thing out of my files, stuck my name in the header of every page and fired it off, with my deepest, humblest, sincerest, most appreciative, and grateful thanks.

'P'tboro Polic' called about ten minutes later. I didn't pick up. I could listen to Les' obscenity-riddled rant later. Plus, it would give him time to cool down. That's how considerate I can be.

Late that afternoon, the telephone rang again. And again, caller ID said "Ptboro Polic." I thought maybe Les had gotten over his hissy fit and was calling with more info on Bromley's fatal night.

"What the fuck do you want?" I answered.

"I beg your pardon," said a very startled, very female voice.

"Sorry," I managed. "You're not Les Macgregor."

"No, I'm not. This is Inspector Wilson."

"Inspector, glad to hear from you again."

"I'm calling you to request your presence in my office tomorrow morning at 9 AM."

"May I ask what this is about?"

"You may. But you'll find out tomorrow. 9AM."

Click.

CHAPTER THIRTY

The next morning, I drove to Peterborough unable to escape that ol' familiar feeling of being sent to the principal's office.

There was nothing matronly about the inspector as I faced her across her desk. She dove right in.

"I understand you've been putting a lot of demands on our office," she stated.

"Les ratted me out?"

"Les told me about all the tasks you were giving him."

"Nobody likes a snitch."

"In fact, we do. But that's not the point. He doesn't work for you. *You* work for *us* and, frankly, we don't have much to show for whatever you're doing. Other than a big printing expense. Your book? Seriously?"

"I need it. Trust me."

Reasonable guy that I am, I could see where the Inspector might not see the point of that printing exercise. I had to explain that it was a key part of my effort to get inside the literary world of Truscott, Blake and Morland.

"You shouldn't be doing any of this," she said.

"Did you not just remind me that I was working for you?"

"Not as a fucking on-the-job detective, for fuck's sake!" Wilson exploded.

The Inspector's angry outburst surprised me. I think it surprised her. I got the impression that Wilson did not routinely, if ever, use the word 'fuck' in any of its wonderful derivations. Such are the limits I can push people to.

At that moment, I should've admitted that I had overstepped some boundary, apologized, and swore—in a legal sense only—that I wouldn't do it again. It would've been the diplomatic thing to do. Turns out, no government would ever hire me to represent them overseas, oh and I really do hate apologizing and, while we're at it, I don't much care for boundaries.

"Look, Inspector, I'm pretty sure I'm onto something. I have to play out. If we catch a killer or two, that would be a good thing, wouldn't it? That's what we both want, isn't it?"

"Yes," she said, because what else could she?

"That's why I need your resources."

"You should know that those resources are getting spread a little thin."

"Because of the murder I just read about?"

"Yes."

"Care to fill me in?"

"Not really. Guy was a bottom of the barrel dealer. It's not related."

"That's what you folks thought about Bromley's death and Thompson's lecture," I dickishly pointed out.

"We had no reason to think they might be linked. Now we do."

"Thanks to me."

"And thanks to you, I've got the Chief leaning on me big time because of the deal we made to not go after Jan Morris or this whole fraud. He's worried—I'm worried—that it'll get out before we release it."

"Tell him to relax. I went to see her. She's not about to squawk. And she gave me some interesting facts about Ryan Loffler."

"Don't try to distract me with that. The Ryan Loffler killing is not my concern."

"I don't want to tell you your job but maybe it should concern you if his killer and Bromley's killer is the same person."

"I need to know what you know—or what you think you know. Right now."

There's something in me that just has to make a deal, some 'do something/get something' dynamic that just kicks in, even if I'm holding fuck-all in the way of cards.

"Tell you what: I'll explain the situation as I see it, give you my theory—because that's all it is right now—and you tell me what you got about this week's murder. Deal?"

"Speak."

I had to back up and lay out my whole grand scheme.

She didn't take notes, but she was listening intently. She offered no comment.

"Talk to Les about this week's murder," was all she said.

I left the Inspector's office, if not sympathetic of the pressure she was under, then at least cognizant of the fact that I should be more of a team player. That all but faded at the front counter where I saw Les standing there, with one hand resting on a huge, neat stack of paper and a shit-eating grin on his round face.

"Thanks for the printing job, you fucking squealer," I said.

"Got your pee-pee whacked, did you?" he wanted to know.

"Yup. But nothing like the shitstorm you're about to walk into."

"What do you mean?"

"For the life of me, I can't understand why you told me that you thought the Inspector was incompetent...*and* a lousy dresser."

His grin vanished, replaced by a momentary look of terror.

"...You didn't!" he sputtered.

"No, I didn't. Yet. But doesn't that sudden rush of shit to the heart make you feel alive?"

"You bastard!"

"Hey. C'mon, buddy. Inspector said we have to play nice. So play nice."

"Take your crappy book and get out of my face."

"Gladly. But before I go, tell me about that latest body in the morgue."

"Why would I do that?"

"Because the inspector said you have to. Go ask her. Or I'm going to march right back into her office and let her know you're being a dick. Now, where were we? Right. Inspector said he was a low-level dealer."

"Darren Nelson, forty-five," Les reluctantly began. "We've had him on the radar for years but, so far not much—a couple of priors for possession—pot only. Definitely small potatoes."

"What happened?"

"Alley behind the pawn shop on George. Delivery guy found him early in the morning. Throat slit. Nobody heard anything."

"They never do."

"In this case, they wouldn't have. Cut from ear to ear and deep. Big ass knife. Serrated. Would've severed his larynx."

"Pro job?"

"Maybe. Or maybe the perp just got lucky."

"Any chance he was Bromley's connection?"

"Maybe."

"Oh, Les, there you go again, not playing nice."

"We found the numbers for a lot of his customers on his burner phone. One number was Bromley's. That's it. That's all we got."

I left and trotted my ass down to the Post Office where I watched with horror as they determined the tonnage of my manuscript. For what they charged in shipping, I figured I could've rented a limo and drove down there with the pile of book sitting beside me in the plush back seat while I sipped Tanqueray and tonics.

Another plate was set in motion on top of my theoretic bamboo pole.

Stumbling home from AA with Carl a few days later, I found a box on my front steps. The UPS slip said it was from Jameson & Lord. Blake had been a busy lanky beaver and edited his brains out. The ball was back in my court. I now had to review his changes and either agree with them or brawl.

His cover note was succinct:

> *Jake - Here are my suggestions. I had a head start by already marking up the hard copy of the book. I haven't really got at the line-by-line review. We need to agree on my ideas for the major edits and re-ordering first. Please consider them carefully, as well as the mandatory direction that you excise <u>at least</u> 150 pages that will make a good book better. Get back to me. Soon. Henry*

It was a major effort to contain myself as my dismay turned to rage seeing page after page marked with a big red 'X'. When you sweat out big sections that you've been able to convince yourself move the story along or grow characters or relate to themes you were interested in and then see them just thrown out would, under normal circumstances, make me bat-shit. But these were not normal circumstances. I had to keep telling myself it was all bullshit, a shadow play. So play along, Jake.

I waited a day and e-wrote to him.

I hate to do it, but I agree with vast majority of changes. I'll make them and send you the soft copy. We have to talk about the re-ordering you want that'll turn the book into a series of flashbacks instead of telling a straight-ahead story, even though the main character is a straight-ahead guy. But if you absolutely insist, then I might be convinced.

I held my nose and went into full stenographic mode, transposing all his changes (well, most of them) onto my Word doc. I sent it back to him along with a brief note:

'Tis done (almost). We need to talk – hopefully in person – about switching things around.

A new plate was now spinning. And another one was slowing down and wobbling on its pole.

Terrence Childers. His calmness when I flat out named him as Bromley's killer was bugging the shit out of me. It had been like he was waiting for the accusation, just so he could trot out his iron-clad defense.

Let's see if we can find a few holes in that defense, shall we? First up, some internet searches, figuring distances on a map of Peterborough, learning about bus companies and such. Then it was time to talk to a real live human being—specifically the owner of Al's auto repair shop. I decided to take the Vibe. I get the sense that tradespeople always look at the wheels someone's got before they figure how helpful they're going to be and how much they're going to charge if they land you as a customer—a sort of ways and means test.

Al's was an old school garage like the one in Florida where I got my old man's Caddy fixed, except without the surrounding palm trees. The yard in front and along the side of his battered old concrete block building were littered with vehicles waiting for some veteran oily hands to heal them. The business sat on a corner lot with cars and trucks threatening to spill onto the sidewalks on two sides.

Time again for a little bit of bullshit.

"Al?" I asked of the skinny old guy at the battered counter.

"You got him."

I introduced myself as Larry Childers, spun him a tale of my wayward son who was constantly hitting me up for money with his hard luck stories getting more outlandish by the day.

"Last time, he claimed his car was busted and that he desperately needed it for school and work. Have you, by chance, worked on a Suzuki Samurai lately? He said you did."

"Yeah, I fixed one. A few months ago. Big guy dropped it off, a real old-timer. The car, I mean. '86 or '87, I think. Don't see many of them on the road, sorta like yours," he said, eyeing the Vibe with a heartbreakingly cruel and clinical stare.

"So you can see by my car why money matters to me. Was it a big job?"

"Yeah, radiator had sprung a couple of big holes. Original parts aren't easy to get but I found an after-market aluminum jobbie that fit. Not the best answer but it'd last longer than the rest of the car. I called him to let him know, asked for the payment for the part before I ordered it."

"You usually do that?"

"No, but that rad, what am I gonna do with it if he bales? Bastard said he didn't have the money but to hold the car until he did. Guess he got it from you because he dropped by with the go-ahead and the cash a few days later. Had it ready in three, four days."

"How much was the bill?"

"Don't remember."

"Can you check?"

Al wasn't at all thrilled, but he went looking. Not on his computer—I didn't see one—but through a stack of greasy invoices. While he was thumbing through them, I speculated out loud on how some new technology stuff might make chores like that one go easier.

"Mister, you think I'm goin' to be doin' this much longer? Cuz I ain't. Can't keep up with the new cars and any nickel I spend on goddamned computers means a nickel less towards buying bait for my fishing which I intend to do every goddamned day for the rest of my life."

"Makes sense, Al."

"Here!" he announced. "$486.70."

"Son-of-a-bitch!"

"Look, Larry, that's what it cost! Parts and two hours on the lift."

"No. Sorry. I'm not doubting you, Al. He hit me up for 700."

"What can I tell you?" he said, shaking his head. "Kids."

"Kids," I echoed, shaking my head in agreement."

"When was that?"

"Lemme see…brought it in March 16, didn't order the part until March 20 when he brought a deposit in. He picked it up and paid the rest on the 25th."

"Could anyone have driven it in that condition?"

"Couple of miles, *maybe*. Holes that big would've drained the coolant pretty quick. It'd get overheated right away. Then you got a cracked block, mister."

"Would you have put that money into it?"

"Hell, no."

"Was it worth anything?"

"Maybe to a rust collector. Duct tape was pretty well the only thing holdin' the body together. Funny thing though."

"What?"

"Somebody took pretty good care of the guts. Engine clean, brakes, tranny all in good shape."

I thanked Al and walked back to my recently disparaged automotive wonder with a smile on my face. Even though he didn't know it, thanks to ol' Al, the world had just become a lot clearer to me.

CHAPTER THIRTY-ONE

I played and replayed the mini-movie in my head. I argued with myself about virtually every scene. Does this bit make sense? What about that shot? Is it plausible; is there another possibility? Will someone stand up in the theatre and yell: "C'mon, stop fucking around! It just couldn't happen like that in real life!"?

Now what to do about the puzzle I had pieced together.

Why, confront the big, extremely fit man who had been trained to extinguish human life, of course.

Are you out of your goddamned mind? Not a chance I'd do that.

My first step was to go into my full chickenshit modus operandi. Then I trotted my cowardly ass down to the police station and asked for Inspector Wilson.

"It's all circumstantial," she said after I laid out my theory. "It makes sense, don't get me wrong. It *could've* happened that way. But without a shred of evidence, there's no way it'll stick."

"Isn't that what you guys do? Get proof?"

"Not easily now. Think about it. The murder was almost six

months ago. We'd need a witness or two who could swear to seeing Childers driving out to Trent on the night of. Oh, and here's
another thing crown attorneys like: a motive. You *might* have the
how and you *might* have the who, but I can't see the why."

"How about: He's disturbed and a former professional killer."

"So you can pin every murder anywhere on anybody who's
ever seen active duty in the military?"

Sometimes, reality checks really suck, but I had to admit the
Inspector was right. There was every possibility that I'd spent way
too much time on the how, walking step-by-step in my mind ac-
counting for every moment of that night that I hadn't backed up
and settled on a why.

Why would Terrence Childers murder an academic who obviously admired him?

All the think-think-thinking in the world about how he
could've done it wouldn't get me any closer to a motive. I needed
more information about Terence Childers, recent information. I
could go back to his wife and get a little more in-depth. Assuming
she'd even agree, anything she might tell me would be four years
old. His classmate had indicated that Terrence was a loner, bereft
of any friends that he could see, which didn't surprise me.

It struck me that the person closest to him at that time would
very likely have been Professor Bromley. And he wasn't talking.

But, Jake, you moron, maybe his journals had been speaking
volumes and you just weren't listening.

I dug out Ted's most recent diary which covered the school
year and found the longest account I'd found so far of his dealings
with Childers.

I went back to that entry:

*TC is grim. Deadly serious. One always sees the heart in one's
writing. TC showed me some short stories he'd written (I was not
aware of JL writing anything beyond that which he had been assigned). All four of his sordid tales began bleakly and progressed*

through to utter despair, punctuated by callousness and grotesque violence. He did not care for my observations. At all. There is menace in his darkness. Perhaps I know why. He needs help. And I shall ensure he gets it. I will stop abetting him and I will contact the authorities if I must. I must preserve his unique genius. Despite his dingy vision, TC has done nothing but exceptional work for me. If my gift-giving rite is to have any integrity I must set aside his issues and reward him.

Well, that'll teach me not to skim-read. There was a ton of information, perhaps useful information that needed exploring. This section of it now grabbed my attention where I'd skipped over it the first time that I read it, too busy focusing on Bromley's critique of Childer's writing:

There is menace in his darkness. Perhaps I know why. He needs help. And I shall ensure he gets it. I will stop abetting him and I will contact the authorities if I must.

Bromley felt if not fatherly towards his star student, at the very least mentor-y enough to care about his condition. I thought back to my barroom conversation with Childers. Something he had told me stood out. He confessed to being a coke and heroin user in Afghanistan. But Eleni, his nurse and bride-to-be, had helped him kick it. Now, there was no Eleni in his life anymore. Would he have returned to his nasty habits? Maybe. And if he had, and he was a new kid in town, who could connect him to a source? Bromley could; Childers could probably recognize him as a fellow user. That must have been what the *abetting* was all about.

But did he actually put an end to his abetting or was it all just big talk in the safety and anonymity of a private diary? I retrieved the most recent journal. Shit was moving so fast that I had referred to it only to confirm that Thompson had never set foot in Ted's house anytime in March. On February 21, I read this: *There, it is done. Henceforth, I shall no longer be a party to TC's impairment. I informed him. He was, to say the least, not pleased. But I*

am confident his ire will dissipate, and he will come to understand
my action was driven by the purest of motive and for his betterment.

OK, Jake, it's not conclusive; I could understand why Bromley
might not record in detail his dealing with dealers but suppose
Bromley did have Childers cut off and suppose he did threaten
him with a call to the cops or some social services agency. What
would Childers have done? Kill both Bromley *and* his drug dealer? That made no sense to me. Bromley was being concerned for
his welfare and, for sure, Darren Nelson wouldn't have been the
only dealer in Peterborough. A 'thanks but no thanks' to Bromley
and a few hours spent making another connection and he'd be
back in the business of getting fucked up.

So, once again, loomed the elusive why.

It's at times like these when you've got to make an effort—
as best you can—to see the world through someone else's eyes,
someone else's mind. Good cops and good shrinks can do that.
The guiding principle is to abandon what I would have done—or
you or any "normal" person would have done. What would *he*
have done? I didn't need a *good* reason; I had to find *his* reason.

Assuming that he was back using, and his drug addiction was
the overarching factor, what did that look like? I obsess over a
bunch of people and things that I can't possibly imagine my life
without. It's a long list: Alexandra, the Stones, NFL football, the
sun, writing, beer, books, tobacco, laughter. Oh, and bacon; bacon's in there somewhere.

But no matter how much I love those things, I just don't understand—and most people don't understand—what it means to have
a complete I'm-willing-to-throw-everything-away-for-this one-
thing type of addiction. We are unable to grasp the extent of the
all-consuming craving because it's so far outside our experience.
Same as a repeat astronaut riding on top of a giant goddamned
missile saying: Boy, oh boy, there's nothing like being shot into
space. I'll take your word for it, buddy, but I can't possibly know

what it's like.

But the grasp of addiction isn't made up. How many more stories do you have to hear from addicts—recovering or otherwise—describing how they would—and did—toss aside spouses, kids, careers, houses for that brief rush. How their day consisted of thinking about getting high, getting high, coming down from being high and then planning to get high again.

As you inch farther out on the limb of possibilities, you have to combine the general sense of what you've learned with the specifics of that individual's situation. What else about Terrence Childers's background and experience could've played into what happened that night in the university parking lot and weeks later in a city back alley? First off, look at the question of how he could be a stone addict and still manage. Simple fact: Terrence Childers was a high-functioning human. His intellect, rigorous training, and discipline likely prevented him from being a useless, ambitionless, inert puddle of a man.

Now mix in the effects of the horror show he'd lived through in combat and the resulting demons running around his brain wreaking havoc. I'd read about the intense and intensive training he'd undergone. What'd that do him? At a guess, a lot. The goal is to tear down the individual's sense of self and build him back up as an element of a team, part of a self-sufficient unit that comes to matter more than anything, mostly because your life, their lives depend on cohesion and support and everybody carrying the weight. It's an amplification by a factor of about a million of my high school experience as an excessively mediocre football player when you celebrated a win or mourned a loss together, as a team.

We are told, largely by Facebook via block capitals on coloured backgrounds, that we must treasure friends who have our back. Have our backs from what, for fuck's sake? What dire situation are most of us ever in that we need protection and from whom? But that phrase has real meaning in a hostile country with bullets flying from an unidentified enemy. You fucking better have some-body watching your back.

I continued my unfettered speculation, trying to imagine what life in the field would have been like for his self-contained unit, adrift and in the thick of it.

Best guess: they would have made up their own rules, had their own set of ethics they'd fashioned on the fly to handle their other worldly reality. I had had a taste, a mere soupçon of that when I thought back to my less-than-glory days of high school football. Our three-man linebacking corps was close. We did shit on and off the field that we'd likely never do individually (except our left corner linebacker; he had a future turning up on police blotters).

Think, Jake, think back to your last conversation with him. What had Childers actually *said*?

I remembered the matter-of-fact way he described how hu-mans became not-humans to them, transformed into mere "tar-gets" that either stood in the way of your mission or were them-selves the mission. And when the mission was impossible to carry out, then then they occupied their time "settling accounts," loving nothing beyond each other and their dogs and driven by the urge to survive.

Can someone actually argue that anyone could just file away all that crap when they returned to civilian life, that you could just turn in your deadly ethos at the door along with your rifle when you left the military?

Put those two influences together—addiction and horrible combat experience—and do some more supposing, Jake. Suppose Childers came up with a couple of 'accounts' that, to his bent way of thinking, needed settling. Bromley because he threatened his desire to fulfill his mission of getting high and Dealer Darren be-cause he dared get in the way of that mission by cutting him off.

It didn't have to make sense to me; it had to strike Childers as completely defensible.

But still, I now had more information and a more detailed plausible theory than I had before. Let's see what those gosh darned authorities think.

I laid it all out for Inspector Wilson and Les Macgregor in her office.

Wilson got her rank because she was a damn good cop. She immediately pounced on a weak link along my chain of suppositions.

"It makes no sense that Nelson would refuse to sell to Childers just because Bromley asked him to," she pointed out. "He was a much better customer than Bromley was."

"I'm betting Dealer Darren was content with his low-level business. He had been operating that way for years. Sure, Childers could offer more reward but that would've come with a whole lot more risk. You haven't sat across from Childers. He can be one big, intimidating son of a bitch. Nelson probably thought: "I don't need this in my life.""

"I think you've got it," the Inspector finally said. "But it's still all circumstantial. And we've got the same problem with evidence. It's a flimsy case."

"What do you need to make it unflimsy?"

"Witnesses, a murder weapon or a confession."

More often than I care to remember, I blurt shit out, then have to live with it. This was one of those times.

"What about me wearing a wire?"

"Not a chance!"

"Look, I think I can get him to talk. Last time, he told me stuff. This is a guy trained to shut the fuck up during torture. No way he's talking to you, and you said that finding evidence now is next to impossible."

"We don't send civilians into those situations."

"Sorta like hostage-taking?"

"Smart ass. Sometimes, we do wire confidential informants.

Most of the CIs are facing charges or awaiting trial; they'll take the risk for reduced sentences or immunity."

"So, if I was a felon, you'd let me go in?"

"Maybe."

"Here's an idea: why don't I go up to Les over there and hoof him one in the gonads? That's a crime, right? Although it really shouldn't be."

"Nice try."

"Inspector, I have to arrange to see him again. It may be a tad tricky because last time I might have accused him of the murder."

"To his face?"

"And large body. But leave it with me. I'll call you."

During a hugely satisfying and fattening meal at Harvey's— best hamburger chain on the planet—it came to me. I rushed back to the police station. Well, not really rushed, more like waddled.

"He'll talk to me! I got a publishing contract, and he wants one. I can suggest I can get him in the door."

"OK, you win," the Inspector said. "Set it up then come see me and we'll get you ready and go over the rules."

"Rules? There are rules?"

"My rules. Just set it up and let me know. Give me three days after that to arrange things at my end."

I wanted to get this over as quickly as possible, but there was a planning element that went way beyond my 'let's wing it and see what happens' approach to life. The SWAT team, which didn't have a lot to do in generally sleepy Peterborough, had to be briefed. That apparently involved a couple of drive-bys to take pictures, then pair them with city maps, and Google satellite images. They even would hunt for architectural drawings of the house lay-out inside.

I had a sterling excuse to write to Childers and to sit down with him. I really did have big-league publishing connections. A high-powered agent and a two-book deal replete with signed contracts and an advance cheque (that I still hadn't cashed) and everything. The fact that all of it was bullshit didn't matter.

I wrote to tell him about my publishing touchdown, told him I had spoken to my brand spanking new agent about him as well.

What did you say about me? He wrote back.

Let's talk. I replied.

He sure didn't play hard to get. His new mission was to get published. He wanted to see me as soon as possible. I had been told that the cops needed three days to get ready, so I got to keep him dangling for a few days. We set an evening date at his place. Not a chance I'd invite him up to the hovel in the wilderness.

While I was waiting for my play date with Childers, I voted to get another plate spinning. Henry Blake. I had insisted on a face-to-face editing session. Holding it at their office was a non-starter owing to its great distance to a piece of sidewalk I could smoke in. I also didn't suggest he come up to the lake so we could have some peace and quiet while he disemboweled my book and maybe me. If Henry was a killer, I'd rather not supply him with a location where he could practice his new-found profession without being disturbed, any more than I would Childers who had had a lot more practice.

I wasn't being theoretical about the threat posed by being alone with a possibly dangerous man. Just last summer I had invited a murderer up to my place. If Carl and his trusty shotgun hadn't turned up, all of what was now transpiring this year would be coolly academic as I would've died that day a year earlier.

CHAPTER THIRTY-TWO

On the day of my meeting with Childers, I went back to the police station to get mic'ed up.

Inspector Wilson ushered me into their 'tech room' and I started to take my shirt off.

"What the Sam Hill are you doing?" she asked.

"Getting ready for you to tape the wire to me."

Inspector Wilson almost laughed out loud.

"You watch too many old movies."

She produced what looked like a hearing aid.

"This works just fine. With your hair, nobody is going to see it."

Feeling foolish, I buttoned up my shirt, a classy number smothered in pink orchids.

"And now the rules," Wilson said.

"Shoot."

"We don't want any shooting."

"That's a cop joke, right?"

"Rule #1: You have to get him to admit to a crime. Verbally. Not the nod of a head, not anything that's qualified. If he's our guy, he would've committed several offenses he can be charged with: conspiracy to commit murder, assault with a deadly weapon, the murder itself. He has to admit at least one of them."

"Got it."

"Rule #2: You can't put words in his mouth, and you have to be clear. You can't be vague about the details or be satisfied with a 'maybe.'"

"What else?"

"Rule #3: You'll blow it if you walk in there and accuse him right away. You have to get him relaxed and talking, lead up to it. That means you might be in there for a while."

"Anything else?"

"Sergeant Macgregor disagrees with me on this one, but Rule #4 is: your safety comes first. At the slightest hint that he might be suspicious, I want you out of there. We need a password. All you have to do is say it and we're through the door."

"Who's we?"

"The SWAT team."

"Been thinking about that and I dunno if they can get that close. He's been trained to listen."

"And they've been trained to not be heard. Getting back to the password."

"Whaddya got?"

"No, *you* have to think of one. It'll be easier to remember if things get hairy."

"Boxwoods," I offered.

"Why boxwoods?"

"He must've hidden behind a row of boxwood shrubs to get close to Bromley in the parking lot. I'm a gardening guy."

"Boxwoods it is. One last thing."

"Enough with the rules! You're making me nervous."

"It's not really a rule, more of a suggestion. We don't think he's armed but he could be. Military hardware does go missing. So, *if* the shooting starts, get down on the floor and stay there."

"OK, now I'm nervous."

"Jake, you don't have to do this."

"Yeah, I do."

They sent me outside to test the earpiece. As instructed, I talked to myself for a while alternating between whispers and an old man loudly arguing with himself.

"How were the levels?" I asked when I returned.

"Just fine. It would've been more helpful if you had something beyond "Les is a dick, Les is a dick.""

It wasn't a fun drive over to Childers' place. My problem—one of my many problems—is that I play movies in my wee brain all the time. In this case, the various scenes all ended badly for yours truly. That's another of my problems: I always think the worst.

Note to the anonymous cinematographer: The sun was low in the sky which had started to redden as I pulled up to Childers' house. Sound guy: Some ominous cellos rumbled away.

It was one of those so-called war homes, built after WWII to shelter returning vets. Small, square, a story and a half with a simple pitched roof, one of maybe eight identical houses along the street.

I parked behind the old white 4X4 and, as instructed by the cops, knocked on the side door that led directly into the kitchen.

Childers was courteous, almost friendly.

"Beer?"

"Why, yes. I think I'll give one of those a try."

I looked around while he went to the fridge. The small kitchen was spotless, counters empty, no dishes in the sink or drying rack, towel folded neatly on the oven handle, appliances old but gleaming. The only mess, if you could call it that, was a line of three plastic gallon jugs on the floor. But overall, not exactly the way a bachelor student usually lives. I couldn't imagine that Childers went to that effort for little old me and assumed his military training had carried over to civilian life. Keep your space clean, soldier.

We sat at the kitchen table, and it was immediately evident that he wanted to get down to business.

"So what can you tell me?" he wanted to know.

I went through the details of how I supposedly got my contract. He was polite but impatient. Like anyone else, he was eager to hear the part about him. I piled it on, describing the fictional way I had extolled his writing to my new agent and publisher.

"Did you pass along the stories I gave you?"

"No. Neither of them wanted to open with a short story collection. They want to see a long sample of your novel."

"You had that too. Did you send it?"

"No again. That's what I want to talk to you about. You need to be sure you want to turn that bit in. Is it as polished as you'd like?"

"Maybe not."

"Oh, and they want to get their hands on an outline for the whole thing. Do you have that?"

"No. Most of it's up here," he said, tapping the side of his head. "Did they give you a deadline?"

"I have to finish editing mine by the end of September. I said you could probably have something for them by then as well."

We shot the shit for a while about the format, the things he had to cover off in a submission, the need for a pro-looking document. I impressed the fuck out of myself by sounding like I knew what I was talking about.

It was clear that Childers was thinking about the effort ahead of him.

"So you can see," I said, "you've got some work to do. Could you collaborate with someone to get it in shape?"

Sidebar: Collaborate. Fuck, I hate that word, unless it's applied to the Nazi enablers in the countries that the little failed artist/madman invaded.

"Doubt it."

"I'd offer to help but, like I said, I've got to finish mine...Too bad Ted Bromley isn't around."

"Yeah, too bad."

I bet even Google would have a hard time coming up with an answer to typing the phrase 'segueing conversation to murder accusation.' There was a lull in our chat as I thought about how to introduce what I assumed would be a slightly awkward discussion.

"What?" he asked, as if on cue.

"I was wondering if Professor Bromley gave you a prize of some kind for being a good student. Maybe a Viking meat skewer."

"As a matter of fact, he did," Childers said, without missing a beat. "Want to see it? It's in the living room."

"No, no," I said, in no particular hurry to put a pre-used murder weapon into his hands.

"Why did you ask me that?"

"You know, Terrence, I just can't shake the idea that you had something to do with his death."

"You're back to that, are you? It's getting old...and irritating."

"Hear me out."

"I'm listening."

"You believed you had to get rid of him."

"Why would I want that?"

"Because he made sure his dealer cut you off and he was trying to get you into rehab."

Childers straightened up. Direct hit. Now press the attack, Commander Jake.

"He really liked you. Even gave you one of those Viking things as his secret prize. His big sin was that he just wanted to help you," I added.

His expression darkened. He stared into some middle distance before turning to me.

"He wouldn't mind his own business."

Childers seemed to catch himself and snap out of thinking

about why he did what he had done. He settled back in his chair.

"Your word against mine. You can't prove anything."

"That's where I think you're wrong. Follow along with me, won't you, boys and girls?" I said, doing my best Mr. Rogers' impression.

I took a deep breath.

"What stumped me was why all the elaborate planning? The easiest way to do that would be at his place. He'd let you in, probably at any time, and even if somebody saw you come and go, they might recognize you as a frequent visitor. Plus, the murder weapon was right there if you decided not to use yours. Then it occurred to me: Hugo wouldn't let you anywhere close to Bromley. You'd have to kill the dog and you couldn't do it, could you?"

"No," he said quietly.

Another direct hit. Pour it on, Field Marshall Jake.

"And that presented real problems. Bromley was a virtual recluse; he just didn't go out much. You figured you maybe had a shot at the main campus after he announced two weeks before that class would be out there. That's when you arranged for your car to have a busted radiator. I wondered why you picked Al's. There are at least two garages closer which sorta matters to someone with a blown rad. But you took it to the one shop that was two miles away."

"….That Al guy said he was an expert at fixing old foreign 4X4s," he offered.

"That'd be horseshit. You picked him because he didn't have either a fenced compound or any security cameras. I checked, just like you did."

Terrence got real quiet. I couldn't tell if he was mentally scrambling for an explanation to challenge my theory or just thinking of ways to eliminate me in the next few minutes. I had come this far so I kept on laying out my reasoning.

"That night, it was crucial to not be noticed. You bummed a

ride out to the campus and back with Richard and made sure everybody knew about it. This is where the timing got tricky. You estimated that you'd have about a two-hour window while Bromley was at the lecture then the reception. As soon as you got back to Peterborough you walked to the garage with your extra set of keys and a big jug of water—take you maybe half an hour double-time. You temporarily sealed the leaks with gum or something, filled the rad up, and away you went. After years in the desert, you'd know all about DIY vehicle fixes. After that, you went back to your place for more jugs of water—probably the ones right there—in case your patch didn't hold," I said, motioning to the five-gallon water bottles.

I imagined Childers wanted to curse himself out loud for leaving them in the kitchen. I ploughed on.

"You ditched your car off the main road or, more likely, the service road to the north of the lot. You knew Bromley had parked there because he bitched about it in class. Then it's over hill and dale to the lot. You were used to night hikes in hilly terrain, so the drumlin would be a piece of cake. How am I doing so far?"

"Oh, do go on."

"You couldn't take a chance by hitchhiking out there and back. No guarantee you'd get a ride in time and sure as shit whoever picked you up would remember you. Same with a cab. You could've just taken the city bus out there. I called and they have cameras inside now and there'd be other riders who would remember you. You also knew you couldn't hang around the Champlain buildings waiting for him after Thompson's lecture and reception for the same reason. And you couldn't walk by the closer parking lot with him because it has a camera and was busier. Campus cops patrol the lots, mostly looking to write parking tickets. They wouldn't bother with a single car out there and, if they did show up, they wouldn't be looking on the other side of those shrubs on the east side of the lot by the river."

It was weird. It looked like he was replaying the events of that night in his head while I supplied the voice-over narration.

"Once you were out there, it didn't matter to you how long Bromley took to leave. You're also used to waiting—for hours, if you had to—because you'd have been trained to be patient and silent. Then you sprang into action as soon as he went to the trunk of his car. Most people would probably want to get rid of the murder weapon as soon as possible and the fucking river was right there. But you're not most people. You couldn't be sure if they'd fish the skewer out, have it rise out of the water like Arthur's sword, or if other people knew about you getting it from Bromley so explaining why you didn't have it any more would be real difficult. Along with everything else in this house, I bet it's just sitting there all shiny and clean and blood-free as if it just came out of Svend the Smithy's forge a thousand years ago. Does all this sound about right?"

"It does."

"I do have to hand it to you. That's some good plan you worked up in short notice. But then again, you're smart and you would've been trained to figure out all the angles, usually, I bet, on the fly."

"Well, first, I suppose I should congratulate you for figuring it out."

Bingo! I thought, almost said it out loud. I didn't have time to pat myself on the back for getting him to finally admit to the crime.

There was a brief period when Childers just sat there looking dumbfounded. He had spent hours, days, concocting and carrying out his fool-proof plan, the plan I had taken it apart in minutes.

"….But you should also have been able to figure out what happens next," he said, recovering and starting to get up.

I didn't think he was on his way to the fridge to get me another beer. I don't know about you, but I find it truly unnerving to be stared at by the murderous eyes of someone who is younger, bigger, meaner, and smarter than you are. Particularly when that someone has shown remarkable ease in taking human lives. I panicked trying to remember the code word.

"Boxwoods," I said finally as I got up too.

"What?" Childers said, momentarily frozen.

"Boxwoods!" I yelled. "Boxwoods!"

He lunged for me and missed while I was busy ducking out of the way, being scared shitless, and throwing my chair at him to slow him down, in that order.

I retreated further into the house. I gazed wildly around the living room until I saw the skewer, slightly gleaming in the darkened room, just as the front door behind me and the kitchen door exploded at the same time. A bunch of black-uniformed cops poured in.

Childers put up a helluva fight but there were at least eight SWAT guys who swarmed him and tazed the fuck out of him until he was a flopping, frothing mass on the floor.

I had seen enough and gingerly stepped over the collapsed front door into the night. There to greet me was Inspector Wilson.

"Are you alright?" she asked, in full matron mode.

"Couldn't be better," I answered, my nerves shot and my legs shaking like a human being. "You folks cut that awfully close," I noted.

"*We* cut it close? You had one word—just one damn word—to remember."

"I'm old, OK? I forget stuff. Just a minute."

I went back into the house to see Childers on his feet but trussed up like a Christmas turkey. The most he could do to me now was glare as he was hustled out of there. Even that stung.

I got a beer from the fridge and rejoined the Inspector.

"Seriously?" she asked as she watched me take a swig.

"I'm thirsty. And he owes me at least one more beer. Did you get it all?"

"Circumstantial no more," she confirmed.

"One more thing, Inspector," I said, as I drained my beer.

"Oh, don't tell me," she smiled. "Keep you out of this."

"If you don't mind."

"No, I don't mind. In fact, I don't have a choice; you're a confidential informant. But if I didn't know any better, I might think you're shy and humble."

CHAPTER THIRTY-THREE

The press conference the next day announcing the arrest of Terrence Childers went the way all police media scrums seem to go these days. More than half of its time was spent on self-congratulations as everybody evenly remotely connected with the case (who were all standing in line behind the Chief of Police) got thanked for their "co-operation and support." Dysart of the OPP and Inspector Wilson got piled with accolades which was fair. They even thanked the security company that supplied the campus cops whose only contribution I could fathom was not seeing anything and not doing anything. Towards the end of the self-congratulations-a-palooza, the Police Chief recognized the role a confidential informant had played.

But, to the Chief's credit, I did get a call from him the next morning to thank me, "just between you and me."

Later that day, Halley called.

"Heard the news up there," she said. "Any chance you had something to do with the arrest?"

"I may have played some small part in pointing the cops in the right direction," I allowed.

"You must be relieved."

"As fuck. Tell me: how are you making out with the Ryan Loffler case?"

"Not too well. We've got eight other homicides on our dance card."

"Maybe you need some help. I got time on my hands before I fuck off south."

"Maybe you need to not even think about stumbling around down here and just fuck off."

"Daughter dearest, that's no way to talk to your father."

"I'm not kidding, dad."

"Fine. At least tell me what you've got so far."

"The leading theory is a random killing. It doesn't matter how rare it was; stuff like that still happens."

"What about Henry Blake?"

"I've got three witnesses at Jameson & Lord who will swear that Blake was at his desk at least an hour before the crime."

"Truscott?"

"A little less certain. His wife said he was out for his jog that morning, like every morning. Neighbours confirmed seeing him leaving and returning about an hour later. He might have had time but it's highly doubtful."

"And Patricia Morland?"

"Two other agents from her company called and talked to her at home in Rosedale that morning."

"So what do you have?"

"Dad, you have to understand that a murder like that is messy. It was a bloodbath in that stairwell. The perp would have been splattered. And before you ask, of course we searched dumpsters and alleys in a three-block radius for bloody clothes. We canvassed the usuals all around there for anything unusual. Nothing."

I was thwarted. I hate being thwarted. There's altogether too much thwarting going on these days, if you ask me.

I suppose, after all that thwarting, I could've just cancelled my editing session with Henry Blake. My trio of suspects—for a different murder now—were still suspects in my books, but Halley had gone some way in convincing me that I was yet again, *plein de merde* (everything *does* sound better in French, doesn't it?).

And that meant that there was the off-off-off chance this whole publishing dealio was legitimate.

Or that the cops had missed something.

Later that night, I got another call from Halley.

"Twice in on day? What's the occasion, daughter dearest?"

"Dad, something's been bothering me. You have to tell me why you're so interested in those three."

There was nothing daughterly in her tone.

Damn! I was afraid she might ask. If she hadn't, I wouldn't have revealed anything about the literary fraud and kept it quiet for the meantime. I wasn't about to start lying to the cops. Plus, it sounded like she already knew exactly why I was interested.

"How's your time?" I asked.

"Plenty. What's up?"

I took a deep breath and laid out as much as I thought I knew about how Henry Blake had pillaged unpublished manuscripts for the choicest bits to fold into Clayton Thompson's book. How Patricia Morland and maybe Truscott knew about it.

Silence.

"Halley, you still there?"

"How long have you known about this?"

"A while. A week or so," I said, trying to convince myself that "or so" meant four weeks since Loffler shuffled off his mortal coil.

That's when it got loud.

"Bullshit!" she yelled. "I just got off the phone with Inspector Wilson! She said you told her over four weeks ago!"

"Calm down, Halley."

But my only offspring wasn't done.

"Calm down?! Calm down?! You selfish bastard! You kept this quiet so you could play amateur detective! And meanwhile, we could have saved a ton of time we spent chasing our tails, instead of looking at those three. That's giant fraud and that's motive; we would've torn their lives apart, if you'd told us."

"When you put it like that—"

"There is no other fucking way to put it!"

I was glad she was on her cellphone. All I heard was the same 'Click' you get at the end of all such conversations. With a clunky landline phone, she would have likely perforated my eardrum when she slammed the phone into the receiver.

I felt like shit.

I twisted myself into knots trying to justify my willful silence, but facts are facts. I had fucked up big time with a person I deeply love. But another fact occurred to me. What's done is done and here we all are. Now what do you do, Jake?

The best piece of advice to someone who has dug themselves into a hole is to stop digging and put down the goddamned shovel.

I chose to ignore that sage wisdom and, instead, went with the second-best piece of advice: try to fix the hole. First off, I scanned and sent all that I had to her. Pages from Bromley's journal, his e-mails to Thompson and Loffler, print-outs of the bolded sections in his manuscript with the corresponding pages from Thompson's book that I had highlighted.

Now, on to the second stage of my fix-it campaign. I had set the cops off in the right direction once. I was sure I could do it again. I was going to see Henry Blake.

CHAPTER THIRTY-FOUR

Blake had given me his address. I googled it and saw that yet again I was headed into the darkest wilds of downtown Toronto. Rather than risk my health in the Vibe, I took the Tucson, so no matter how unpleasant it was to be back, yet again, in a big city, the ride getting there was comfortable. Kudos to me, I had even figured out how to turn the fucking radio on. Good tunes through a great sound system went some distance to erasing my usual aggravation with insane drivers, congested roadways, and deliberately misleading signs. The fact that I was going into the city at a time when most people were fleeing it for the suburbs may have helped.

Blake lived in the almost laughably named Canary District. A real canary would've keeled over instantly in that atmosphere—a deadly combination of old-time industrial emissions and New Age smugness.

His condo building was a modest eight-story affair, with a bricked ground floor housing stores selling all the things I could never with a straight face bring myself to buy.

Blake greeted me at the door. He was polite and efficient as hell as if he was ushering me into a business meeting, which I suppose he was. This despite the fact that his bare-footed self was wearing a torn old Tony Hawk T-shirt and tattered jean cut-offs.

His place was small and eclectically decorated. A many-coloured surfboard hung above the camel-back sofa. I saw no evidence of a TV but a sleek bicycle, probably worth thousands, stood prominently where the big screen ought to be.

I asked the question every nicotine addict asks in new surroundings.

"Can I smoke out there?" I said, indicating the balcony outside the floor to ceiling window and sliding door.

"You're not supposed to. It's a smoke-free property."

"In the middle of a smog-filled city?"

"Condo rules."

"Oh, come on. How about you take a walk on the wild side?"

Reluctantly, he agreed after insisting that the patio door had to be shut while I was outside polluting Toronto the Clean.

"Now, can we get back to the business hand?" he asked.

"If that business is offering me a beer, then yes."

He went to the fridge and retrieved two bottles, wildly labelled and unrecognizable to me. Of course, craft beer, I thought, likely named Moderately Amused Hyena or Gala Slum or some other fucking cutesy ironic thing or other.

Beer in hand, we sat at the dining table. Driving down there, I had decided to be as infuriating as possible (you may find this hard to believe, but that's not a big leap for me).

True to form I got up not five minutes after we sat down, fishing a cigarette out of my pack.

"Really?" he asked, the exasperation obvious in his voice.

"Beer. Butt. Goes together like yuppie and pretentiousness."

There followed a division of labour. I stood on the balcony and slowly smoked my lung dart down to the filter while he sat inside and fumed.

"Now, where were we?" I asked.

"We need to talk about *The Sixth String* first. It could be problematic."

"It's fucking history! What's problematic about that?"

"The subject matter. Nazis, concentration camps, the Holocaust."

"I have no fucking idea what you're talking about."

"You're…not Jewish, are you?"

"So fucking what?"

"There might be some issues dealing with this."

"Anybody has an issue with this can go fuck their hat! Jews, Gypsies, Ukrainians, Russians were all innocent human beings, having monstrously evil things done by other human beings. It didn't matter a good goddamn what religion, race, or nationality they were. The Nazis just used that as an excuse to act on the very worst human impulses. And those impulses are what interest me as another human being, OK?"

"Maybe settle down," he advised.

Oh, that always works with me.

"I'm not going to fucking settle down about this! I just have to be right on the facts. Research is taking longer than I thought because—above all—I've got to be accurate."

"Alright, alright."

"Look, Henry, if you don't believe in the book, maybe you shouldn't be working on it."

"I resent that!" he sputtered.

"Trust me when I tell you I couldn't give two shits whether you resent it or not. It's my book; *that's* what matters to me."

That seemed to stifle his reaction to my insult. We turned our attention to the task at hand, editing the first book. I had the hard copy of the draft he'd marked up; he had his laptop. Before we got into the re-ordering of the book, he wanted to discuss the changes to the text he'd suggested and I had rejected. We went through them one by one. And I fought every one of them in between frequent smoke breaks and asking for more beer. I won most of them which I attributed to wearing him down. That part of pissing him off wasn't an act. I make it a habit, whether right or wrong, to vigourously defend every goddamned word I write.

I got down three beer while he nursed one. So in addition to my smoking interludes, I added a few bathroom breaks whether I needed one or not. Strangely coincidental, I'd excuse myself just as Blake was about to make a point.

On my first trip to the can, I looked around, as everyone does. Hard not to notice the Lady Schick razor in the shower or the jars and tubes of moisturizers, facial scrubs, toners, cleansers, and god knows what else on the vanity. The manufacturers didn't hide the fact but rather bragged that their products contained enough shit to outfit a small chemistry lab. BHA Liquid Salicylic Acid Exfoliant, Retinol, Hyaluronic Acid, Pure Glycolic Acid Serum, Kojic Acid, among others. They had also apparently raided grocery store shelves so that you could slap aloe, cucumber, green tea berry, yogurt, carrot, kiwi, eucalyptus, honey, avocado, turmeric pomegranate and something called cica on your face. Either Henry cared more about his appearance than I thought, or he and Patricia had progressed well past the kissy-face stage.

The undercard over, we began the main event: moving massive chunks around as flashbacks instead of an uninterrupted story.

In the first round, we danced around, feeling each other out, probing for what was pushback and what was pushover. About midway through the second round, the jabs started landing when I flat-out refused to go along with him. Angrily, Henry closed his laptop and pushed away from the table.

"This isn't working!" he declared.

"Why, whatever do you mean?"

"You're being a prick."

"Maybe. Are all your authors just wimps?"

"No. They respect what I can bring."

"Even Clayton Thompson?"

His eyes narrowed and he sat up straight.

"Patricia was right."

"About what?"

"You're not going to let this Thompson thing go, are you?"

"Now why would you say that?"

"She said you're going to be a problem," he said, ignoring my question.

"Have you seen anything about your little fraud—sorry, I mean big fraud—in the press?

"So you *do* know!"

"Yup. But a deal's a deal. You won't see anything in public from me. So you can fuck off with your worry. Tell Patricia that. Excuse me, but I need a butt."

I left him rattled and fuming as he reached for his cellphone.

I lit up, leaned over the balcony railing, and contemplated my next move towards pushing every button he had.

It's clear in my mind what happened next. When I had reached the half-way point of my cigarette, at that very moment, I discovered I was in love with office buildings, specifically plate glass-clad buildings at least four stories tall and, more specifically, the building directly across the narrow side street from Blake's balcony. I could plainly see moi in the glass's reflection. And the patio door sliding slowly open behind me, although I hadn't heard it. A pause and the lanky Henry Blake rushing through the doorway.

My reflexes are pretty good. Youthful years as a high school hockey, lacrosse and soccer goalie helped. As did decades of tennis. But I really give credit to some more recent years of boxing training where I had the great motivation to move quickly. If I didn't, I got punched in the face, something I didn't much care for.

I am able to twitch-respond to threats like a chipmunk on cocaine.

I automatically dropped into a crouch, then straightened up a bit as I felt his body above me. I want to say that I then executed a perfect judo flip, but more accurately I acted like one of those stationary vaulting horses they make you jump over in high school. My slight upward thrust and his momentum carried him over the railing. A small scream of surprise and a large thud.

I looked over the balcony, expecting to see an inert and squashed Henry Blake. He lay beside the maple tree that had obviously cushioned his fall. But he was moving and moaning. One leg and one arm were bent in positions most human limbs don't assume.

I called 9-1-1.

"What is your emergency?"

"I don't have one, but the guy who just fell off the balcony of apartment 402, Canary Condominium sure looks like he does."

"Excuse me?"

"There a guy lying on the sidewalk of Cooperage Street near the corner of Rolling Mills Road who took a header off his balcony while he was trying to kill me."

"What?"

"The busted-up guy is Henry Blake. He's alive. My name is Jake Lydon. My daughter is Halley Lydon of Toronto Homicide. You might want to call her too, after you give the EMTs a dingle."

I waited, but not very long. Within a few minutes, sirens tore up the hipster calm. I watched from the balcony as the paramedics tried to put Humpty Henry back together again. I had debated going down to the sidewalk but understood that, without a shred of emergency medical knowledge but with my astonishing clumsiness, I'd just fuck it up as I did most repair jobs.

A few minutes later there was a godawful pounding on the condo door, accompanied by shouts of "Police!"

Rather than have them bust down the door, I let them in. Two cops rushed in like they'd been first in line for an hour of free bar at a wedding.

There's nothing charming about being handcuffed. It had happened to me a lot over the last few years—and not for sport. I didn't much enjoy it, but I didn't blame them. They didn't know what had just taken place. I could've been fixing to toss them over the railing too.

We sat around in an awkward silence until Halley arrived. She breezed in, large and in charge, a crime scene unit in tow. She looked at me with a mixture of pity and anger. I used to get that same look from her some years after Beth died, when I was still drinking heavily, and she'd come to retrieve me from whatever bar I was shit-hammered in.

She told them to uncuff me and then dispatched them to tie off the sidewalk which Blake had recently been smooching. We went into the bedroom and she closed the door.

"What the fuck are you doing here?!" she said, turning to me with fury.

"I'm fine; thanks for asking, honey. That murder attempt didn't bother me at all."

"Oh, spare me! We talked about this. You've got no business being here."

I was now getting a little pissed off.

"If you'd let me explain. I *did* have business with Henry Blake. And it had nothing to do with anything beyond the fact that he's my fucking editor. I got a book deal. Take some time and look at all the goddamned paper on the goddamned dining table. That's what we were talking about."

That slowed her down. But it didn't stop her.

"Congratulations, dad. I mean that. So can you explain what happened? You're working away; I bet you get up to have a smoke on the balcony and, out of the blue, he decides to kill you? Help me understand."

"It's a poser, for sure. I intend to ask him."

"There you go again. That's our job. Butt out."

"I have to see him, Hal."

"Not a chance."

"C'mon, where's the harm? Five minutes."

"Why?"

"Call it a personal victim impact statement."

"You've got to do better than that."

"Look, I lie, you lie, we all lie. Part of what makes you a good cop is you know when a suspect or witness is bullshitting you. I do too. The difference is: you guys have a great big book somewhere that you have to go by. I don't. I might find out something."

I could see she was wavering.

"Can I wear a wire? Huh, can I? Can I?

"Absolutely not. I'm not going to risk fucking up this investigation."

"I've done it before."

"What? Fuck up an investigation? Yeah, I know."

"No, wear a wire."

"When?" Halley asked, her voice full of dubiosity.

"Recently."

"When?" she asked again, then stopped herself. "That's how they caught that guy who murdered Bromley, isn't it?"

"Maybe."

"Well, this ain't Peterborough."

"I know. Traffic's worse, buildings are real big, and there seems to be a bad smell I can't identify."

"The answer's still no. We couldn't use anything he might tell you. Defense will argue that you were acting as a police agent. Especially with your last name. You can't question him without a lawyer."

"There's a grey area there, Hal, and you know it. I can suggest an avenue you *might* pursue without getting into specifics."

I had her on the edge and played my final card.

"Halley, as a favour to your old man?"

I was in full cajoling mode. In a way, I was pulling rank. I may have been a shitty father, but I was still her father.

"Five minutes."

"Thanks, Hal! One more favour?"

"I'm starting to envy Little Orphan Annie. What?"

"Can you pick up Patricia Morland?"

"We're doing that tonight. Ron's on her for the plagiarism fraud. We think she's involved."

"Can you keep her? At least until late tomorrow?"

"She'll get bail right away, but we could lose the paperwork for a bit. Why?"

"Why, why, why. Just like when you were a kid. Because of that one thing that's not in that great big book I mentioned. That's why."

"Call me tomorrow morning. We'll know where Blake is and what kinda shape he's in."

I didn't think Blake would be in a talkative mood for a bit, what with his life-threatening injuries and all. Where to sleep? I considered staying in Blake's apartment, but the crime scene cops didn't think that was a swell idea. I could just drop in on Steve and his lakefront condo. Our fractured relationship ruled that out, so I checked into the Royal York on Front Street.

It was after ten, the magic time when you can actually bargain over the price for a room that otherwise was going to net them zero dollars for sitting empty. I credit my winters spent bartering and negotiating in the Dominican for browbeating the front desk clerk into giving it to me for just a bit more than a no-tel mo-tel outside of Cleveland in February. But they made up the difference with the fucking room service charge—forty bucks for a cheeseburger and a beer? What?

The next morning, I actually slept in. Without a goddamn cup of coffee, I called Halley.

She told me that, surprisingly, Blake wasn't in too bad shape. No brain damage, no messed-up organs or internal bleeding. Busted arm, busted leg, fractured wrist, broken collar bone, fucked up pelvis. All stuff that would heal. He was out of ICU at Toronto General, just up the street from the Royal York.

"Room 607. I'll let the guard at Toronto Gen know," she said. "Five minutes."

"Thanks, Hal. You might not regret this."

CHAPTER THIRTY-FIVE

I don't like hospitals, starting with their sky-high parking rates. The last time I'd spent any time in one was twelve years ago when my wife was dying. Oh, then there was my stay in Punta Cana after I got shot. And then there was a brief stint in a Boston hospital when I went in for a—surprise, surprise—another gunshot wound. But other than that.

The cop seated outside the room door got up to intercept me, but let me pass after I proved I was me.

None too surprisingly, Blake didn't look up to running even a half-marathon. One big-ass plaster cast-encased leg was raised up by a pulley of some kind. Ditto for an arm, also frozen in plaster but at a 90-degree angle at the elbow. His other arm rattled the handcuff attached to the bed railing. He must've done a somersault on the way down because his face was bandaged in various places—souvenirs from the tree branches that had slowed his fall. Various wires and tubes ran into him.

"Hank, old buddy old pal, just how the fuck are you?! No, don't get up."

"What do you want?" he said, his voice groggy.

"Look, I'm sorry I didn't bring flowers, but I thought I'd at least sign your cast. I mean casts. Got a pen?"

"Fuck off."

"Henry, we should finish our little chat."

"Why would I say anything to you?"

"Because there are certain realities you should aware of," I said.

"Such as…?"

"Such as I don't think you had anything to do with Ryan's death—that's what I told the cops anyway."

"Because I didn't!" he said, painfully summoning up some vigour in his voice.

"But I think you know who did."

Silence.

"The cops are likely gonna charge you with the attempted murder of me, so you're looking at least ten years, maybe more. Oh, did I mention that my daughter's the Toronto cop investigating this? She just might want to lean pretty hard on anyone who tried to hurt her dear old dad."

Silence.

"Anywho. You plead to assault, on the other hand, and you get six months and a fine. Maybe just the fine."

"I'm pretty messed up. Doctor said I'll probably never walk normally."

"Sucks to be you. But maybe you shouldn't've tried to kill me. Whaddya think?"

One of them silences again.

"Look, Henry, do what you gotta do. But I'm telling you, you're on your own."

"What do you mean?"

"Patricia come to see you yet?"

"No…but…"

"The cold hard truth is she probably won't. She'll stay as far away from you and this mess as she can."

"She will not!"

"For Christ's sake, think about it. Jameson & Lord is fucked. Depending on the choices you make, you're fucked too. But she's got a business that's far removed from all this and Jameson. That business means the world to her and she's going to be absolutely fierce about protecting it. You gotta face the fact that there's no 'til death do you part here, Henry."

Yet more silence. Maybe it was the pain meds, but he was clearly thinking about what I'd said.

"Oh, by the by, I also think she's moving on up from an editor to a CEO," I added.

"What?"

"Room 408, Peterborough Hilton, March 23. She checked-in with a certain dapper-looking older gentleman who looked, for all the world, like the head honcho at a publishing house."

"No!"

"Yes."

That last tidbit clinched the deal.

"But…it was her idea."

"What was?"

"All of it."

"The copycatting?"

"Yes."

"Tell me more."

"She knew that what Thompson had turned in was awful. I knew it too."

"Why didn't she just get a ghost writer to tart it up?"

"There's a reason they're ghost writers. They're not that good and she wanted great."

"Where'd you find great?"

"I couldn't use any stuff from my authors, so I enlisted Ryan. It wasn't hard. He was hungry. He found the sections in manuscripts in his slush pile. He's smart. He tuned them up and I stitched them in. And it worked. The home run Patricia was sure of."

"You did all this at work?"

"No. Ryan's place. Air-gapped computers and memory sticks."

"So what happened?"

"The money was rolling in. Ryan actually made the most because he'd found the new sections and because we needed his silence. I was paid on the back-end on commissions and stock sales when the book took off. Patricia had stock too, and a slice of all the speaking fees."

"But Loffler kept demanding more."

"And more."

"After he blew all that coin on that condo down the street."

"Fuckin' idiot! I told him not buy it. But he said he deserved it. He was pissed because he said I was crippling his career. And he was still mad at Patricia because she turned him down as a client for his novel a couple of years earlier."

Sidebar: Is everybody writing a goddamned book?

The pain killers were really dripping into him at that point. I couldn't help but notice that Blake had become quite the Chatty Cathy, as if he wanted to tell the tale that had been weighing on him. Or maybe just to prove how fucking smart he was setting the whole thing up. But more than anything, I suspected he was in full ass-covering mode and pissed at Morland.

"Ryan wouldn't give up his place, even after he found out how much it cost to furnish it, and then cover the monthly fees and taxes. So Patricia and I were paying for it all with cash. But Patricia was positive that he wouldn't ever be satisfied."

"So she killed him, and she told you to do the same to me when you were on the phone with her last night?"

Henry didn't say anything.

"No, forget I asked that. Let me guess. Want to hear my bet? She arranged to have an early breakfast meeting with him at his condo, said she was reconsidering representing him. She stayed over with you the night before he died, didn't she? It's only a few blocks from Ryan's. Of course she had a bag with a change of clothes. Oh, and a knife. You both have read enough mystery or thriller manuscripts to know about the mess these events leave and how to clean up. She had her meeting with him, followed him down to the stairwell or left earlier and was waiting for him. Stab, slash, stab, and out the side door after she changed. Strolled down the side street around back to your place, where she did the final bit of clean-up and waited. Maybe drove to her office or went to a coffee shop. Or even drove back to her place to take the phone off call forward."

"I haven't said a word," Henry said. "And I didn't know."

"That's fine. But don't you see what a great bargaining position you're in? Confirm my little story to the cops and you fucking skate. Think hard about that, will you? It's OK; I'll show myself out."

The cop guarding the door stopped me.

"Got a message from somebody. You're supposed to go to Lucy's Kitchen on St. Clair at Atlas."

"Female voice?"

"No."

I was mystified as I got my wheels out of hock from the hospital parking lot. I was also sure that anything Blake had told me about the plagiarism would get tossed out of court and that he likely knew it. I didn't give a shit. Toronto cops already knew about it. There could only be a couple of possibilities and I had both Bromley's e-mails and his book manuscript. Inevitable discovery, your Honour! And even if it was inadmissible, it didn't really matter to me. The arrests and resulting media coverage would fuck up thems who needed fucking up.

But the murder? Blake had been careful not to say a goddamned thing. And I hadn't asked him about it, except for one question that I had immediately withdrawn.

I parked on a side street (for free!) and entered Lucy's. Now this was my kinda place, I thought. One big room with booths lining two sides. A raucous lunch-time crowd, their laughter and conversation almost drowned out by the loud clink and clatter of cutlery and plates. Middle-aged waitresses buzzing among the fake wood tables, taking orders and yelling them into the frantic cooks in the open-end kitchen. And nary a maître-d in sight. A place built to serve the vast army of tradespeople and municipal employees who kept the city running and who couldn't afford or wouldn't ever pay twenty-seven goddamned dollars for a god-damned cheeseburger.

"Daughter dear, how great to see you again!" I said loudly after I spied her in a booth. "It's been too long!"

"Cute," she said as I slid into the genuine Naugahyde bench across from her.

"Oh, don't start. Speaking of cute: that was Farisi who called for me at the hospital."

"On a burner," she said, smiling, it seemed, for the first time in a long time.

"What'd you learn?" she wanted to know.

"I'm not telling you."

"Fuck off, dad."

"So what's good here?" I said, studying the laminated menu. I was encouraged because I hadn't found the words "reduction," "artisanal" or fucking "bouquet garnis" anywhere on the diner menu.

"Dad….?"

"Let me order; I'm starving."

Club sandwich, fries with gravy, and a Diet Pepsi on the way, I settled back.

"How about we play a game of what if?" I said.

"What are the rules?"

"I ask a bunch of wildly theoretical questions and you shut the fuck up while I'm asking them. Instead, you go away and think about the possible theoretical answers."

"OK. Start."

"What if Ryan Loffler and Henry Blake both had home computers that showed how they stole from other manuscripts to put into Clayton Thompson's book?"

"What if you found store receipts for high-end furniture and appliances that Blake bought, but that the stuff was delivered to the 28th floor of Loffler's condo building and not to his place?"

"What if you found out that Blake has made cash withdrawals of about thirty-five hundred dollars every month for the last three years or so?"

"What if you told Detective Farisi about all this?"

"Now. What if Henry Blake had no connection to Ryan's death but that somebody he knew—maybe a lover or recently ex-lover—did the deed?"

"What if a thorough search of his place and his lover or ex-lover's house in Rosedale—closets, bathtubs, sink drains and such—turned up something like Loffler's blood stains?"

Halley sat there quietly, thinking and grinning.

"Any other questions?" she asked.

"One more....What if Bill Wyman had never left the Stones?"

"I have no idea how Alexandra puts up with you," she said.

"You should ask her. I'd give worlds to know the answer. And speaking of significant other, do you still have one or are you just co-workers again?"

"Still going steady," she answered.

"Hal, I'm really happy for you."

"But?"

"There is no but."

She was smiling again. Father and daughter then pleasantly shot the shit about everything except crime and people dying violently while we had lunch. Although I can never figure out how you can consider ordering salad as having a meal.

A massive hug on the sidewalk.

"Thanks, dad," she said as she pulled away. "You saved us a lot of time, but we would have got there."

"I know, Hal. I know."

"And I'm glad you survived Blake."

For lots of reasons, I was happy as hell to be getting the fuck out of the city. But I knew I was in for a major business deal when I got home.

CHAPTER THIRTY-SIX

Carl must have some kind of natural distant early warning system built into his giant frame. He knows when I'm away from the hovel and when I return.

I had just parked the Tucson when I saw him emerging from the lake onto my shoreline.

"Where you been, boss?" he asked as he toweled off on the deck.

"None of your fucking business."

He looked almost hurt.

"Alright, alright. If you must know, I was shopping for a cottage on another lake, way the fuck and gone from this one."

"Thank Christ. I might get some neighbours who aren't arseholes. Want to go to AA to celebrate?"

"Yeah, but have a beer here first. We got some business to take care of."

Beer in hand, I led a puzzled friend to the Vibe.

"You want it?" I asked, slapping the hood.

"How much you askin'?" he asked, suddenly becoming all

business-like and suspicious.

"Welllll...I did a bunch of research on-line, called a few deal-erships..."

"How much?" he demanded.

"How about nothing?"

"Stop fucking around. How much?"

"For fuck's sake, I'm not. I could get maybe three hundred bucks from a junk yard. *Maybe*."

"So will you take five cases of beer?"

"You goddamned horse trader! I can put you behind the wheel of this baby for three cases. And I'll throw in the snow tires. Worth more than the car. That's my final offer."

"I don't know."

"OK, OK, two cases; take it or leave it."

"Done!" he said, finally breaking into a smile.

I'm glad we did the deal just then. Any longer at it, and I'd've been paying him.

After a wonderfully hazy afternoon with him at the Angler Arms, I caught up with my insulin injections, a chat with Alex, the news, and my sleep in roughly that order. I was delighted, even thrilled to be back home, looking to get entrenched once more in my boring, solitary routine.

The following afternoon, just after my suitable mourning peri-od for the loss of the Vibe, the plagiarism scandal became public. Very public. Patricia Morland and Henry Blake were officially ar-rested and charged (Blake from the comfort of his hospital bed). I was surprised that Truscott was charged too.

There was a built-in worldwide audience for news of the big-league copycatting. The millions of people who bought the fuck-ing book would be the core spectators, but it would go much far-ther than that. Even though everybody everywhere gets tricked by politicians and businesspeople every goddamned day, there was something obvious, self-contained, and delicious about the plagiarism that upped the level of fury and disgust. For one brief shining moment, the world was united in its outrage over the scandal.

The mid-September days passed and I was furiously—well, for me—working at *The Sixth String*. It didn't matter if my publishing contract was all bullshit or even if Jameson & Lord existed or not. I was completely convinced it could a good book. Now, all I had to do was make it so.

Mornings were spent racking up the pixels until my brain hurt, with most afternoons occupied by research into all the elements I knew I had to get right. I decorated the screened-in porch with the yellow post-it notes I habitually fill out with tidbits I might include. All fascinating stuff about the origins and mechanics of flamenco in Spain, about East European Gypsies (and why you shouldn't call them that anymore), and about how 500,000 of them were slaughtered by the Nazis wherever they were found or in their incomprehensibly barbaric concentration and death camps.

I quickly understood that, on the days I spent finding out more about the Nazis and their enablers, I ought not to talk to Alexandra or Carl. I was black and speechless at both the individual acts of cruelty and the industrial-scale inhumanity.

This writing and reading ritual thoroughly engrossed me for three weeks, until I got one of my rare non-telemarketing phone calls. It was Steve.

"Just tell me," he said. "Were you the confidential informant the Toronto cops cited when they announced their arrests in a major plagiarism scandal? And while I've got you on the line: did you have anything to do with the Peterborough cops picking up Bromley's killer? Oh, and one more question: did you know about the plagiarizing a long time ago?"

"Yes, yes, and yes," I said, done with bullshitting my friend.

"That's what I thought."

Click.

Way to go, Jake! That'll help patch things up.

Friendship's an odd and wonderful thing. I've never had a lot of friends and I treasure the ones I do. In a very particular order: Alexandra, Carl, and Steve. They have common elements, most prominently trust and ease. Oh, and sarcasm. All three give as good as they get and make me laugh. I'm pretty sure I supply them with the same commodities. The result is a comforting warmth, a sense of fairness, and the complete lack of fucking drama. Alexandra easily gets the edge because she makes my heart race when I look at her and she's willing to sleep with me naked. I'd have turned them down, but the other two have never so much as asked.

Steve and I had been under radio silence since the night after Clayton's suicide. He was pissed because I had clearly lied to him, and he had trusted me not to ever do that. I was pissed at him because I had trusted him to understand why I had lied. Whatever chance there was of this feud dying down had vanished with his sleuthing out my bargain-basement investigating.

Sidebar: I had lied to Alexandra by either omitting or downplaying the seriousness of a few near-fatal encounters thrown my way since we got together. But that's not what had nearly blown us up. It was her—rightly—questioning whether she wanted to be around all that aforementioned fucking drama or not.

I hate simmering gravy until it's burnt away and caking the pot. Bring that shit to a boil quickly and get it settled—or not.

I sent Steve a short e-mail:

How about you come up to the hovel, drink some beer, and listen to the fucking loons?

He wrote a shorter note back: *Friday*

CHAPTER THIRTY-SEVEN

Like everything else involving big money and big crimes, the fall-out from the plagiarizing scandal rolled on for a while.

Jan Morris had been arrested, and I was sorry about that. She hadn't done any of the defrauding, but she had conspired to keep it quiet. I didn't think she was in for a stiff penalty and, with Inspector Wilson's approval, there would be no charges filed against her for her role in the faked hostage drama up here.

"Let Toronto have her," the Inspector said. "I called her to tell her we wouldn't be laying charges."

I figured that the Inspector was back to being a kind matron on that call. But I also reckoned she probably would've shown the knife by letting Jan know that the Peterborough police had years to file charges in case she was thinking about yakking to Toronto in the hopes of leniency down there.

The plagiarism scandal was soon overshadowed, at least temporarily, by the announcement of Patricia's arrest for the murder of Ryan Loffler on top of her pending trial for fraud. The press tried to outdo each other with screaming headlines. As usual the tabloids won, with "Agent of Evil?" nudging out "Murder She

Wrote." Also as usual, the word "alleged" was used frequently and the lawyers were going to "vigorously defend against these false and baseless accusations."

Halley called, just to let me know that those "false and baseless accusations" were sure to stand up. In their search of Morland's home, they didn't find the murder knife, but they did discover a few drops of Ryan Loffler's blood on the bottom of her gym bag.

"She's going to have a tough job explaining how they got there," she told me.

To no one's surprise, Jameson & Lord quickly became the pariah of the publishing biz. In short order, Daniel Truscott was turfed by the board of directors—even though he had had the charges dropped against him because there was no proof he had known about or participated in the scheme. Their stable of writers bolted, all proclaiming their shock and disgust. The company stock cratered. Court-appointed auditors moved in to determine if they would ever again be "an on-going concern," as the once-proud institution circled the drain. Lay-offs and lawsuits sure to follow.

Closer to home, I got a call then a registered letter from the new and very temporary CEO at Jameson & Lord cancelling my contract with them. Oh, happy day, they wouldn't try to recover my advance in return for me not suing their ass off.

Steve pulled up around seven on the Friday. It was awkward as hell from the get-go. No warm greeting at the door, no handshake, no hug. Gruff agreement that we convene on the deck. We settled into the Adirondacks.

"Beer?" I offered.

He didn't answer. Instead he said:

"I guess we should deal with this…this thing that's going on."

"I guess we should. But not without a beer, we won't."

When we both had an ice-cold Ex in our mitts, we got down to it.

"Let me start." Steve said. "You played me."

"I did. And I'm sorry."

"You fucking played me."

"And two murderers are behind bars."

"They would've been sooner or later."

"You don't know that. If you did, then tell me, Monsieur Clairvoyant, who's winning the Superbowl this year?"

"You are fucking lucky. If I revealed the name of a confidential informant, I would be completely fucked with the cops."

"What did you lose here—professionally?" I asked. "You didn't get the inside story from the guy you *coincidentally* knew who *coincidentally* happened to be involved."

"That's not the point. You lied to me."

"I said I was sorry and I meant it. You're gonna have to get over this, buddy. Or not. Your choice."

We fell quiet.

"How about another beer?" he asked.

I took his request as a major move forward, sort of like a tremendous breakthrough development in international nuclear arms negotiations. But things slowed down as we thoughtfully drank. Those two beer weren't enough. Neither was the next one or the one after that. Maybe five bottles later and the stalemate started to melt. It didn't disappear altogether, perhaps it never would, but we started talking and then grinning and then laughing. And we talked out the plagiarism scheme until we couldn't anymore, thanks to the continuous flow of ale.

"This is all deep anonymous background, you parasite," I said, wanting to get that ground rule on the books.

"Agreed. The way I figure it, the thing had to fall apart as soon as Loffler lifted those sections of Bromley's book."

"No question, that was Loffler's mistake. Ripping off a Trent English professor who had spent his life parsing the fuck out of books. First, because he should've known Bromley might read a

book by his former student and, second, that he'd instantly recognize passages he'd written years earlier."

"But I understand that there only two plagiarized bits Bromley complained about. If there were more, he would've mentioned
them.

"There were. He found them, of course. I did too. Six in all.

"So, total was what? Two or three pages? Doesn't make sense.
There are a ton of other parts written by Thompson that are every
bit as good—if not better. As far as he knew, there were only a few
paragraphs that had been copied from Bromley. He kills himself
over a couple of hundred words?"

"He must've suspected there were more. Lots more. And not
just from Bromley. If you understood literature at all, you could
probably pick out every decent passage in Thompson's book and
figure that somebody else wrote it."

"But, still, murder for that?

"Think about it. It's not for the copycatting, although the stink
from a plagiarism bust follows you around. That crime is bad
enough, but the real problem is hiding it."

"But good writing didn't make that book a hit."

"So it turns out they didn't really have to do it, so what? The
fall-out from getting caught was always the issue. Everybody's
douched if that happened. Watergate really *was* a shitty 'third-rate
burglary.' Until you looked at who ordered it, who organized it,
who knew about it, and who and how they lied trying to bury it."

"I'm guessing at most of it," he said. "Halley filled me in, but
not the whole thing. Tell me how they did it."

"Everything's by e-mail these days. Cut and paste from a word
doc. How do you prove it was yours? You've relied on your publisher not to do shit like that when you submitted it. And they
don't. Their reputation would be fucked. And, anyway, it's usually
too much of a pain in the ass to discreetly steal from somebody
else."

"Usually?"

"Just rare to unheard of. Blake or Morland anointed Thompson as the next big literary sensation and convinced Truscott to bet big on it. Sales and Marketing would've been onside because Thompson was already known to millions. How often does that happen with a first book? And Jameson & Lord had a ton riding on it. Big advance, big promotional investment. This was Truscott's moon shot. Blake wasn't going to take any chances. But when he saw that first draft, he realized it was less than OK, nothing like he needed to blow away the public. He believed he had to juice it up. They get thousands of manuscripts a year, pretty well all of them as Word docs. A lot of publishers use the same plagiarism recognition software that universities have. Schools use it to stop cheats from lifting shit that's already in print. Publishers use it to protect themselves from the same thing. Blake ran the doctored draft through it. The new and improved *Returning* came up clean because all the copycatted manuscripts were unpublished. There was no trace of them anywhere in the public domain."

"But they existed. Surely, they could establish that."

"Let's say they stole from fifty submissions. How many novelists do you figure would've read what's essentially a self-help book? Take Bromley. He didn't read *The Returning* until three years after it came out. And he picked it up only because Thompson, the Trent grad, had been appointed writer-in-residence. So, some of the, let's say, fifty pirated unknowns maybe read it too. A very small number, if any."

"But still, that's a big gamble."

"Yeah, but let's say a couple of the real authors who were victims discovered the theft of their work and called J&L on it. Can you hear their response? "Wanna go to court? Are you up for expensive litigation that lasts forever, during which *you* get accused of stealing from one of *our authors*? Wanna take on a PR machine that'll turn you into pond slime by the time they're done?" And, after it's over, who wants to publish a nobody who might turn around and sue you? So you take the settlement they offer because you know it's still way more than you'd likely make if you self-published the book. You may grumble, but you sign the non-disclosure agreement promising to shut the fuck up forever."

"I can't believe all this elaborate scheming was worth it."

"Are you fucking kidding me? Of course they'd think it was worth it. *The Returning* sold something like five million copies. At thirty bucks a throw, Thompson would've seen at least four bucks a copy. Ka-ching! Twenty million. Jameson & Lord would get to keep even more after producing the book. It was only around 70,000 words. Not a big book, so no big paper costs and smaller shipping charges. Once you have a big press run, your per book cost drops like a stone but the cover price stays the same. All those reprintings were gravy because they mostly had orders for them. The e-book costs fuck-all to produce; Thompson would've seen a quarter of those sales. Same deal with the audiobook which Thompson also got paid to read."

"Wasn't there a movie deal?"

"I forgot about that. What's not to like about an engaging story with most of the dialogue already written by a world-famous guy? Sure, the film had to be shelved—although the new controversy might kickstart it again—that's what happened, for different reasons, with *A Million Pieces*—but they'd already shelled out at least a million for the rights. And then, of course, there's a built-in audience for the follow-up book." And let's not forget all the speaking engagements. At least fifty grand an appearance. Say he does just fifty of them a year, one a week. Gidday, another two and half million smackeroos—minimum. And a cool $250K for his agent. I did some math on the total take. It'd be something like a quarter of a billion. So, yeah, it was worth it."

"Everybody involved stood to make out like bandits," Steve said, shaking his head at the magnitude of the scheme.

"And it didn't stop there. Jameson & Lord took a lot of that profit to their bottom line which goosed the stock. Bonuses all the way around based on market performance. Truscott benefitted the most. I went back and read the IPO filing. He got a ton of share options at the issue price. Stock's almost doubled since then. Henry Blake did pretty well too; he's listed as an officer under the Executive Compensation section. Then, he also got paid his editor/copycatter salary *plus* what had to be a hefty commission based on book sales."

"That's a lot of gravy was spilling off the plate. Forget the lone writer toiling away in an unheated attic; this was a fucking conglomerate."

"Better yet, imagine Clayton as the fatted calf at the king's banquet."

"Meat skewers optional. Are you sure Loffler was in on it?"

"No question. Henry Blake couldn't have been ripping off the manuscripts that got sent his way. He was top editing dog, and his writers were all established. In this little copycatting cartel, Loffler was a mule, likely their star mule. He carried the choice bits of prose that he came across in the slush pile of unpublished manuscripts to Henry Blake who was quite skillful in assembling, slightly paraphrasing, and stitching them together."

"Why would Loffler do it?"

"Same reason as Blake and Morland. Money. What else? He had a lifestyle in mind that he dearly wanted to become accustomed to. He'd also be smart enough to know that they could afford to pay him a shit-ton—say, enough for a pricey condo—and still do well. Everybody was happy with the arrangement. Until they weren't."

"What we don't know is if the rip-off ring stopped there. Were other editors or past editors doing it? Not just with Thompson, but other writers as well?"

"Not that they can tell. It's gonna take a while but they're reviewing every e-manuscript Jameson & Lord received in the last three years, loading them into the anti-piracy software to see if anything turns up. So far, nothing, and I doubt there will be. I think this was the single perfect storm of opportunity."

At about the same time, I think we both realized that we'd flogged the fuck out of the copycatting caper. That dead horse wasn't going anywhere.

Our conversation turned to the state of affairs with his book. I didn't bring it up. I may not be all that smart, but I'm not stupid enough to raise the subject like it was some kind of bargaining chip and that he better fucking realize he somehow owed me enough to let all the current mess slide.

He had worked his ass off, finished the first draft of *High Stakes* on time, and got it back with minor revisions. Cover art done and approved; promo blurbs written.

"Wanna hear their big sales pitch?" he asked.

"Sure."

"*High Stakes: The true inside story of the gambling swindle that shook America.*"

"Wow! I might even read that....On second thought, I'm going to wait for the movie."

"Arsehole. I'm a little surprised you didn't ask to see it."

"Why would I? You're a pretty good reporter. And besides, you wouldn't have sent it to me if I had asked, would you?"

"No," he said, smiling.

He stared off into the dark. That time of night, the only hint of civilization were a few distant faint lights from houses across the lake. On cue, a loon started up.

"I'm tired, Jake."

"You know where your room is."

"No. I'm tired of the daily grind. This book does well and I'm going to quit chasing stories about shitty people doing shitty things every day."

"And do what?"

"Just write books about shitty people doing shitty things every once in a while, and take it easier. I see what you've got and, although I hate to admit it, I'm envious."

"Oh bullshit. You give up the city, your fancy condo, and go on up the country? You'd last about a week in the bush. You'd either go cabin crazy or cut your fucking arm off with a chainsaw."

"Maybe."

"One more beer?

Our little post-mortem and his retirement dreaming soon descended into drunken lapses punctuated by nonsense non sequiturs as "one more beer" wasn't the end of it. We resurrected our tried-and-true shtick developed decades ago when Steve used to drink almost as much as me. In sober times, we referred to it as the long-lost *Chip n' Dale Get Shit-faced* Episode.

All it took was a minor disagreement over something or other, I can't remember what. And who said each line is immaterial and untraceable. It went like this:

"Don't be a dick."

"No, *you* don't be a dick."

"No, you don't."

"After you."

"No, I insist, after you."

"Well, you, sir, may indubitably fuck off."

"No, you fuck off."

"No, you."

And so on.

I know; cute, right?

He stumbled inside while I had one last butt as I drained my bottle. I was happy and relieved that we'd repaired our old jalopy of friendship. Once in bed, I fell asleep/passed out quickly, feeling goddamned contented. Judging by the deafening snoring sifting out from Steve's room, he was feeling pretty relaxed too.

CHAPTER THIRTY-EIGHT

We woke up not exactly feeling or looking our best. After a quiet, almost catatonic morning and a good-bye hug, Steve was off to chase down the dirty deeds being done dirt cheap in the big city. And I was off to do sweet fuck-all.

Except for the book writing, I had joined the emotional DIY craze by deciding that sweet fuck-all was exactly what I needed to undertake some of that self-care. A summer of too much driving, too much of a big city, too much thinking about bad people, too many attacks on my person, and way too much talking to humans other than myself had taken its toll.

And then there's the asterisk for Carl. He is a delight to me at any time. We became regulars again at the Angler Arms and my late afternoons/evenings with him arguing over the early season NFL developments were almost as much fun as watching the games again in front of my big screen. They and he were also a welcome antidote the horrors of Nazism.

One fine mid-morning I heard the beep, beep, beep of a big truck backing up near the hovel. Outside, I watched the flatbed drop off big bundles of lumber onto Carl's mainland strip of land across from his island home.

"What the fuck are you doing?" I asked as he was supervising the delivery.

"Got some building to do."

Carl never asks for help in any of his outdoorsy activities. He knows that my total ineptitude would just slow him down. But pressure-treated wood? That was right up my narrow alley of competence.

Wordlessly, we started dividing up the pile of 12-foot deck boards, 2X10s and 2X6s into boat-sized loads that took the rest of the day to raft over to Isla de Carl.

"You building a whole new fucking house?" I asked as the last pile was assembled on the ground in front of his place; he'd already torn down, chain-sawed, and stacked the old deck for squared firewood.

The next morning, I heard his saw start up at eight o'clock. Jack snap, I packed my tools in the canoe and paddled over.

It was a sweaty but pleasant as hell day, our bickering drowned out by the whine of skill saws then two hammer drills screwing the boards down. Carl's island is just a big rock that wasn't going anywhere so he didn't need anything in the way of a foundation.

Unless you're building a deck vertically—in which case I guess it's called a wall—you spend the day doing nothing but bendy work. With the sun sinking, I was in meal planning mode: Naproxen and tequila were on the menu.

The finished product was darn smart-looking and mostly solid and level. We regarded our handiwork over an inaugural beer or two as the sun set.

"What colour you gonna stain it?" I asked.

"No colour, already got one."

"It'll turn grey."

"I like grey."

There. That's Carl in a nutshell.

I got a call from Inspector Wilson. She wanted to e-send me some money.

"We haven't paid you. Any number you have in mind?" she asked.

"Whatever you think's fair. If I charged my going hourly rate, I'd wind up owning the cop shop and all your cars. Can I get a cheque?"

"Sure."

"Can you have Les present it to me."

"You are relentless."

By the end of September, I was happy enough with the first chapter, one other, and the outline for the whole thing to send it off to a bunch of places. I made mention of my ill-fated contract with Jameson & Lord in my covering letter but doubted it would tug any heartstrings or establish my creds. The flood of writers deserting J&L would fill up the publishing schedules of everybody else. But who knows?

Halley and Detective Ron came up to see me for a weekend in early October just as the leaves were changing colour. They went for long walks amid the fiery reds, oranges, and yellows which must have been a welcome change from their strolls along the grey mean streets of the city amid all sorts of human nastiness.

I didn't relish blowing up their bliss, but I needed some clarity about the future, specifically my future. I had to know if my involvement in the shit just passed would become public. Halley was as reassuring as she could be. Morland's defense team was pressing for details about the investigation into Ryan's murder.

"We said we had a confidential informant," she said. "And now her lawyers want you named. We'll fight it and probably win because we can prove inevitable discovery and also, we'll argue that our CI is a valuable future asset who we can't afford to out."

"Valuable future asset? Sounds like I'm on the payroll! Can we discuss salary? What kind of benefits package do you have?"

"How about this: you'll get fully compensated by me not pressing obstruction of justice charges."

"You drive a hard bargain, but OK. What happens with the fraud case and Blake's heinous assault of this valuable asset?"

"Looks like we've got a deal with him. We drop the attempted murder of you and offer leniency as a murder accessory in exchange for his testimony against Morland. If he refuses—and I don't think he will because he's still mightily pissed at her—victims have to agree to be identified and I'm thinking your disagreeable self won't allow that."

"And the copycatting?"

"We got a tip on the plagiarism from those wonderful cops in Peterborough which is true, courtesy of *their* confidential agent who they don't have to name but who, I understand, is a complete—what did Inspector Wilson say? Oh, yeah—a complete arsehole."

"Nice, daughter. Real nice."

I needed just one more answer. Halley, that smarty pants, guessed what it was.

"And if you're wondering about Alexandra…"

"I am. More than anything."

"Like I said, we can keep you out of all the court stuff. And you have my word I won't tell her."

"You'd do that?"

"To have my old man be happier than I've seen him in years? Yes, I would."

"Thank you, Hal. Thank you."

"Oh, I didn't mention my small fee."

"Blackmail! Ron, you're a witness. Whaddya want, you pirate?"

"Free access to this place when you're away."

"Done. But why the fuck would you want to shiver your asses off up here?"

"We're thinking about taking up cross-country skiing."

"Oh my Christ! Cross-country skiing? Where, oh where did I go wrong?"

With the last details of my messy summer cleared up, I slept like a baby. By that I mean I slept a lot. When beer failed me as a sleep aid, largely because my mind was jogging along thinking about the next day's e-scribbling, I discovered a sure-fire coma inducer. Nature documentaries! On many a night, I drifted off to beautiful images and Sir David Attenborough's soothing voice—he deserved the knighthood just for those narrations—but was invariably disappointed the next morning because I never stayed up long enough to see how things turned out.

I now know how the many different kinds of animals coalesce into organized herds setting off on the Great Migration across the Serengeti, but did they get to wherever they were going? Beats me. Ditto for all those green sea turtle hatchlings along the Mexican Pacific Coast. Looked pretty dicey for them as they madly scrambled across the sand, but I sure do hope they made it to the ocean.

My remaining time was spent fooling with my baby on the telephone. And planning. Road trip! I hadn't been on one of those for a long time. We fixed a date for me to pick her up. I mapped the route: eight hours to Boston, twenty hours to Indian Rocks Beach. With two drivers, we faced just one overnight stay—Fayetteville, North Carolina, I reckoned.

I was going to be setting off on my personal Great Migration south with two outstanding gifts. One came in the form of an envelope that contained a cheque for $100,000 and a note from Steve instructing me to renovate my ass off, (which I would add to my advance and the two grand Les begrudgingly turned over to me, making a nice kitty to overhaul both my hovels). But the bestest present was Alexandra informing me she would be present in Florida for the whole winter.

The news was a welcome surprise. On the sly, she'd been slowly extricating herself from the day-to-day operations of the boutique brokerage house she had founded years before ethical investing was the raging fad that everybody was now insisting they operate by.

She had herself appointed CEO, restricting herself to media appearances as she was in demand as an insightful and smart commentator (and darn smart-looking on camera). She would also write the occasional report and chair the Board of Directors, all of which she could do without leaving the comfortable—OK, OK, the claustrophobic—confines of the Hovel-by-the-Sea.

While I may have had the wonderful image of us lazing around under palm trees in the land of cheap beer and smokes, Alex had a different vision. My Type-A lover was itching to get back at the renovations to our hovel. I promised to shout words of encouragement to her every time I went inside to get a frosty Yuengling. In return, the little witch threatened to take up pickleball on the new courts right beside the Hovel. So we reached a stand-off.

I finished my fall outdoor chores—raking, pruning, digging up bulbs, pointlessly trying to strengthen the barricades to stop the invading horde of mice—all the activities that would guarantee I'd be achy as fuck when I started my drive south.

Packing an SUV, even a small one, proved to be a challenge. For my previous trips south, I brought only my shitty laptop and my trusty bowling bag. I added a few more Hawaiian shirts, extra shorts and some work clothes in a garbage bag, a few beach books, and some gardening tools, but all that would still fit in the passenger seat. I easily had room for the case of Molson Ex that would delay my heebie-jeebies over Canadian beer for a week or so.

The last job—a ritual, really—was to load my big screen and the canna, calla, and dahlia bulbs onto my boat and sail them over to Carl's island.

Carl was pouting, the big baby. He was unsettled and unhappy about the abandonment of another ritual—him taking me to Toronto airport in return for me putting the NFL and NHL Networks onto his cable package. Even after I assured him it was still a fair deal because he would be opening and closing my hovel for Halley and Ron and their cross-country skiing insanity, he was still sulking.

It was odd to say our good-byes from his dock, but I was comforted by his one-fingered wave farewell. I saw his big goofy smile when I returned it as I floated away.

Despite the drive ahead of me, despite the masses of people and vehicles I was about to encounter, I was elated as I pulled out of driveway.

Full tank of gas, great tunes lined up, and me, profanely massacring a Leonard Cohen song:

"First, we take Boston, then we take Indian Rocks."

ACKNOWLEDGEMENTS

Profuse thanks to a bunch of people who, after five Jake Lydon books, now officially qualify as a gang of usual suspects.

Glenn Torresan for his wonderful cover and page design (and his obstinacy).

Publisher dude Ron Corbett for putting out the mysteries.

JoDee and Lou Costello, late of Indian Rocks—her for her enthusiastically dogged editing, him for his encouragement and tequila. I hereby pledge to perfect a mobile margarita canteen.

And my beautiful Maggie for her love and astounding patience.

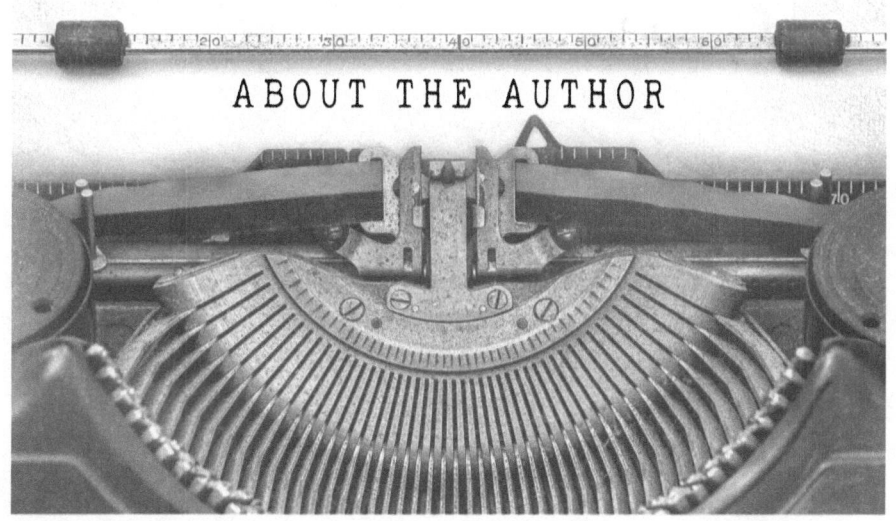

ABOUT THE AUTHOR

John Owens has written five books in the Jake Lydon Mystery series and two works of historical fiction. You can find out more about them on the johnowensauthor.com website that the lazy bastard occasionally updates or by going to ottawapressandpublishing.com

Owens lives in Morrisburg, Ontario with his wife, Maggie, and some place closer to the Equator when the snow flies.